Fluently Speaking Baron

The Starling Legacy
Book 1

Ava Devlin

ARE YOU SIGNED UP FOR DRAGONBLADE'S BLOG?

You'll get the latest news and information on exclusive giveaways, exclusive excerpts, coming releases, sales, free books, cover reveals and more.

Check out our complete list of authors, too!

No spam, no junk. That's a promise!

Sign Up Here

www.dragonbladepublishing.com

Dearest Reader;

Thank you for your support of a small press. At Dragonblade Publishing, we strive to bring you the highest quality Historical Romance from some of the best authors in the business. Without your support, there is no 'us', so we sincerely hope you adore these stories and find some new favorite authors along the way.

Happy Reading!

CEO, Dragonblade Publishing

*For John Schudel, who was so much more than an English teacher.
Thank you for believing in me. The world misses you.*

Prologue

Brighton, England, 1802

WHEN HARRIET FRENCH was eleven years old, she said a naughty word in Italian.

Followed by one in French.

And a third in German.

The fourth thing she said was not so much a curse as a crass self-rebuke, in a language she only thought of as "Fishmonger Talk," due to only ever hearing it down at the wharfs on the days they bought fish for the kitchens. It was still coarse enough that, had anyone understood it as it had come out of the mouth of an eleven-year-old girl, it would have caused gasps.

In Harriet's defense, she had just burned her hand touching a hot pan, sent the pan flying, and then knocked several more dishes onto her little body as she'd toppled to the floor, bruised and scalding.

Unfortunately, the hot pan had contained part of the day's main course.

Worse, the day's main course was dinner for the master of the house's funeral.

And perhaps most unfortunate at all was that Harriet's flurry of vulgarity happened to explode from her mouth as the widow herself was walking past the open door of the kitchens, with the late baron's sister-in-law and his nephew in tow.

Even at eleven, and clutching a hand that still sang like fire,

Harriet was not certain it could have been timed any worse.

They had all turned to stare at her, with her skirt up over her tatty stockings, her bruised knees on display, and her hand turning pinker and angrier by the second.

"Was that Norwegian?" the baron's sister-in-law asked, her narrow, brown eyes sweeping over Hattie's disheveled appearance.

"Danish, I think," the dowager baroness had replied, turning and stepping into the kitchen with a curious little click of her black heel, her auburn chignon glinting in rows of contained curls as she moved. "Like the fishermen from whom we buy our catch. Was that what it was, little maid?"

Harriet stared, awestruck and horrified. "It's the Fish Tongue," she blurted out, blinking away the sounds of the rest of the kitchen staff exploding in a panic around her. "I don't know its real name."

"Remarkable," said the baroness, her dark eyes flicking up once, impatiently, at the staff. "Is no one going to get this child a poultice?"

The cook huffed, her cheeks pink. "She can dip it in cold water once she gets off her wagon, my lady. 'Twas just a scald."

"Scalding would require water," Harriet said, a little dazed from the pain. "There was no water. The pan was dry. No steam. No water."

The cook's beady eyes had narrowed and her thick neck was turning pink. Harriet knew it, even without looking at her. "My mistake, little madam. I didn't know they spoke so proper at the foundlings' home. Get up. You've distressed the mourners on a somber day!"

"I am not distressed." The baroness turned over her shoulder to the young boy who was watching from just beyond the door. "Elias, are you distressed?"

He blinked his dark-blue eyes, hugging his arms around his plump body, and shook his head.

"See? We're all in fine form," the dowager baroness declared, ignoring her sister-in-law's pinched lips at not having her own potential distress acknowledged. "Except for this little scullery maid here, who is blistering. If you aren't going to help her, then I will."

"Oh, we'll help her," the cook muttered.

Harriet knew what that meant.

Tonight she'd have to tell the mistress at the foundling home that she'd lost her job. She liked this job. She had enjoyed her many months here, listening to the fancy people who came in and out of the Rest, even if they did not look at or speak to her. She had liked the baron too and was sad that he had died.

"Come along with me, girl," the baroness said suddenly, snapping her fingers toward Harriet's face. "What is your name?"

"Hattie," she said without thinking. "Harriet. I mean Harriet. It means *head of household*. But I'm not. I'm not one."

The baroness's lips twitched. "Let's get that hand wrapped up. Lucky for you, a surgeon cared enough about my late husband to be sad that he died. He's just in the drawing room. Come now."

Hattie hesitated, glancing at the cook, who actually appeared to be steaming well enough now to cause a scald in the proper sense of the word.

"Don't mind anyone else," the baroness instructed. "I am in charge here and I say come with me. You will not be punished for obeying your mistress."

Hattie pressed her lips together, her cheeks warming—though not as much as her hand—and scrambled up to her feet, wincing at the way the blood rushed down her arm and into the burns lingering along the pads of her fingers.

"Poor thing," murmured the baroness, placing a hand on her shoulder and guiding her outside. "Did you learn your other languages at the orphanage, my dear? Are there orphans from elsewhere on the Continent there?"

Hattie winced, glancing back at the other boy for help, but he was watching her warily, like he did not trust her or her sudden presence in their little coterie at all.

"No, my lady," she said, pausing and grimacing at how common and coarse her own accent sounded against the baroness's. She wondered if she could improve it if she tried.

She tried.

"I hear those languages during the carnivals," she said overly carefully, enunciating entirely too much. "And you have an Italian groom."

"Do I, indeed?" the baroness asked with a little chuckle. "There's a Russian diplomat in the foyer, you know. Have you ever heard Russian?"

Hattie shrugged. "If I have, no one told me its name."

"I am very curious to hear your thoughts about it once we get your hand wrapped up," the baroness told her. "Tell me, Hattie, do you live here in the house with us or do you return to the orphanage every night?"

"I go back," Hattie said, frowning. "I'm only new."

"Yes, I suppose I ought to have guessed you were not a seasoned servant at your advanced age," the baroness quipped, tittering to herself. "And can you read and write, Hattie?"

She nodded. "A little. My penmanship is poor, though."

"Penmanship never defined anyone of note," the baroness told her, switching to French. "*Unless you can think of someone famous for their handwriting?*"

Harriet shook her head. "*I can't,*" she said, also in French, which made the other woman grin.

"My dear girl," she said, "I fear you are wasted in the kitchens here."

Hattie thought about that sentence quite a lot as the surgeon clucked as he slathered and wrapped her hand.

The word *wasted* hovered in her mind. It spelled itself, the letters warm and fragrant on the empty canvas behind her eyelids. What did it mean?

Wasted in the kitchens.

Like kitchen waste? Like scraps?

Why did the word taste sweet, even without letting it escape off her tongue? Why did it taste so sweet?

She was brought into the drawing room, the only person not clad in black and the only person with holes in her stockings. No one seemed to mind. She was ushered forward to meet a gentleman with heavy wrinkles under his eyes and a mustache that gleamed like polished wood.

"I want to play a game," the dowager baroness said immediately, by way of introduction. "I've a suspicion this little girl is a polyglot, and you've the most confounding language in the room. How shall we test her?"

"Russian is beautiful," he assured her, his vowels deep and thrumming. "It has more rhythm and passion than English."

"You could tell me a poem," Hattie suggested, which made the man's head snap to her, brows lifted, as though he had never expected her to speak. "Or a story, if you prefer?"

He narrowed his eyes, considering her. "You are not a guest," he observed, eyeing her clothes. "My dear Lady Selwyn, what is this?"

"A game," the baroness said, still grinning. "Go on, then, a story. Folklore from your frigid homeland."

The man sighed, setting aside his drink, and turned to face Hattie, meeting her eye. And then he started to speak.

He was right, Hattie thought.

It had rhythm. It reminded her of the big bass drums at the end of a military parade. It reminded her a little of the way the baroness's heels clicked on hard floors. She listened for the words that repeated. She watched his hands move and his expression change.

"*Baba Yaga*," she repeated, mimicking his accent as best she could. "A witch?"

The man froze, staring at her with his mouth hanging open.

"I am being teased," he guessed, looking up at the baroness for confirmation. "Are you teasing me, Willa?"

"I am not," the baroness said, sounding utterly pleased.

"Hattie, my girl. I'm afraid I'm stuck attending this funeral for the next several hours, but would you be a dear and fetch a footman for me? He can take you back to the foundling home to gather your things and bring them here."

"'Bring them here'?" Hattie repeated, her hand still throbbing, her mind still muddled and dazed. "To live in the kitchens?"

"No, my dear girl," the baroness said with a grin. "You will be living upstairs with me. You see, death sometimes does funny things to our lives. I suppose you already know that, as an orphan?"

"Willa!" the Russian man balked, wrinkling his nose in distaste and stalking away, muttering to himself.

Hattie gave an uncertain lift of her shoulder. "Well, yes," she said. "If I had parents, I suppose things would be different."

"Precisely," the baroness said with pleasure. "When my husband the baron died, my life changed too. I've been wondering how I ought to change with it, and then I walked past you, screaming profanity that would sober a demon in mine own kitchens. Perhaps it is fate."

"Fortuna," said Hattie, teetering a little on her feet. "Isn't that funny? There's Fortuna and then there are the Fates. Do you think they get along?"

"No," said the baroness with a laugh. "I do not."

"I'll just go get the footman," Hattie said, turning and wavering as the room turned further, even after she had stopped.

The last thing she saw before she slumped to the floor was that other child. The boy, Elias.

He had a valise with him, she saw. He was holding a valise.

Americans called it a 'grip.'

She opened her mouth to tell him that, because he clearly was expecting her to say something, the way he was staring.

But the words didn't come out.

Because she fainted.

Part I
The Rule of Seven

Chapter One

London, Fifteen Years Later

THE JOURNEY FROM Saint Petersburg to London was meant to take five weeks.

Because of the weather, it had taken seven.

Harriet French supposed that was appropriate, given the circumstances. Seven, in her estimation, was a canary-yellow color that sounded of viola strings and smelled of sun and sea.

It had been seven years since her adoptive mother, warden, and proprietress, the Dowager Baroness Selwyn had gone missing. Seven weeks from her receipt of the letter in the tsar's palace to the day they turned into the Thames port alley. Seven steps from the deck to the pier.

And she touched seven fingers with the curve of her thumbnail as she surveyed the awaiting crowd on the embankment, looking for a flash of silver hair and a well-tailored black suit. Later, she would guess it took her exactly seven minutes to find him.

"Miss French!" the baroness's steadfast, lifelong friend and devoted barrister had called, booming and certain, his hand waving over the crowd. "Miss Harriet French! Over here, if you please!"

"Oh, Mr. Harcourt," she breathed, turning with a sag of relief and waving back. "There you are. For a moment, I feared you'd forgotten me."

"I've an ironclad memory, I assure you," the silver-haired barrister said fondly, trotting up to meet her. "Are your trunks still aboard?"

She nodded, reaching up to brush the salt-touched strands of her brassy curls. "I thought some of the others would be with you," she confessed. "At least Malcolm, as we are in London."

The barrister turned and lifted two fingers to a porter he had evidently secured prior to their business, pointing to the ship with the implicit instructions to retrieve Hattie's things. "I've secured rooms for you tonight at an inn in Bloomsbury," he informed her as he offered his elbow and nodded toward the path to the street. "My thinking was that you should rest before you set off again straight away for Brighton, but after my arrival here, I realized I am going to need your help, anyhow."

"My help doing what, sir?" she asked, following him toward a gleaming black hackney coach that awaited them beyond the throng. "I confess, your letter relayed your urgency effectively, but not so much anything else. I'm not entirely sure why I am here."

He heaved a heavy sigh, shaking his head a little mournfully. "I did specify," he reminded her, "that the passage of seven years since anyone has seen the dowager baroness means that the law now considers her deceased."

"Yes, of course," said Hattie, pausing to be assisted into the carriage. She waited until the doors closed to speak again, watching Mr. Harcourt settle in across from her. "That doesn't mean that she is."

"For my purposes, my dear, I'm afraid that it does," he told her seriously. "Which means that her estate has entered a state of bequeathment escrow until such a time as her last will and testament can be read, a stipulation that requires the physical presence of all her heirs. I did not realize until I started tracking you all down how elusive the group of you has become."

"The seven of us," she said, with a wry, little twist of her lips. "Isn't that funny? Seven heirs. Seven years. Did you know King

Henry VIII and Anne Boleyn wore canary yellow on the day Catherine of Aragon died? Yellow is believed to have been a color of mourning in Spain, from whence she hailed."

He blinked at her, clearly a little taken aback. "Did they, indeed?"

"Many people thought they were celebrating her demise," Hattie said, settling back as the carriage began to move and gazing out the window. "They were not through their clothing, though I suppose they might have been otherwise."

There was a beat of silence, a lingering shift from the port sounds to the streets as the wheels of the carriage turned onto the street proper.

Mr. Harcourt cleared his throat. "Eight," he said, politely.

Hattie turned back to him, frowning. "Pardon?"

"There are eight of you," he said to her. "Not seven."

She shook her head, her brow wrinkling as she ran through the list of wards who had been raised alongside her at Starling's Rest, her thumbnail tapping on those seven fingers again. "Myself," she said, remembering them in the order in which they'd come into the home. "Malcolm and Libba. Ruby, Errol, Monica, and Rhys. Seven."

"Ah, Libba," said Mr. Harcourt, grimacing. "I should mention we are headed to Giltspur Street Compter before we move onto the inn, to retrieve Miss Elizabeth. Or Miss Liberty, I believe, as she is now called."

"Giltspur Street!" Hattie balked. "She is in jail?!"

He nodded. "I would have gotten her out yesterday, when I found her, but I'm afraid I was under explicit instructions to contact you and only the executor of the baroness's will first and foremost, which, of course, is you. My hands were tied, so to speak."

"It sounds like Libba's are too!" Hattie exclaimed. "What has she done?"

"She was caught with some smuggled goods," he told her with a grimace. "French textiles and spirits, I believe. Nothing half the households in Mayfair don't also have in their pantries. I will represent her and clear it with the magistrate before we start back to Brighton. We can also retrieve her brother while we are here. For the others, I will be relying on you to locate and contact them."

"The six others," she said again, tapping that thumbnail. "Seven."

"Eight," the barrister corrected with a sigh. "You are forgetting Elias Selwyn, the new baron and rightful heir of all the land under Starling's Rest."

Hattie stared for a moment, her mind whirring.

Eight was very different.

Eight was dark blue. Somber. Stormy. Eight smelled of fire.

"Elias," she repeated slowly, flashes of a taciturn, pudgy boy with rosy cheeks and a frowning demeanor in the corners of Starling's Rest flickering into her mind. "Yes. I remember him. He was already baron. He's been baron this whole time."

"More or less," the barrister agreed with a shrug. "But his inheritance was complicated and contingent while the dowager baroness still lived. All will be explained in Brighton, I assure you. Ah, here we are. Shall we retrieve Miss Lennox?"

"Smuggled goods," Hattie tutted, waiting for the door to be wrenched open. "What is she about these days? I thought she was an actress."

"You will have to ask her," Mr. Harcourt said as they entered the cavernous foyer of the holding chamber. "I will have to ask her too, I suppose. Ah, there's the clerk now. I'll only be a moment."

Hattie nodded, turning and looking for a place to wait.

The only option was a long, mean-looking wooden bench. It had no legs. Instead, it had been nailed directly into the brick wall, as though anyone who might come here and sit on it would also be just as likely to make off with it down the street.

She cleared her throat and frowned, giving the bench a little wipe with her kerchief before she settled onto it.

Oddly, she was certain she could still feel the ocean waves moving under her feet, even here, on perfectly solid land and in the embrace of a place meant for holding people still besides. She closed her eyes and pressed her feet firmly to the uneven stone floor beneath her boots, reminding herself that she was ashore again, that she was home again.

England, she told herself. English. The King's English? Or the Regent's? Had it changed because of the Regency?

She would have to ask someone who might know.

When Mary and then Elizabeth Tudor had reigned, after all, it had been the Queen's English.

Clerk was a funny sort of word, wasn't it? Why was it pronounced as though the vowel were an *a* rather than an *e*? When English had shifted, and the ligaments had been replaced with single letters, most had retained their phonetic vowel. This particular word, it seemed, was a matter of contention. Hattie preferred a lack of contention in matters of phonics, and often thought English was perhaps the most unfortunate language to have been born into, with its many roots and borrowings and eras. *Clerk*, she thought again.

"I'm not leaving without Lem," came Libba's voice from the hall, shrill and animated and entirely familiar. "You'll bail him out too or I'll sleep here for another week."

Hattie smiled, her eyes still closed.

She couldn't make out exactly what Mr. Harcourt said in response, but she supposed that Libba won the argument, because a few moments later, in the darkness behind her eyelids, she felt the bench creak and smelled Libba's favorite jasmine hair oil as it sprinkled into the air.

She didn't speak. Instead, Liberty Lennox just reached out and took Hattie's hand, linking her fingers through the other woman's.

Hattie sighed and opened her eyes then, turning to look upon a face she had missed very much. "You changed your name," she said by way of greeting. "The new one is a little ironic, given the venue of our reunion."

Libba grinned, the constellation of beauty marks on her face dancing along her lip and cheek. "I knew you'd say something like that," she said. "By way of greeting."

Hattie gave half a smile and a shrug, admiring this version of Libba, who appeared to still be partially in costume from some performance she'd given before arrest. There was white talc in her dark, tight-coiled hair and her gown was more of a toga than respectable dress. Her skin, dark as oiled beechwood, sparkled with a layer of glittering cosmetics that caught in the light.

"Who is Lem?" Hattie asked, tilting her head curiously. "Did you marry?"

"Marry Lem? Absolutely not," Libba said with a laugh. "He's my muscle."

Hattie blinked, reaching forward instinctively and poking at Libba's bicep, which made the other woman snort and slap at her hand.

"Stop being so queer."

"I can't," said Hattie with a lazy smile. "Smuggling?"

Libba scoffed. "All the best things are French. You know that as well as anyone. Wine, silk, cheese, shoes, men. Where were you this time, by the by?"

"Russia," said Hattie. "They have very nice shoes as well."

"Russia," Libba repeated with a wistful little sigh. "Living with a king again?"

"A tsar," Hattie said. "And tsarina. Or empress, depending on who you ask. Her, you would have liked."

"And him?" Libba pressed.

"Pious," said Hattie with a shrug. "Or blessed, depending on whom you ask. I thought I was there to teach or to translate, but I think I was primarily something like a centerpiece for dinners."

"Put you right on the tablecloth, did they?" Libba asked with a grin as Hattie immediately shook her head. "I know. I do that to Lem sometimes, though. We oil him up and surround him with fruit as the patrons file in. It does draw a particular crowd."

"Because of his muscle?" Hattie asked, blinking.

"Because of his muscle," Libba agreed. "Ah, here he is."

Both women stood as Mr. Harcourt emerged with an extremely tall, extremely muscled bald man, dressed in a costume like some manner of sultan or pasha. He was even darker than Libba, gleaming closer to ebonwood and wearing the same layer of sparkle as he trudged out. "Lem, meet Hattie," Libba said. "Hattie, Lem."

"It is a pleasure," Hattie said, drawing nearer, offering her hand to shake. "Is 'Lem' short for 'Lemuel'?"

"Short for 'Lem,'" he said, each word clipped at the end.

Mr. Harcourt sighed. "Why don't we go to the inn presently?" he suggested. "I can get an extra room for Mister … Lem here. I'm sorry, sir, do you have a surname?"

The big man blinked down at the barrister. "Lem."

"Right," said Mr. Harcourt, giving his head a little shake. "We'll go to the inn and gather our thoughts, unless we ought to go grab your brother on the way, Miss Lennox?"

Libba made a face. "No. Let me wash and change before I face Malcolm. And if either of you tells him about this jail business, I'll make hell for you. Understand?"

Hattie nodded immediately, while Mr. Harcourt just looked weary, the circles under his eyes seeming darker and heavier than they had been back on the docks.

Lem did not react at all.

"Good," said Libba, brightening. "Off we go. Good God, Harriet. What on earth are you doing back in England, anyway?"

"Well," said Hattie. "It's been seven years, you see. And there are seven of us."

"Naturally," said Libba in an amused, fond way that always meant she didn't understand at all.

"Eight," corrected Mr. Harcourt as they walked toward the carriage. "There are eight of you."

Harriet French frowned.

Dark blue, she thought, counting her fingers. *Stormy, dark blue*

and the smell of smoke.
Eight.
She had forgotten Elias Selwyn.

Chapter Two

I T HAD TAKEN a lot longer to get out of London than Harriet had anticipated. Almost an entire month.

A month! And the trouble had not been entirely because of Libba's legal muck, either. While Julian Harcourt, Esquire had handled the matter rapidly and cleanly, with details Harriet was happy to never know entirely, there had been the matter of Libba's acting troupe and their contract with a Seven Dials playhouse that would not end for another half dozen performances.

Libba's brother, Malcolm, had also thrown a wrench into the works. He worked as a junior banker at a respected institution near Bow Street and evidently also required quite a bit of preparation before he could simply step away from his life, though he'd reacted with immediate enthusiasm at the idea of returning to Brighton.

"I'll have to write ahead to the lads!" he'd exclaimed after lifting Hattie fully off her feet in an embrace of greeting. "They'll toast me properly the instant we set boots to pebbles. You'll come, of course."

"Oh, of course," Libba had replied with a roll of her eyes, even though the invitation had been directed at Hattie, actually.

Next, Hattie had written a letter directly to Starling's Rest, where one of them still resided. Errol Cagney would prepare for their imminent stay and further, she entrusted him with tracking down one of the other wards, Ruby Little.

Errol and Ruby had long been inseparable, both as whispering, giggling friends when they had been children, and as shrewd and passionate business partners in adulthood. Ruby traveled to sell and market their wares, but he would know how to find her and how best to convince her to leave whatever she was about and return to the Rest.

While they had hoped Monica Thresher would be in London for the High Season, as many well-known modistes were prone to be, she had not been seen in St. James's or on Regent Street in some time. It had taken quite a lot of gossip and questioning, but eventually, the other modistes had been able to provide her whereabouts.

Berlin, apparently. On commission.

"She always goes back to Brighton to visit her mum by autumn if you just want to wait," they had told Harriet and Libba. "She's a very good daughter."

"I wish we *could* wait," Hattie had said sincerely. "But we require her now. Do you have the address?"

"Well, no," the narrow-faced modiste had said. "But I imagine if you write *Royal Opera House* on the envelope, it'll find her."

"'Royal Opera House'!" Libba had gasped, at which point the conversation had devolved past the point of productivity, with Libba far more interested in the theatrical pedigree of the commission than her foster sister's ultimate whereabouts.

That left Rhys Caradoc, who was always going to be the most impossible of the seven to track down.

"Have either of you heard from him?" Hattie asked the Lennoxes over dinner, her distress growing at the glance they exchanged. "Anything at all?"

"Well, he's always somewhere," Libba said cryptically. "Up to something."

"Maybe he went back to Wales," Malcolm speculated, seemingly on nothing but pure whimsy, popping a roasted fingerling potato in his mouth. "Or maybe he's dead."

"Mal," Libba said, frowning. "He's not dead. There would've been trumpets."

Malcolm chortled at that. "And fireworks."

"All right," said Hattie, waving her hand. "We do need to find him. Nothing can happen until we do."

Libba groaned, dropping her head into her hands and shaking it. "Fine. I will go inquire with the Illusionists' Guild out of Covent Garden. They're likely to have heard something. I hate them, though, and they hate me, so you owe me a dessert."

"Why?" Malcolm asked, on his third potato. "It's all a little similar, isn't it? Acting, dancing, and magic?"

At which point, his plate magically ended up in his lap.

By the time Mr. Harcourt had provided confirmation that Rhys had indeed been located and contacted, Hattie was simply ready to begin her journey south and get the next stage moving. There was a will to be read, a house to be opened, a new chapter of their lives to begin.

And there was also …

"Did you write to the baron?" Mr. Harcourt asked, frowning at her. "Why do I get the feeling you did not?"

"Oh, him," she said, frowning at the scent of smoke in her nose. "Would you do that, Mr. Harcourt? Would you mind it horribly? I've no idea where to find him and it seems like you do."

He had nodded, frowning at her like a disappointed papa, and clipped away from her, his silver hair glinting in the sunlight.

Hattie had watched him go.

They both knew very well that he'd told her that Elias Selwyn was stationed in Hunslow. She simply did not wish to address it.

Somehow, it was both a relief and more damning than a rebuke that he'd chosen silence in response to her avoidance.

Julian Harcourt had sported white hair all of her life, she thought. He must have gone gray as a student. Thinking about it, he must have only been early in his forties by now, still quite young for that shock of snowy hair.

What an odd thing. Perhaps he had been born with it.

She counted her fingers again, her thumbnail grazing against the pads of them, and turned her focus toward Brighton.

Why, after traveling to Russia and back, it was nothing at all from London to the coast. Nothing but the bat of an eye.

Libba, Malcolm, and Mr. Harcourt all traveled alongside her, all reacting with quite a bit more enthusiasm and relief when their destination drew near than Hattie thought appropriate, given how manageable the travel had been.

But she didn't say so.

"It almost feels like a pilgrimage, doesn't it?" she said to Mal. "Except we are not on foot."

"I'd make a terrible pilgrim," he told her with a nudge to the ribs, "and we both know it."

She smiled, imagining him in rags, leaning on a walking stick, caves and forests around him, and yet still somehow smelling of excellent cologne and shaved to a clean, shiny cut of his square jaw. "Terrible," she agreed. "Yes."

Starling's Rest sat beyond the fashionable terraces and well beyond the Royal Pavilion, deeper into the part of Brighton that was not necessarily for the footfalls of the late summer rush. It sat on a little hill, high enough that one could sometimes hear the sound of the Channel, when everything else was very quiet. The main building was surrounded by a variety of outbuildings and amenities that had been installed and expanded throughout the whole of Hattie's life.

The walls were gray, but in the bright summer sun, they looked black.

She *thought* they looked black.

The doors were thrown open the instant their carriage had halted, but it was not Errol Cagney who came bursting out of the house to greet them. At least not first. Errol lagged slightly behind their one-man reception party.

It was Rhys Caradoc, grinning broadly and loping down the

entry steps, his dark-brown curls tousled in the breeze, with Errol's paler, slower figure behind him only emphasizing the sprite-like energy of his greeting.

"Hattie!" he cried. "Libba! Mal! Come give us a *cwtch*!"

"A what?" Mal muttered.

"*Cwtch*," Hattie replied softly. "Snuggle. Cuddle. Embrace."

"Absolutely not!" Mal boomed back, holding his finger up at Rhys's wide-thrown arms. "You will not!"

It was too late. Rhys threw his arms around Malcolm first, winning a resigned groan from the other man.

For all his protesting, he did not seem to truly mind it. At least not to Hattie's estimation.

Libba was next, and then Hattie herself, and they returned the *cwtch* in the spirit with which it was given.

"The girls are inside," Rhys told them. "Monica just landed yesterday. It took you three ages to get here! Ages! So she's dead, then? Gone off to the great beyond? Do you think she's unseated Lucifer yet?"

"Rhys," Hattie hissed, catching the eye of a quietly amused Errol, a gentle smile playing on his lips as she passed by him. "Errol," she added. "Good to see you."

"Hattie," Errol replied in his gentle Irish brogue, turning and guiding her into the house. "You're looking well. My da has asked after you."

"I'll visit him soon," she promised, patting his arm.

Errol, like Hattie herself, had started life as part of the staff at Starling's Rest. While Hattie had been employed directly as a scullery maid, Errol had been the groom's son and had lived, even after becoming one of the baroness's wards, in the groom's cottage outside the stables.

His father had always been very proud.

"My goodness, is that Mr. Harcourt?!" Rhys's voice echoed from behind her. "Why have you been the same age for twenty years? Tell me your secrets!"

Hattie sighed, increasing her speed as she walked farther into the house.

She could hear feminine chittering from farther in and the click of porcelain teacups alongside the tinkle of liquid being poured therein.

She was dusty, exhausted, and more than a little bit rumpled from the nonstop work and travel of the past three months, but she could not imagine waiting to see the others any more than she could fathom having lived a life without them in it.

"Oh, it's Hattie! Hattie!" Monica cried, coming to her feet with her sweet, round face in her hands. "Oh, you look so elegant!"

"She looks like she was tossed into the sea and dried out on the mast," Ruby Little tittered from her reclined place on the chaise, her teacup still held aloft. "But a sight for sore eyes, all the same. Welcome, Hattie."

"Ruby," said Hattie, opening her arms for Monica's quick and warm embrace. "Monica. You both made excellent time."

Ruby flashed a little smile. "It is among my talents, you know," she said. "Physics."

Monica blinked, stepping away from Hattie with a look of puzzlement narrowing her eyes and rounding her cheeks. "'Physics'? I thought you favored chemistry."

"I think you will find that one often begets the other, Monica, my love," Ruby purred.

"She is jesting," said Malcolm, striding in from behind with his sister in tow. "Greetings, all!"

"My, my," said Ruby in a little cooing voice, looking him up and down. "You managed to stay neat all the way here."

"Don't flirt with me unless you mean it," he chided, throwing her a wink that immediately made her grimace. "You never do."

"I never do," she agreed.

"Good," said Libba with obvious distaste. "Disgusting."

"Who's disgusting?" Rhys asked, bouncing in around a sighing Errol and plopping onto the chaise so quickly that Ruby had to pull her legs up with an undignified squeak. "Still me?"

"Always you!" Ruby snapped back. "Good afternoon, Mr. Harcourt."

"Oh, Mr. Harcourt," Monica said, suddenly even pinker than she had been before as she patted at her hair. "I did not know you would be joining us today."

Hattie watched her curiously.

Evidently, some things never did change.

"So shall we get started, then?" Ruby asked, raising her brows. "Here we all are. Here you are, Mr. Harcourt. I haven't stolen any jewelry yet. Let's get on with it."

The barrister glanced at Hattie, tightening his lips, then turned back to the others. "We are still waiting for one more."

"'One more'?" Ruby repeated, furrowing up her brow. She turned and counted the heads, mouthing to herself, "Five, six, seven …" Then she said, louder, "No, sir, we are all here."

"Eight," Mr. Harcourt said, much to Hattie's distress. "There are eight of you."

And at that moment, another carriage pulled up on the drive, the pebbles and gravel crunching and popping from outside the window, drawing everyone's attention around to observe it.

"Eight," repeated Hattie, blinking away the stormy blue that had settled over her mind. "That will be Lord Selwyn."

"Lord bloody Selwyn?" Ruby repeated, aghast. "The dead husband?"

"No, Ruby." Monica tutted, her fingers at her lips. "Elias is Baron Selwyn now."

"Oh, Elias," Rhys said, his big, green eyes widening. "I'd forgotten all about him. Is he coming, then? Involved in all this?"

"Evidently," Libba snapped. "Aren't you listening?"

"Never," Rhys replied with a gloating smile.

"Is that him, then?" Monica wondered, breathy and clearly nervous. "Lord Selwyn?"

"Yes," Hattie confirmed, floating in slow, absent footsteps toward the window as the coach driver hopped down and made his way to the door. The crest on the outside of the coach was unmistakable. The embellished letter *S* for House Selwyn was painted on the door in stark gold and green. "Elias is here."

⁂

Chapter Three

ELIAS SELWYN BRIEFLY considered turning the coach around and going directly back to Hounslow. He had a nice life there, he reasoned. He was respected. Well-liked. Happy.

He certainly never felt the doom and weight that was currently sitting on every single one of his ribs like dangling iron weights back in Hounslow.

Starling's Rest rose up on its pert, little hill beyond the coastal townhouses of Brighton like a crow's eye, glinting and smug and still so very, very tall.

Yes, he thought as they turned into the drive.

He should just go back to Hounslow. He'd made a home there, hadn't he? He just wanted to go home.

The only reason he couldn't was because as far as the law was concerned, *this* was home now. If Willa Selwyn was truly dead and gone, then there was nothing left between Elias and the full burden of his barony.

This was home now.

Or something like it.

He sighed, resisting the urge to rub the anxieties that prickled over his face, and straightened his shoulders as the driver's boots hit the pebbled drive.

He was not a child anymore. And neither were any of the people inside.

It would be different now.

They were all going to be different now.

Still, the instant his body had moved from the cushioned embrace of the carriage to the windy landing of the house, Elias was certain he was no longer the man who had ridden here from Hounslow.

He had been that man, in the carriage. And as soon as he had stepped out, he'd been half as tall, still swaddled in baby fat, trembling in a coat that was a little bit too tight about the arms because his mother had refused to spend what had been left of their pin money every time he'd grown, either taller or wider.

He shivered, despite the glorious, shimmering sunlight, his very person flickering between the man and the boy. The tall and the short.

He ran both hands over his dark-brown hair and gave himself a shake.

"They're waiting," he said out loud, though the driver was gone to unbridle the horses and he was alone here, boots digging into the tiny, pebbled drive. "Aren't they?"

If Willa's ghost was there to hear him, she did not answer.

That was very like her.

The doors opened and a figure emerged, casting a long, slanting shadow opposite the sun. It was, mercifully, not one of Willa's little prodigies, but the staid and familiar Julian Harcourt, Esquire. The barrister. The friendly man who had always had a warm hand for Elias's shoulder.

He exhaled, lifting his chin and giving his best smile of greeting. "Mr. Harcourt!"

"Lord Selwyn," the older man called back, breaking into a smile. "I have not seen you in some time! You are looking very well. Very well, indeed. And I must congratulate you on your recent promotion. A baron and a captain both. You do your house proud."

"Not that house," Elias joked, nodding toward Starling's Rest. "But maybe another one, somewhere."

Mr. Harcourt gave him a wry, little twist of the lips and turned, gesturing at the door. "You are the last to arrive. Won't you come in?"

"Oh," said Elias, trying not to frown as he followed the other man to the doors. "All of them are here? Already?"

"Indeed. I've only just arrived myself, along with the Lennoxes and Miss French. The others were here waiting."

Elias blanched, flashes of children bouncing in his mind. Of Malcolm, dark-skinned and charming, leading games of make believe on the lawn while his sister had become heroes and villains, damsels and brigands, breath after breath.

And Hattie.

He winced, hearing a splash of water and a crack of thunder in a far-tucked corner of his memory.

He flexed his hands. The hands that had pushed her into the ocean, so bloody annoyed by her endless prattling and following and chattering and questions. The attempts to mimic his accent, the way she'd repeat everything he'd said.

It was no wonder he'd shoved her.

They had still been children back then.

Did she still hold a grudge over it? Did she remember it at all?

Somehow, he imagined she did.

But if it haunted her … If that day on the pier—and off it, for that matter—revisited Hattie French, Elias knew for certain that it looked very different to the memory as it played for him.

Very different, indeed.

He sucked in a breath and turned the corner into the parlor, a room so silent, he would not have expected to find anyone in it at all.

When he walked in and found all their eyes on him, all seven pairs, he understood.

He had caused the silence.

Again.

He'd spent almost three years in this house. Amongst them. And then, finally, he'd been allowed to leave. He'd left and had only come back twice: once for Christmas that first year, and once more to collect his papers before he'd made the change from Eton to Oxford.

He'd made that second journey when he'd known the household had been on holiday elsewhere. He'd avoided them then. He'd avoided them since he had been still growing into his body and learning who he was, away from all of this.

"Good God," said Ruby Little, still dark haired and bright eyed, fluttering up from her lounge on the chaise with a hand to her chest. "Elias Selwyn, look at you! My goodness, who knew what was hiding under all that youthful pudge. Come sit by me."

"Ruby," Errol chided, softly and frowning.

She stood, her red gown crinkling around her, still the type of beautiful that gloated over the fact in every move she made. "I can't believe it," she said again, her shining, rouged lips parting in a grin. "You really are gorgeous. Welcome home."

"Well, what about the rest of us?" the little Welsh shit who used to steal Elias's desserts and his socks said from the window, grinning widely. Rhys Caradoc, Elias reminded himself. Greasy Rhys. He'd been the last addition to the wards, perhaps even the final straw on Elias's tolerance for staying here. "Aren't we all gorgeous too?"

Ruby turned and looked at him, flicking her eyes from his scuffed shoes to his open collar. "No," she said, slumping back into the chaise in a flutter of skirts.

Elias frowned.

Willa hadn't taken in any other wards after he'd left this place. Had that been related to his leaving? Surely not.

Mr. Harcourt cleared his throat, still standing formal and stiff near the entry. "I suppose I ought to ask," he said politely, "if you all wish to settle and rest before we begin the reading or if you wish to have it done with immediately."

"Done with," several voices chanted right away, with only one deviating.

"Oh, I wouldn't mind a nap," said Harriet French, bronze

curls glowing in the afternoon sun from where she stood near Rhys Caradoc at the window. She blinked, her eyes glinting like amber in the light. "I suppose I'm the outlier."

"Usually," said Ruby, making Rhys snicker and soft, little Monica Thresher frown.

"Oh, Ruby." Monica tutted under her breath.

Hattie nodded, her eyes moving slowly to settle over Elias as her narrow shoulders straightened. "Then I suppose I will stay," she said, as though speaking directly to him. "I shouldn't like to be the cause of everyone's irritation."

He inclined his head toward her, using the opportunity to admire the ways she'd changed in the years since he'd seen her last.

And the ways she hadn't.

Judging from that last little comment, she remembered him as well as he remembered her.

It seemed, for that brief moment, that neither of them had changed much at all.

She was still brassy inside and out, a perfect little pedant with impeccable posture and strange affectations, and he still felt like an idiot in her presence.

He wasn't two inches shorter than her anymore, of course. Nor was he quite as soft as he had once been. The miracles of transitional adulthood alone couldn't be the only things that had changed, though, could they?

She had, perhaps, gained some control over the incessant questions and chatter, though Elias supposed that remained to be seen.

She had finally mastered that posh, perfect accent she'd wanted so badly. Every syllable was refined.

She was taller now. Shapelier.

Though of course that shape of hers had already started to blossom that day at the pier. He could see her now, sputtering and aghast and confused, lurching out of the water with her muslin dress translucent and clinging to her. He could feel the shock of it. The heat and confusion and instant regret.

He cleared his throat, shifting and looking for somewhere to sit.

Heat or confusion or instant regret would not suit him right now, at a damned funerary rite. He turned his back to Hattie and hastened toward the chair in the rear corner of the room, shadowed and cool, apart from the wards.

Elias had never been one of them, anyhow.

Mr. Harcourt was already thumbing through his folio, pulling a pair of well-worn silver spectacles from his pocket and perching them midway down his nose.

"I've a letter for each of you," he began, "though I would ask that you wait until I've read the preliminary statements to open and read them."

"You can keep mine," Rhys said immediately, grimacing at the envelopes and crossing himself. "I can't read."

"Shut up, Rhys," Malcolm suggested.

The Irish boy, Errol, settled into the chair next to Elias, shaking his head with what seemed a fond exasperation at the exchange between the other two. He glanced over at Elias and gave him a little nod of greeting, friendly and brief.

Elias nodded back, grateful that of all of them, this was the one who had taken that chair.

Errol had always been easy. Quiet. Even as a lad, when all the other children had been playing knights and bandits on the lawn, Errol would be off to the side with his vegetables or his birds or his flowers or the horses.

The only person he ever seemed to like as well as his natural things had been Ruby, who could sometimes coax him into play or otherwise join him in his naturalist idyll apart from the others.

This had always puzzled Elias, who found Ruby overwhelming and exhausting, even when she didn't speak.

But, he reminded himself, he did not care. It did not matter. He was not curious about these people.

He had moved on.

Though it was still worth noting that Ruby had not changed a whit. Two seconds into seeing him again and she was already trying to unsettle him with barbed flirtations that felt like a lure on a hook into some unseen trap.

These bloody people.

Mr. Harcourt cleared his throat, withdrawing the first pages of the will. "'In the Name of God, Amen. I, Willa Selwyn, of Starling's Rest in the County of Sussex, Widow, being of sound and disposing mind and memory, do make and publish this my last Will and Testament, hereby revoking all former wills by me made. My soul I commend to Almighty God and my body to the earth. To ensure these wishes are executed in both letter and spirit, I appoint Harriet French of Brighton, daughter of my heart, to be the Executrix of this my last Will and Testament.'"

"Oh," said Hattie, coloring and covering her mouth.

"Hattie?!" said Libba, frowning. "I was always the organizer. Willa knew that."

"Hush," said her brother, patting her knee.

Libba swatted his hand away. "It's true! Hattie has no mind for logistics. She is brilliant but scattered. We all know it."

"I shouldn't decline your assistance," Hattie said softly, blinking at the observation that had been made. "If this is your way of offering it."

It was enough to make Libba pause and flush a little, giving a quick nod and a wince. Mr. Harcourt did not look at them or otherwise acknowledge the outburst. He did glance up, however, and grimace at Elias directly before continuing.

"'To my nephew, Elias, Baron Selwyn, I bequeath the lands and fields of the Selwyn barony of in perpetuity: all natural soil and rights appurtenant thereto.'"

"Good show," said Rhys, looking bored.

"'To my ward, Harriet French,'" Mr. Harcourt continued, a little louder, "'I bequeath the dwelling house known as Starling's Rest, together with all furnishings, chattels, revenues, and appurtenances thereof.

"'These two inheritances shall remain separate and distinct unless and until the said Elias Selwyn and Harriet French are lawfully joined in matrimony, whereupon the property shall be reconciled and united under one settlement. Should they decline, the manor and lands shall be broken and sold in parcels, the proceeds distributed at my discretion as described in the remainder of this will.'"

There was an extremely long pause, during which the only sound was the rustling of paper as Mr. Harcourt lowered the will and sighed very heavily, as if he'd already had this conversation many times in his mind.

Elias could do little more than laugh, a bark of astounded, incredulous bafflement. "What in God's name?" he managed. "The house is part of the barony."

Mr. Harcourt winced. "Shall I explain the legalities here first or continue with the will?"

"Continue," Ruby said, examining her cuticles in pointed avoidance of her fellow wards' wide-eyed expressions.

"Please explain," Hattie said, louder and more strangled than she'd intended. "Please."

Mr. Harcourt nodded. "The late Lord Selwyn was destitute at the time of his engagement to Miss Willa Starling, who came into the marriage with a sizable dowry and allowance from her father," he began. "She initiated construction of the home during their engagement, which means the deeds and completion of the building were drawn up before she joined the baron in matrimony, under her father's legal ownership. When her father died, rather than inherit the house directly, the dowager baroness moved its property deed into a trust so that it would not merge with the barony. This was, I'm afraid, very deliberate."

Elias blinked several times. His chest felt like it might cave in.

"But then Lord Selwyn could just purchase it from me," Hattie said reasonably. "There is no need for matrimony at all."

Elias stared at her, unable to form words. He supposed he ought to be agreeing with her. He *did* agree with her, but there was something a little offensive at how quickly and easily she'd found a way out of the decree to be his.

"I'm afraid not," said Mr. Harcourt with a sigh. "The rest of the will outlines a dissolution of the house and outbuildings, save for the Cagneys' cottage, greenhouse, and livestock environs, should matrimony fail to occur. The baroness would rather have seen the house torn down than her will subverted."

"Her will?" repeated Hattie. "Or *her Will?*"

"Oh, here she goes," muttered Rhys, shaking his head and stalking away from her. "Willa's willing will. Will she?"

"Rhys, stop," Libba said softly. "Sit down."

In this interlude, Mr. Harcourt had nudged the stack of letters forward on the low glass table that sat in front of the chaise and sofa. Monica had retrieved them and begun to hand them to those to whom they were addressed, her expression solemn and heavy.

"So we get nothing, then?" Malcolm asked, sounding more curious than offended. "If the land is his and the house is hers."

"Not at all," Julian Harcourt corrected, a faint smile on his mouth. "There is a third element of wealth, Mr. Lennox. Money itself."

Elias pressed his lips together.

He had always known she would spend it all before he could inherit it. He had known because she'd told him so before he'd even turned thirteen. Still, it wasn't pleasant to hear again, stark and writ in legal binding.

She would force him to come along and watch her pour funds into this investment or that expansion, trying to explain to him how interest compounds or funding automates with symbiotic structures built in tandem.

He'd been too young and too stupid to really listen, at the time, and she'd known it.

"Elias, all I will leave you when I am gone is legacy, not coin. And if you understand it, you will thank me for it, so pay attention!"

He rubbed his fingers over his eyes. He could hear her so

clearly, even now. Could see the sun bouncing off her coiled, auburn hair and the way the tip of her nose turned red in unhidden frustration at his ambivalence.

Was she really dead?

"Money with stipulations, I'd wager," said Ruby Little, glancing up from her fingernails. "Isn't that right, Mr. Harcourt?"

"Of course it is," the older man replied with a chuckle. "Shall I proceed?"

Elias nodded his thanks to Miss Thresher, accepting his envelope, which felt heavier than a vessel for simply paper. He ran his fingers over it, feeling inside something metallic and round. Those weights pulled at his ribs again.

Mr. Harcourt was listing gifts for the others, properties she had bought around Brighton. A playhouse for Libba, a pavilion for Rhys, a conjoined shop for Monica and Ruby with an attached laboratory and workshop, a quarter share in a shipping company for Malcolm.

It was odd, but the barrister's voice almost seemed to melt into Willa's own shrill delivery as he read her words.

As it went on, Elias was certain she was speaking directly to them, her tone and timbre ringing out loudly in the room.

"'To Errol Cagney, I leave the greenhouse, gardens, and kennels of Starling's Rest, with my admiration. You were the only one who never needed reminding where home was,'" she said, through the mouth of Mr. Harcourt. "'And all of these things are freely given, on the basis of the following stipulations, met and attended in full.'"

Elias glanced up, frowning, and tore the end off of his own envelope, tilting it forward into his open hand.

The item inside landed, leaving the letter still nestled in its wrapping. It was a ring. A man's ring. Gold, by the look of it, and poorly kept, dented and tarnished.

It was a simple gold band.

Inside there was an inscription. Elias had to tilt it toward the light, squinting down at it to make out the words etched into the inner ring.

Mea Culpa, it read.

My fault.

"'And lastly,'" said Willa as Mr. Harcourt, "'it is my express wish and command that there shall be, in the year of my decease, a Carnival and Exhibition at Starling's Rest in the manner of those summer showcases once held under my direction. Each of my prodigies, to whom I have given so much, shall contribute their talents to this entertainment, that Brighton may remember me not with mourning, but with marvels.'"

"Oh, for the love of God," Malcolm said, frowning.

"The showcase?" Errol repeated, blinking rapidly, his voice gone hoarse. "Truly?"

"A carnival for a funeral," Rhys said, sounding thoughtful. "It is a nice idea."

Mr. Harcourt smiled despite himself. "'Furthermore, I direct that each of my said wards, together with my nephew the Baron Selwyn, shall reside within the town of Brighton for one full calendar year following my decease, the better to cement their fortunes, their reputations, and their affections. Should any fail in this, or absent themselves without due cause, their inheritance shall be forfeit and divided amongst the others who remain faithful to both my memory and my mischief.'"

That last part hung in the air.

Monica immediately burst into tears. "Oh, but Berlin," she moaned. "Oh, my work!"

Libba shot to her feet, shaking her head fervently. "My entire company is in London! Is that not due cause?!"

"A quarter share is lovely," Malcolm put in, mostly to himself, "but I still have to put in notice at the bank in London."

"I still belong to the Crown," Elias put in, closing his fist around the golden ring. "I cannot simply abandon my commission."

"No," said Ruby, batting her lashes at him, "but you could sell it, couldn't you, handsome?"

He grimaced at her.

The only one who was not reacting at all was Harriet French, who stood frozen by the window, glittering in sunlight.

She was staring not at Mr. Harcourt, nor at her fellow wards, nor at the Last Will and Testament, which now sat dormant on the glass table. Her letter hung limply in her hands. Her eyes, that stunning clash of bronze and brass and hazel and gold, were on Elias.

"These matters can be mitigated," Mr. Harcourt said, raising his hands as though to stamp down the flurry of discontent currently rising in the room. "You have your letters from the baroness. You have heard her will. Perhaps it is time that we all retreat for a moment and rest and reconvene at dinner to discuss the specifics. Does that sound reasonable?"

It didn't, as far as Elias was concerned.

None of this sounded reasonable.

But he did it, anyway, because this was Starling's Rest, and reason was never part of the equation within these walls.

He did it, anyway, because he was home.

Chapter Four

I T SEEMED TO Hattie that she had lost some time.

She was aware, of course, that Mr. Harcourt had continued speaking after the business about her being compelled to wed Elias Selwyn, but it seemed to her it had lasted only a moment.

She had watched Elias, across the room, trying to catch his eye, to communicate something of the shock they must both have been feeling and had utterly failed to capture his attention in any way. It made her wonder if she was truly standing in the room at all.

She did not come back to herself until the room had begun to empty of the others, making her utterly certain that she was standing in it, because she was about to be the only one left doing so.

"Ah, look what I found," Malcolm exclaimed, withdrawing a little wooden sword from behind a cushion. He spun and pointed it at Ruby. "Saxon or Dane?!"

"Both, you nit," she tutted, flicking the sword away with two upturned fingers. "Do you think our rooms are still in living condition?"

"They are," said Errol quietly from the dark corner where Elias had been sitting, his eyes gentle and fixed on Ruby. "They've been ready for any of you to come home at any time."

Ruby softened, turning to give him a tilting, half-smile, no flash of teeth or bat of her lashes. "That's good, then," she said. "Isn't it?"

He nodded, putting his hands in his pockets and giving her the same little smile back.

"Ugh," said Malcolm in disgust. "I'll take my sword elsewhere."

"That's been half the trouble with you all your life," Libba quipped, snatching it from him and ducking under his arm before he could take it back as she turned on her heel out of the room. "You can't be trusted with it!" she called over her shoulder, giggling as she took off down the hall.

Hattie blinked again.

Now she was uncertain she'd ever left Starling's Rest at all.

She looked down at her hands, stretching her fingers wide, and peeked down at the toes of her boots emerging from her yellow skirt.

She was an adult now.

Yes, this was all real.

The other parts had been too. She had seen the Continent. She had translated treaty negotiations and taught children fairy tales in a dozen languages. She had seen royal courts and remote villages and everything in between. She had walked sandstone paths in blazing sunlight and padded over snow deeper than two men standing foot to shoulder, with glittering palaces on one side and mud huts on the other. She had sailed and walked and ridden between idyllic meadows, towering mountains, dunes of sand, and even war-torn urban throngs.

And somehow, none of that had changed a single thing about Starling's Rest.

She needed to speak to Elias.

"Are you all right, Hattie?" Errol asked, still standing in the doorway with his hands in his pockets. "Do you need anything?"

She swallowed, dropping her hands at her sides, and shook her head. "No. No, I am well," she told him. "Are you?"

He nodded, still looking unconvinced, but didn't stop her as she walked past him out into the halls, turning left instead of right, toward the boys' rooms.

She passed by Rhys's bedroom, the door flung open as he was already making a mess of the linens.

"I know I left it here!" he cried to no one in particular. "Where the devil is it?"

She passed Malcolm's room, which was shut.

Elias's room was at the end of the hall.

She hadn't stood in front of this door in a very, very long time. If someone had asked her, some weeks ago, if she'd *ever* stood in front of it at all, she might have said *no*.

That was how long it had been.

She could almost hear the arguing behind it, echoing through the past. She could almost feel the sting of salt dried on her eyelashes and the chill of wet shoes that had picked up grit and rocks on the walk back from the pier.

"I don't want to study here! I want you to send me to Eton! Or Harrow! Or to bloody Cheapside, for all I care! Not here anymore!"

"Elias Selwyn, you are an ungrateful, spoiled, little fool," Willa had chided back. *"What's gotten into you?"*

"I can't bear it anymore. I hate it."

"You hate what?" she'd demanded. *"All the best tutors? The most brilliant minds of your age learning alongside you? The challenge?"*

"Whatever you need to believe!" he had shouted back. *"Just go away. And let me go away too!"*

Hattie blinked, the world hazy and blurred in front of her.

She shifted, half-expecting to still find sand in her shoes.

"Just come along with us after dinner," Malcolm said, emerging from Elias's door so suddenly that she startled, hopping back a step. "It'll do you some good to get out of this house."

"I'll consider it," Elias replied, sounding neither committed nor dismissive as Mal grinned and shook his head, turning back toward the hall.

"Oh," he said, spotting Hattie and hesitating on closing the door behind him. "Come to see your fiancé?"

"I need to see Elias," she replied, instead of answering.

Mal raised his dark eyebrows, stepping to the side and gesturing for her to go in.

So she did. And she heard him close the door behind her.

Elias was seated on the edge of the bed. He'd taken off his jacket and cravat and was slumped forward, staring at the carpet between his shoes, his dark hair flashing almost white where the sunlight hit it from the window.

He looked very different, Harriet thought. It wasn't only that he was grown now, or slender, or handsome. It was something else.

She couldn't quite name it.

She folded her hands in front of her and waited until he looked up at her, which he did with a sigh. "Yes?" he said, already impatient.

"I do not want to marry you," she said, quickly and without feeling.

He stared at her for a moment, his bright-blue eyes blinking once, and then he gave a hoarse chuckle, a little bark of laughter, that shook his body. "Well, thank you for that information, Harriet. I see you've still never learned how to properly communicate, despite all the languages you've mastered."

She frowned. "You do not want to marry me, either," she added, hoping that was what she had missed the first time.

It made him stare at her, incredulous. "I don't?" he said, sarcasm dripping from every consonant.

"Well, I know I am not … I am not of the usual pedigree for the likes of a baron," she reasoned. "And even if I were, I do not think you would have chosen me."

He gave a humorless chuckle, tossing something glinting and small between his palms. "Do you know anything about this?"

She took a step forward to accept something he was holding out toward her, clenched in his fist. Into her palm fell a heavy, gold ring, clearly sized for a man. She drew it close to her face, inspecting the antique pallor of its finish and tilting it to the side.

"'*Mea Culpa,*'" she read aloud, from the engraving inside the ring.

"Yes," he agreed, tightening his jaw and straining his neck from side to side. "Somehow, I suspect it is."

"What is this?" she asked, looking at him over the top of the ring. "Something Willa put in your envelope?"

He nodded, sighing and running a hand over his hair. "It was probably my uncle's. That would make the most sense, wouldn't it?"

She shook her head. "No. The baron did wear a ring, but it was silver. I don't know whose this was, but it wasn't his. He never wore gold. He used to jest that he was allergic to it and that was why the baroness handled the coin."

He grimaced, his face pulling taut in the motion. "Is that so?" he managed, sounding a bit clogged as he pushed himself to his feet. "Maybe there is an explanation, then, if I read the damned letter it came wrapped in. I haven't yet. Did you read yours?"

"My letter?" she repeated, realizing she had left it somewhere. Back in the parlor? "No. Not yet."

He nodded, reaching out to accept the ring back from her. "I suppose it will just be more of the same, anyway. 'Marry or else.' Did you know she intended this?"

"Of course not," Hattie answered, finally returning enough to herself to feel a spark of offense. "I hadn't an inkling. But that is what I came to talk about."

He twisted his lips, looking almost amused. "To express your disinterest?"

"To come to an accord," she said, taking a step toward him, as though proximity might make her better understood. "Neither of us wish for this match and we both know it, but that only provides us with the basis to enter into it with a set of clear understandings. Isn't that right?"

"'Understandings'?" he repeated, his brows ticking up a notch as she drew closer to him, close enough that he had to tilt his head down to continue to meet her eye. "Such as?"

"I don't know," she admitted, wrinkling her brow. "But it seems there ought to be some, doesn't it? I have never been married before. I have observed many marriages; all of them appear very different. Why, there is a tribe in Siberia—"

"Please do not," he said, holding his hand up between them, his palm almost to the tip of her nose. "God, you have not changed a single whit."

She huffed, twisting her hands together in her skirt. "I do not know if you have!" she shot back, her voice gone shrill. "I barely remember you at all!"

That gave him pause—or seemed to, anyway.

His hand moved slowly away, almost like a coquette's fan, revealing the faces hiding on either side of it. He looked skeptical, once she could see him again, those blue eyes narrowed. "That isn't true," he said.

"It is," she replied, desperation making her hoarse. "Years are like miles, Elias. And you are nothing of the boy I do remember, what little of him does remain. You are a stranger to me. And I …"

"You are *not* a stranger to me, Harriet French," he hissed back, drawing even closer somehow, until their toes collided, until the heat of his words brushed her cheeks as they were spoken in gusts of breath. "You are *exactly* the same."

She breathed out, exasperated as she tilted her face up to try to search for a reflection that made sense in those eyes of his. "I do not know what that means."

"Barren fields," he said, leaning down just an inch, just a breath closer as he lowered his voice. "Don't you recall?"

"'Barren fields,'" she repeated, baffled. But then there was something odd. A sting in her nose. A bleariness in her eyes. Salt in her throat. "No, I … I …"

"It'll come to you," he decided, taking a sudden step back and sending all that cool, static air in the room to swirl around her in place of where his body had been. "Think on it. You're a smart woman."

"Smarter than you," she said, so softly, she might not have said it at all.

Oddly, that seemed to please him, something like triumph flashing in his eyes as he paced backward from where she stood in the center of his room. "There she is," he said, just as softly, shaking his head, like he enjoyed the clash, despite himself. "Do come tell me, when you recall."

"Elias," she said, straightening her shoulders, blinking away the confusing onslaught of sensations and memories that were prodding and boxing her from every angle. "Are we getting married?"

He laughed then. He laughed sincerely, scratching at the back of his neck and breaking into a grin wide enough that she could see all of those even, white teeth.

"Oh, yes," he said, once the first burst of amusement had passed, though he was still smiling, still chuckling, his shoulders still shaking. "Yes, we are. Congratulations to us, my bride-to-be."

"*Mea culpa*," she said, and turned on her heel to flee.

Chapter Five

ELIAS HADN'T EXPECTED another knock on the door. Not tonight, anyway. Perhaps not ever again.

He had flopped onto his back, staring up at the dusty canopy of his childhood bed, trying to blink away the memory of Harriet French standing so close to him, flexing away the feel of the tip of her little nose against the palm of his hand, forcing himself to stay still.

He had come to live in this house on the same day she had. His bags had been from Rottingdean and hers from the foundling home down by the wharf, but their destination had been the same. And for the briefest, oddest moment, he had thought they had been the same.

She had been annoying from the start, of course, the way intelligent children often are. She had followed him, attempting to mimic his posture, the way he held silverware, the gait of his walk. She would repeat the oddest things back to him as soon as he'd said them, trying to capture his accent in her own throat.

And she hadn't been discouraged by his rudeness.

"I am Harriet," she had said to him that first night, after she'd awoken from her fainting spell. "But my people call me 'Hattie.'"

"Then I shall call you 'Harriet,'" he had responded without thinking, and it had only made her giggle.

He had been so embarrassed by that that he'd never been able to bring himself to call her 'Hattie' at all, afterward. Even when absolutely everyone else did.

Her strangeness had been oddly endearing for a time. He could admit that to himself. It had been grating but still somehow musical, because for the first time in his life, he hadn't been the only child in a room.

But then Willa had decided to expand her collection of children. In had come Malcolm with his numbers and Libba with her far-superior skills of mimickery, so startlingly accurate that it had stopped Harriet from attempting such things at all.

Then had come the boy from the stables who could teach a goat the difference between an apple and a pear. And the girl from the laundress's hut who could turn an old kitchen rag into a ballgown in miniature, who had been so, so shy but still bright and quick to smile, which had made her shyness better than Elias's.

And had made him aware of that.

They'd found Ruby peddling perfumes at the behest of the orphanage outside the grand pavilion and collecting extra coins if she could guess the ingredients of any scent a wearer already had on. Of course, she too had been immediately adopted.

By then, Elias already had wanted to vanish. To disappear. To find somewhere else to be, because it was unbearable being so damned ordinary around all these bright, young stars.

He wanted to say Rhys had been the final straw, but he hadn't been.

Barren fields had been the final straw. That day on the pier, as he'd paced and stewed and tried to reason that he was worthwhile too. That he was better than all of them, in the end, and Hattie trailing behind him, refusing to shut up. Chattering, chattering, chattering, and then hitting the sorest nerve.

Splash.

He groaned and covered his face.

Perhaps he could just stay here for the next year, have a vicar come and wed Harriet to him without even mussing the covers, and never face the outside world again.

Naturally, such a thought was immediately interrupted by a rap at the door.

He ignored it.

And it sounded again.

He grunted, pushing himself to his feet and padding over to the door, expecting perhaps Mr. Harcourt, come to talk logistics, or Malcolm here to pitch coming out to the pub after dinner again, neither of which interested him in this moment.

But it was Errol Cagney. It was the boy from the stables, all grown up, hands in his pockets, looking somehow both sheepish and friendly.

"Errol?" Elias managed, blinking twice to make sure he wasn't seeing things.

The other man gave half a smile, as though he knew his own appearance was absurd. "Mal said to come get you," he explained in that soft brogue of his. "We have to sneak out now before Mr. Harcourt starts the preparations for that dinner of his. None of us wanted to go."

"'Sneak out'?" Elias repeated dumbly. "And go where?"

Errol stared at him for a moment, then gave an incredulous little laugh, running a hand over his wispy, blond hair. "Ah, right," he said. "You were gone when we started doing this, weren't you? Off to Eton. We're going to steal out through the root cellar and go for drinks and vittles at the Coin and Cauldron. You're coming."

"I am?" asked Elias.

He was.

If it had been Mal or Rhys who'd come to get him, he might have been able to say *no* and stick to it, but how did one sternly reject the likes of Errol Cagney? By Elias's estimation, it couldn't be done.

And so he found himself shod and jacketed again, following the other man into the root cellar and up its ladder through the open hatches and into the early evening air.

"We're last," Errol said, kicking the hatch doors shut behind him. "And late. I stayed behind to help Da with the fodder and lost track of time. They've all had almost two hours now in their cups, so I imagine they'll all be intolerable. Anyhow, I always go last to make sure our tracks are covered. We used to let Rhys go last because he was the thief, but …"

"But a pickpocket is not a tactician?" Elias guessed, smirking at Errol's chuckle and nod as he followed him down a narrow dirt path that led down the hill toward the beach.

"Spot on," Errol said. "Turns out, Rhys's key aim after a crime is to get away, not to cover his tracks. I suppose that makes sense."

"Lucky for him, too," Elias noted. "Otherwise, he wouldn't be amongst us. I don't believe I've heard of the Coin and Cauldron. A public house?"

"And inn," Errol confirmed, nodding. "It was new back then, and because the owners didn't know who we were yet, we were able to get away with appearing as a group for a while. By the time the barkeep and so on had settled into Brighton proper, they were too fond of us to kick us out. I think the baroness knew, but she never bothered to drag us home or otherwise destroy the illusion that we had a safe haven."

"What about your father?" Elias asked curiously, picturing the tall, seemingly stern groom who had saddled his horses as a lad. "He doesn't seem the indulgent type."

"Doesn't he?" Errol replied with another little laugh. "You might be surprised. Few would have described the baroness as 'indulgent,' either, you know."

Elias tilted his head to the side, considering this. Willa rose in his mind, her sharp grin and oiled curls and quick laugh, and he blinked. "My mother did," he said without thinking. "She thought adopting half a dozen orphans was the very definition of indulgent."

Errol let out a gust of laughter. "If your vices are tolerating and caring for precocious children, I suppose. Not exactly a leisure activity."

"I suppose not," he agreed after a moment. *"Indulgent* is not the word I'd use, certainly. She wasn't lax so much as she was … hm."

"Strategic?" Errol suggested, pointing to a crossroads where they needed to make a left turn. "Unknowable?"

"Unknowable," Elias repeated. "Yes. I like that."

Errol glanced at him out of the corner of his eye. "Do you?"

Elias smirked again, despite himself. "No."

"At least Hattie is easy to know," Errol observed as they walked up toward the door of the pub. "If nothing else, she is direct and open, hm?"

Elias did not have the chance to respond to that, but his amusement quickly melted away as the words left Errol's mouth, even in that charming musicality of his Irish accent. He feared he was halfway to glowering the instant they walked over the threshold, even as a large cheer of welcome arose from the table in the corner, where the other wards were awaiting them, clustered like hours on a clock around a pitcher of ale.

There were a few others with them, Elias noted, hesitating to fall in step behind Errol rather than next to him.

They seemed to be men from the East India offices on the wharf, clustered around Malcolm Lennox like so many barnacles. He only recognized one of them, Malcolm's lifelong best mate Jasper Townsend, whose bright-red mane was unmistakable, even in adulthood.

Elias sighed, softly to himself.

Why had he come here?

"Oh, Elias, you decided to join us!" Ruby Little exclaimed, coming up from her chair with a splash of ale from her glass, her dark hair gleaming in the candlelight. "Come pour yourself a tipple! You can sit next to me!"

He wondered if it would be bad form to turn around and run away.

"That pitcher's almost empty," Malcolm observed from his

clutch of lads. "Shall I go buy us a new one?"

"Let me!" Rhys Caradoc exclaimed, popping up from his seat and rushing forward to grip both of Mal's hands at the wrists as though to stop him from spending more coin. "I'll get more glasses too. You relax and enjoy your reunions."

"Oh," said Mal, blinking a few times. "All right."

Rhys slipped around Elias, a grin spreading on the former's face as he flicked two golden cufflinks over his fingers, tossing Elias a wink in passing as he headed toward the bar, pocketing his take.

Part of Elias wanted to be amused by it, his eyes flicking back to Malcolm, who appeared blissfully unaware that he'd just been robbed as he chortled it up with his banker friends. The other part wanted to tattle on Rhys and ruin everyone's fun.

He frowned.

He had grown up, hadn't he?

He'd thought he had.

He never would have had that impulse back home in Hounslow. He enjoyed a night at the pub in Hounslow. He could relax there, could engage in revelry.

That had been the entire point, hadn't it? Away from this, from *them*, he was his own man. He was perfectly impressive on his own merit. He had gotten good marks in school. He had chosen to enter the service to shine his reputation further, even though a peer in the military rarely gets to actually do very much beyond ceremonial presentation and quill scratching.

He had *tried* to become someone worth being. And all the while, some part of him had always known that no matter what he achieved elsewhere, he would still belong to this odd little constellation. And he would still be its dimmest star.

He gripped his teeth together and turned his head to observe the others, his eye catching Harriet's from where she sat between Libba and Monica in the corner booth, her own ale held still to her lips as she listened to something one of the other women was saying.

"Here you go!" Ruby announced, shoving a pint glass in his hand. "Gulp it down, handsome. Maybe you'll have a bit more fun once you're a glass or three deep."

"Ruby," Errol chided, but without any real heat, accepting a second glass from her with a smile. "You know Rhys just robbed Malcolm?"

"Oh, yes," said Ruby. "Shall we place wagers on how long it takes him to notice?"

"If he notices at all," Errol replied with a chuckle.

"Come sit," Ruby said, placing a hand on either man's shoulders and steering them toward that same corner booth where Hattie was seated.

Elias grimaced and decided to take her advice, tipping the ale into his mouth as he walked and swallowing before he could taste it with any significant detail.

"So are you going to?" Monica Thresher was saying breathlessly to Libba Lennox. "Like old times."

"It's still early," Libba answered with a wave of her hand. "More strangers need to file in first. I wish I'd brought Lem with me. This bit would sell even faster with him in tow."

"Oh, it would, wouldn't it?" Hattie answered, giving a little hiccup into her cup with a curve of her lips. "He looks just like a royal bodyguard from far-flung lands should."

"Who's Lem, then?" Ruby asked, falling into her seat again as Elias and Errol sorted out their own chairs. "And why didn't you bring him with you, you selfish girl?"

"You wouldn't appeal to his tastes," Libba said soothingly to Ruby, who immediately scoffed.

"Nonsense," she said. "I whet all appetites."

"This is a game we used to play," Errol said, leaning closer to Elias, gesturing at the women. "Libba chooses a tourist and convinces him that she is foreign royalty, in Brighton at Prince George's invitation. It's gotten as far as marriage proposals a few times."

"Why would a foreign princess be in a middle-line pub?" Elias replied, baffled.

Errol just shrugged, chuckling. "I don't know if anyone's ever asked, but I suppose the unlikeliness of it only makes her pulling off the ruse all the more impressive."

"Here we are!" Rhys announced, returning with two pitchers. "Ice cold and fizzy. Who needs a top-up?"

"Oh, me!" Hattie said, holding up her empty glass, her cheeks already looking quite pink by Elias's estimation. *"Os gwelwch yn dda."*

"Ah, Hattie," Rhys said, grinning at her and pouring for her first. "Stop trying to ensorcel me in front of your new betrothed, *cariad*, or I'll run off with you."

"He wouldn't mind," she told him in a very loud whisper, then took another sip of her brew.

It made Rhys toss a look over her brassy curls at Elias and frown.

Elias wasn't even convinced that particular man was capable of a genuine frown and took considerable umbrage at having the first one he'd ever seen directed at him.

He looked around for an ally but found only Libba borrowing an earring from Ruby and looping it through a scarf that she'd taken from Monica, then dangling it over her forehead as a sort of royal wrap in an effect he had to admit looked both foreign and convincing.

"Good?" she said to the other two women, who cooed in encouragement.

"Oh, no, you don't!" Rhys called with a chuckle from his pitcher duties. "Not before I've had a chance to do a trick."

"But he's already …" Elias began, only to immediately be shushed by Ruby and Errol.

"You, sir!" Rhys boomed at one of Malcolm's hangers-on while Libba quickly stowed her makeshift disguise. "How would you like to see some magic?"

Rhys produced a rope and a flashing pair of scissors, launching into a diatribe about how he had the power to mend the fibers after they'd been shorn, drawing the attention of some of the other guests, who drifted nearer as he climbed onto a chair to waggle his rope at the group.

Elias blinked, sipping his ale, and tried not to reflect on how odd it was to wander around with scissors in one's trousers.

"Oh, I know this one," Malcolm's friend said, his eyes brightening. "You can buy it in a kit from that shop on the boardwalk. There's a string inside the rope."

Rhys hesitated, narrowing his eyes at him. "What shop?" he snapped.

"Miss Persephone's Oddities and Curiosities," the man replied, slurring in his enthusiasm. "She sells magic tricks there! This one is in the window. Did you buy it from her?"

"Oh!" said Monica, clapping a cupped hand over her mouth while Ruby simply turned her own lips inward as though she were biting them shut.

"Miss Persephone," Rhys repeated, every syllable over enunciated and dripping with venom. "Opened a … a shop. And she sells … She … Where is this shop, pray, my good man?"

Errol cleared his throat, ducking his head as he sipped his own ale, but it was too late, Rhys had already spun around and thrown a pointed finger in his direction. "Did you know about this, Errol?"

"Me?" said Errol, blinking with an attempt at guilelessness. "I barely go into town."

Rhys gave a little snarl, hopping off the chair with his knees so high, he appeared to hover in space for a moment before landing on the ground, as quiet and steady as a cat. "Where is it?" he demanded, prowling toward the exit. "Down toward the grand pavilion? Ohh, I should have known!"

He didn't wait for an answer, stalking out and slamming the door behind him with a little jingle of the pub's bell as he went, muttering Welsh expletives under his breath.

"That means a jam jar that has someone's flatulence sealed inside," Hattie provided helpfully, hiccupping again and then giving a soft giggle. "*Mownt pot jam.* That wouldn't work, would it?"

"Let's never find out," Libba said, patting her on the head. "Now find me a mark."

"What was the other thing you said to Rhys?" Monica asked, tilting her head. "That made him call you *cariad.*"

"*Os gwelwch yn dda,*" Hattie answered, enunciating carefully. "Literally it translates to 'if you see it, good,' but it just means 'please.' And he has always called me '*cariad.*'"

"He has," Monica acknowledged. "That one means 'my heart,' right? He calls all the girls that, except me."

"What does he call you?" Libba asked curiously.

Monica giggled and sipped her ale. "'*Chwaer.*' It means 'sister.' Perhaps he was worried I'd take *cariad* to heart."

Libba pursed her lips. "Or perhaps you're just his favorite."

"Call him '*brawd,*'" Hattie suggested. "It means 'brother.' Even though Rhys is rather narrow."

"Oh, I remember you!" the same man who'd ruined the rope trick exclaimed, his eyes locking on Hattie. "The girl with all the languages! Can you still do that trick? Five ways to say a thing off the top of your head?"

Hattie blinked at him, a little bleary. "Do I know you?"

"Can you still do it?" he asked again instead of answering. "How about … hm … *your mum's a yellow dog with the mumps?*"

Hattie stared at him, blinking a few times and then sighed and nodded, pushing herself to her feet. She swiped up the remainder of her glass, which was only about a quarter full now, and held it as she stepped onto the booth to stand above the others, thrusting it out above them all as they turned their attention to her.

"*Ta mère est une chienne jaune avec les oreillons,*" she announced, stomping her foot once to a wave of light applause. "*Deine Mutter ist eine gelbe Hündin mit Mumps! Din mor er en gul hund med fåresyge!*"

Elias stared at her, stomping and announcing maternal insults in various languages, his heart climbing up to lodge in his throat.

Every new translation drew a louder cheer from the assembled crowd as she grinned, sipped her ale, and swished her skirts around. *"Tha do mhàthair 'na cù buidhe le a' phlàigh nan cnàmhan!"* she cried, raising the glass with its little wisp of foam still swirling at the bottom, stomping again at the cheer. "And fifth ... hm." She pondered, teetering a little on her pedestal, then brightening and holding her glass up in a toast and crying, *"Tvoya mat'. Zhyóltaya sobáka, bol'náya svínkoy!! Vashe zdaróv'ye!"*

The room roared at the final translation and several of the onlookers joined her in knocking back the remainders of what was in their glasses as she collapsed into Libba's and Monica's waiting arms, giggling to herself in a slump of poofed-out yellow skirts and bronzed, bouncing curls falling over her brow.

Elias stared down at his own drink, spitting out the odd, lazy bubble opposite Hattie's effervescent performance, and frowned.

"Cheers," Errol Cagney said, tapping his glass against Elias's with a knowing smirk. "Or *vashe zdaróv'ye*, I suppose."

Chapter Six

HATTIE HAD, EVENTUALLY, worked up the courage to go speak to Elias Selwyn again.

Unfortunately, she had done so after enough pints of ale that her vision was wobbly, and she wasn't entirely sure he was still inside the pub.

She gripped the table, hunched over a cache of empty glasses, searching the crowd for a well-combed top of dark hair or perhaps a flash of those lovely, blue eyes, but saw only Libba, dressed as Princess Xandine of the African Isles, winning a third gift from a group of admirers in a corner near the bar, and Malcolm being hassled to perform his numbers trick from his banker friends.

"Go on, Mal," Jasper Townsend encouraged him, grinning over his own drink, gone almost as red as his hair. "You know you love to do it."

"Oh, all right, all right," Malcolm had allowed, shrugging off his jacket and wiggling his fingers as he prepared to dazzle the masses. It wasn't until his touch fell onto the fabric at his wrist, with the intent of rolling up his sleeves, that his expression fell.

There was a ticking few seconds while his face registered disbelief that his golden cufflinks were gone and then outrage, and then his head snapped up. "Rhys!" he boomed. "Where is that little bastard?!"

"Gone," Monica said wanly from her spot flat on her back in the booth seats, her wisps of blonde hair falling off the edge as she looked at Malcolm from an upside-down perspective. "Gone to slay Miss Persephone, remember?"

"I will kill … I will … maim!" Malcolm was sputtering, as his friends dissolved into guffawing laughter.

Hattie frowned.

It seemed Elias had left as well.

She couldn't find him.

"'*Flatulence in a jar*,'" she murmured to herself, dejected, as she sank back to sitting.

It wasn't until Errol came and lifted her up that she realized she had gone directly to the pub floor, her legs crossed under her skirt, instead of landing in a chair.

"All right, then," he decided, not outright laughing at her but clearly hiding the urge. "You too, Monica. Let's go home."

"Oh, spoilsport," Monica said dreamily, more of her hair tumbling out of its chignon from her head's dangling position over the corner of the booth cushion.

It took him another quarter hour to wrangle the rest of them, especially since he had to do so with Libba by sending her hand signals and meaningful glares from across the room, lest her ruse be discovered, but he did manage it.

They marched back to Starling's Rest after him as the sky turned a yawning violet, the sun tickling under the horizon with all its threats of daylight and consequences.

Ruby yawned heavily from the front, collapsing against Errol as they walked, her skirt sagging and picking up grit from the ground as she wove around on the dirt path. "D'you think Mr. Harcourt is very cross? Is he our papa now?"

"He is *not*," Monica said, as sternly as she was able, which was to say, as gentle as a lamb.

"Oh, no?" Ruby tittered. "Don't want a little discipline from the silver barrister, Miss Thresher?"

Which got Malcolm tittering too until Monica turned the

corner with her face hidden in her hands.

"I'd let him paddle me," Libba put in, if only to immediately silence her brother.

Whether or not he had assumed the status of their new, disapproving parental figure, Julian Harcourt was, in fact, awaiting them at the entrance to Starling's Rest, arms crossed and face unamused as they swayed and stumbled their way back up the drive.

"There's food in the dining room," he said, stepping aside to usher them in. "Soak some of that up before you go to sleep."

"Oh, Mr. Harcourt," Monica said, pink as a peony. "Are you cross?"

He only sighed in response, patting her on the shoulder as he waved her inside.

Rhys was at the table, stabbing a boiled egg with a fork he was wielding like a skewer, and glanced up at them with a glower as they filed in, falling one at a time on the basket of bread and the platters of meat and eggs.

Only Errol hesitated, sighing at the spread.

"Still don't eat meat?" Malcolm asked curiously, stuffing a sausage in his mouth. "Shame."

"There's bread and cheese, Errol," Ruby said, already making a second plate next to her own. "And an egg, if you like?"

"No egg," he said, grimacing at the one Rhys was brutalizing.

"Where is Elias?" Hattie asked, finding a chair and falling into it sidesaddle as she pulled a bun across the table and tore it in half.

No one seemed to know, a series of shrugs going around the table.

"Did you find Miss Persephone's?" Libba asked Rhys, leaning closer to observe the carnage he was delivering on that egg and then sprinkling some salt onto it. "Or better, Miss Persephone herself?"

"It was closed," he ground out, tossing his fork away in evident disgust now that someone had been thoughtful to his egg. "And she's likely still hanging upside down in the cave underneath it, plotting."

"If she were a bat," Monica said thoughtfully, "wouldn't she be awake and open at night instead of the other way 'round?"

"Yes," said Errol.

"Be silent," said Rhys.

"Persephone ..." Ruby was mulling, absently cutting her cheese into little chunks. "That's so familiar."

"She was the little Traveller girl who also did illusions with Rhys at the summer exhibitions, wasn't she?" Malcolm said, raising his eyebrows. "They had a falling out, remember? But we didn't call her 'Persephone.' I believe she went by—"

"Seph!" Monica and Libba exclaimed in unison, both looking delighted as Rhys melted further into his chair.

"I'm going to bed," he announced, flinging himself from the table and stalking away.

"My, my," Ruby observed, watching him go. "Someone's harried."

Hattie realized she was falling asleep mid-mastication, bread still held aloft between her molars, and blinked sleepily at her fellow wards. "Did I eat enough?" she asked, swallowing with some effort and reaching across the table for one of the pre-poured glasses of fruit juice. "I'm so very tired."

"One sausage link," Malcolm decided, "and two cubes of cheese. And you can go."

"Oh, all right," Hattie said, frowning as she accepted her sentence on a small, white plate. "All right."

She forced it down and stood, pleased that Monica decided to walk with her to the girls' wing, and wondered if she could even be bothered to get out of her dress before falling into bed. She said as much to Monica, who shook her own head, tugging at her collar with a sigh.

"So many layers," she bemoaned. "If only I could snap my fingers and be bare, in nothing but a nightrail."

"Bare in," Hattie repeated with a sleepy smile. "Baron."

"Hm?" said Monica.

"Barren," Hattie continued, pausing, and frowning. "Barren Fields."

Monica stopped, turning around with a wrinkle of her brow. "Harriet? You're delirious."

"I … No," she said, shaking her head and holding a hand up. "I'm … almost recalling something. I … think?"

"Hattie," Monica said, her voice gone soothing like it would to reason with a feral cat. "Come on, let's get you to bed."

Hattie let herself be shuffled into her bedroom, but her mind was clawing itself back awake, the words tumbling over one another, climbing over their own syllables, swinging through their vowels, and clambering atop the consonants of each other.

"That man called you 'my lord.' Sometimes I forget that you are the baron now. Baron Elias. That is very fine. You must be proud. Or excited. Or both. I know I would be.

"But baron is a funny sort of title, isn't it? It sounds like 'barren,' which is a bad thing. You know, like barren women or barren fields. And Fields is quite a common surname. Can you imagine if your inherited barony was from an estate called Fields? You'd be Baron Fields!"

She collapsed forward onto the bed, her hands catching in the blankets just the way they had caught in the surf that day, when Elias had punted her right off the edge of the pier and into the water, mid-ramble.

She drew in a deep breath, certain she could taste the briny Channel water in her mouth, her skin erupting in gooseflesh.

Christ, but that had been insensitive, hadn't it?

He had lost his uncle.

He had been born to an unusual family, one where the patriarch spent most of his life waiting to die. His mother had married the baron's younger brother, perhaps anticipating the eventual shift of power, but he too had died while she had been still pregnant with Elias. She'd then married the closest male cousin, Elias's stepfather, Wallace Selwyn, for good measure.

Elias had been born as a placeholder regardless. An expectation of death. Heir to a doomed man.

And she'd called him …

Barren fields.

She moaned, her head throbbing, and climbed into the bed, pushing her face into a pillow.

She'd been all of twelve years old that day, hadn't she? Certainly no more than thirteen. She had wanted nothing in the world so much as Elias Selwyn's friendship back then. His approval. His …

Was he really still upset about that?

Really?

Hadn't he gotten her back in turn by shoving her into the blasted ocean?

Hattie pulled the pillow up around her face and over her ears, as though she could stifle the sound of thoughts that were coming from inside her head, which of course was ridiculous. She squeezed her eyes shut and instructed herself in a dozen different tongues to *sleep*.

Because that always worked.

She sighed, rolling onto her back and opening her eyes a sliver, just enough to glare through her lashes at the cheery sunlight starting to peek in through her curtains.

She was going to have a bottle ache.

She knew it.

Why had she forgotten about that day on the pier? Shame? Anger?

She remembered coming up out of the water, furious and confused and spitting salt water, clawing her way up the shingles and onto the shore in her ruined muslin dress. Elias had just been standing there, staring at her vacantly, like he couldn't quite believe he'd done what he had.

He hadn't apologized or gloated or *anything*. He'd just turned and walked away.

And then Willa had let him go to Eton.

Hattie sat up, groaning and moving to pull the pins out of her hair. At least she'd give herself some small chance of comfort, she thought. She could loosen her hair and undress. She could do that.

She could take the dress off. It felt oddly like salt-starched, soggy muslin against her skin now, anyhow.

When she stood and paced across the room to drop the pins in the little bowl on her vanity table, she spotted the envelope tucked under it.

For Hattie.

Her heart gave an aching, little lurch at Willa's handwriting, her hands trembling as she released the pins with a tinkling series of clinks into the little holding bowl.

She ought to read it, she knew.

She wondered if any of the others had read theirs yet.

The only contents anyone had spoken of, at least in her hearing, came down to that curious gold ring.

Mea culpa.

She frowned, snatching up the letter and marching back over to her bed as she loosened the ties on her bodice. She flicked the wax seal apart and tossed it on the rumpled covers as she pulled the dress over her head and worked at the strings of her half stays, looking at the way the letter peeped tantalizingly over the flap of the envelope, spiky writing showing through the thin paper.

She kicked the dress and stays into a pile, shaking her hair free, and climbed in with the letter, her shift breezing pleasantly over her body underneath. *Bare in*, she thought, twisting her lips as she pulled the sheet of paper from its envelope and unfolded it carefully. *Baron. Barren.*

The handwriting hit her like a gong in the center of her chest.

She'd have known Willa's pen anywhere. In any language. On any parchment.

For a moment, the writing itself seemed to swim, meaningless and narrow, just slashes of ink on the page as memories battled up against the tide of the shapes they made.

Had it really been seven years since she'd gotten a letter from this woman? Had it really been that long?

They had all written to one another feverishly in the begin-ning, when adulthood had pulled them in half a dozen sparkling and thrilling far-flung directions. Weekly, Hattie would rush to the post from her tour of the Continent with that erstwhile chaperone, onto the year she'd spent trading herself as a research subject in exchange for access to study at a Swiss university. They would all write, back and forth, bubbling over with enthusiasm for all the new things life was offering.

It was only as the years had started to pass that the letters had slowed. They'd slowed and slowed and eventually stopped.

And she had not noticed at all.

Hattie gave a shaky little sigh, blinking away the veil of warm, salty regret that had welled over her vision, and shook her head.

Here was one last letter, anyhow, she reasoned.

Whether she deserved it or not.

To My Darling Harriet,

This is the first letter I am writing with the thought that I might someday be dead. It is an odd thing to ponder, isn't it? But I will be, so must we all at some point.

When I met with Mr. Harcourt this afternoon to discuss my wishes for the things I carried in this life and their fates upon my demise, I had only one wish at the outset: that you, my girl, would be my primary heiress.

I told him Hattie should be baroness. I want nothing less.

And he had, of course, laughed in that way of his and told me I was being a ninny. Perhaps he would have kept laughing, if we hadn't gotten to a particular clause concerning the house itself, which holds a deed apart from the demesne.

Ah, but you aren't the only clever one, are you, Hattie? I have my talents too. And you shall be baroness, which was my wish, after all.

I know you might be cursing my name in the wake of the reading of my final wishes and wondering what matter of madness had overtaken me to bind you to my nephew forever. I shall tell you—it is the madness of a life lived long enough to have gathered some degree of wisdom about matrimony.

You and Elias always had a strange dynamic between you. You followed, curious and eager, while he bristled and hid and glowered. I really did not wish to send him away, for I knew it would turn into something else entirely if the two of you were allowed to blossom into young adulthood in one another's company.

But alas, sometimes the demands of necessity force us out of our plans and wishes.

I only take comfort that I can meddle now, from the Fields of Elysium, and that one day, you shall go to my grave, sit upon the bench next to it, and tell me I was right. Below the dirt, on that day, I will smile, as I am smiling now.

Stay strong, my darling girl.

You are going to be a fine baroness.

All my love,
Willa Starling Selwyn—your mother in my heart.

Part II

The Shape of Things

Chapter Seven

ELIAS HADN'T HAD anything more after that first pint, but he had remained for another hour so, unable to tear himself away from observing what must have been some sort of rehearsal for the dowager baroness's imminent funeral.

He remembered their summer showcases very well, of course, though he had only ever attended two of them.

The first two.

Willa had called each of them 'a gauntlet' and 'an opportunity,' a yearly chance to show the world that talent trumps all. There was nowhere else in the world like Brighton to do something so audacious. Prince George had still been young then, but his fashionable exodus to the Brighton shores had already begun to catch, as well as the attractions under the grand pavilion and smaller stages dotted down the coast.

She would spend weeks bringing in experts, hiring propmakers, and rehearsing with her wards so that their showcase would outshine every other act put before the denizens of Brighton that summer. The festivities were, without question, the highlight of the year, not just for Willa, but for every one of her wards, save Elias.

He imagined they had only grown in scale and grandeur during his years away at school. He could close his eyes and see it now, under a shaded pavilion in the summer sun, the surf high and the smell of salt in the air while lanky, adolescent Rhys pulled scarves from his mouth and Malcolm performed unseemly feats of counting and calculation to applause.

Errol had always come with a grange display and a few of his pets to do tricks. It was never something so pedestrian as a dog. No, no. He would have a rabbit sitting and standing on command or a duck hopping through hoops. One very notable time, he'd trained a spider to answer commands.

Ruby, blindfolded, would identify scents and foods and combinations, already flirting with adults she couldn't see from behind the blinders on her eyes.

He shook his head, running a hand over his own eyes as he lay in bed, back to the sun. He might have even enjoyed all of that, if he'd seen it as a guest, rather than as the only child in the house without an act.

"What's my talent?" he had asked Willa once, hoping she might know the secret.

"You are a baron," she had answered, shrugging. Then, perhaps realizing how she'd sounded, she'd put a hand on his shoulder and turned him to face her, amending the statement with, "You are like me. People like us got the luck of birth, so we have to try a little harder elsewhere. It is how the universe keeps balance."

He sighed.

Maybe she'd been right.

He could hear Hattie's boot stomping on that bench tonight as the pub-goers cheered for her nonsense insults in half a dozen languages.

God, she'd been magnificent up there. And it had been nothing at all to her. Just a funny skill she had, a thing she could do without much trying.

Insufferable.

He'd never been quite so irritated by someone before, and he'd met plenty of unbearable people at school. And in the military.

Plenty and more.

A flash of her collapsing back on that bench, her skirts flouncing up around her like an exploded dandelion, played behind his eyes, her brassy hair tickling her cheeks. It sent a spear of heat into his belly that was just as unwelcome as everything else about her.

Insufferable, he thought again. *Perfectly irritating.*

Glorious.

Something about her had always just been … glorious.

He wondered how many languages she spoke now.

He wondered how many foreign men had discovered her brilliance in all the strange and distant lands and royal courts she'd visited.

There again, a spear of heat, though this one burned a little differently.

He grimaced and opened his eyes, his gaze settling on that damned gold ring on his bedside table.

The ring that thought this was his fault.

The ring made him think about logistics. About banns and registrations and selling or at least getting a hold put on his commission with the cavalry. It kept his mind spinning for long enough to begin to lull him into something resembling rest, until mercifully, he blinked and the sun had made its way fairly high into the afternoon sky.

There was next to no staff in this house, after it having been closed for so long, with only a few servants who'd made a life of this place lingering to keep it from crumbling to dust. He'd left his cavalry valet back in Hounslow, not realizing how long he would be stuck in Brighton. As such, Elias saw to his own toilette and change of clothes, shaving himself clean and ensuring that he was crisp and alert to face this new day.

He was going to need to have some unpleasant conversations, both with the barrister and with his bride-to-be. He reasoned that he may as well feel presentable while he did it.

If he expected everyone else to meet him in kind, he was

sorely mistaken.

Those who were awake at this late hour were either slumped in the dining room, picking at an assortment of cold meats and cheeses that had been laid out in lieu of luncheon, or wandering the halls in their dressing gowns, complaining about the brightness of the sunlight.

He realized, in quick order, that he had left far, far earlier than he realized, given the scope of the night that had apparently transpired.

Good. It would be nice to have an advantage for a change.

In fact, he used to fantasize about exactly this sort of thing. He'd lie in bed at Eton and imagine coming back to Starling's Rest as an accomplished, impressive, impervious adult and stunning them all into slack-jawed silence. A childish fantasy, but perhaps still one hiding somewhere in his ribs, regardless.

At the very least, that bent of childishness had kept his marks high and his aspirations focused. It had pushed him to shed his baby fat, hone his mind, and seek commendation. There was something to be said for that, at least.

He'd excelled at almost everything he'd attempted from the first day he'd arrived at Eton. He'd made friends. He'd won fencing competitions. He'd learned to ride for both practicality and performance. For the first time, he had been able to swell with pride at a professor's accolade without suspecting it had been a consolation in the shadow of true genius.

And he had gotten many such accolades.

Many.

It was worth remembering, even if he never told the others about it. It was worth reminding himself that one did not have to be a prodigy to be a success.

And in any event, he was the only one of them smart enough to have gotten through to this morning without the pain of liquid regret.

He strode into the kitchen, feeling brisk and superior, and smiled brightly at the assembled wilted flowers. "Morning, all," he sang, reaching for a strip of bacon. "Is Mr. Harcourt about? Or Harriet?"

Bleary eyed, Rhys glanced up at him from his position near the bread basket and shook his head, standing up as though his stomach had just turned. "Well," he said, palming the side of his head where all his brown curls were completely flattened against his scalp, "aren't you fresh?"

And then he strode out, murmuring to himself.

"That means *'passing wind in a jar,'*" Monica put in helpfully. "We learned it last night."

"Charming," said Elias, rounding the table to choose something from the bread basket. He had his hand outstretched toward one of the butter rolls on top before he noticed something odd about the one at the top of the tower, freezing mid-grab.

It had two golden eyes, shaped suspiciously like rectangular cufflinks, and a jagged smile made of plum preserves.

He blinked at it for a moment, uncertain if he was astounded or amused.

Malcolm Lennox, whose head had been nested in the crook of his elbow, muttered something against the table, then, realizing his voice was not traveling through the wood, sighed and looked up. "Parlor," he said, his voice dry and crackly. "God, I used to be better at this."

"Parlor," Elias repeated, taking up the bun with a face and tossing it in Malcolm's direction. "I think this is yours."

Mal caught it on reflex, surprise registering on his face as Elias turned and strode out of the dining room, grinning to himself as he tore one of the other, unmolested buns in half and popped a piece of fresh bread in his mouth.

A few moments later, there was a booming cry of, *"Rhys!"*

Followed by an impish giggle somewhere in the halls.

Elias allowed himself a light chuckle, rounding down the hall toward the front of the house and passing by Errol, who was fully dressed, and Ruby, who was in a sagging, velvet dressing gown with a steaming cup of tea in her hands.

"Three weeks just isn't enough time to grow anything worthy of a grange," he was saying to her as she yawned behind her hand. He glanced up at Elias, nodding in greeting, just as a series of raps sounded on the door behind them.

"Oh, you were right," Ruby said absently. "Someone *is* at the door."

"I'll get it," Elias offered, stepping around them.

It gave him an opportunity to pass near to the parlor without going in, lest there be something worth overhearing.

Sadly, the only voice he heard was Libba Lennox's, ranting about housing accommodations for a dozen people she apparently had plans to ship in from London for the funeral.

"Lem can stay in the house, but the rest of them will make off with the crockery," she announced.

Elias sighed and turned toward the door, where another series of crisp raps sounded. "I'm coming, I'm coming," he muttered under his breath, grabbing the knob and swinging the damned thing open.

On the stoop was the bright-faced, ginger-haired visage of Jasper Townsend, Malcolm's best mate and lifelong fixture of Starling's Rest, even during Elias's short tenure here. He looked just as fresh and chipper as Elias himself felt, turned out in a crisp, gray day suit.

"Ah," Jasper said, blinking in surprise. "Well, sink me. Lord Selwyn? You answering your own door?"

"We have to hire a staff," Elias said with a shrug, stepping back. "Malcolm's in the dining room. Did you leave early last night?"

"'Course not," said Jasper, hopping into the house. "Why?"

"No reason," said Elias, instinctively retreating inward.

No, he thought. *You're a man now.*

"It's only that all the others look like they were dragged home behind a horse," he added immediately, squaring his shoulders.

Jasper turned to him with a blindingly bright grin. "Really? Even Mal?"

"Especially Mal," Elias assured him.

Jasper chortled. "Well, out of practice, aren't they? Still, must go gloat. Cheerio, Baron."

"Morning," Elias managed to answer, a little dazed by it all as he watched the other man lope down the hall past Ruby and Errol toward his quarry.

Libba emerged from the parlor just as he passed it, nearly colliding with him, and gave him an earful about his carelessness the rest of the way to the dining room.

"My apologies, Princess Xandine!" he answered bombastically as their voices faded down the hall. "Don't have me beheaded!"

"It would take too long to carve off that kettle of yours," Libba snapped back. "My headsman needs his strength."

Elias shut the door slowly and craned his neck side to side.

This place was still a madhouse.

He scratched at his hair, glancing into a hallway mirror as he passed it, just to remind himself that he was not still a pudgy, uncertain child, and sighed, shaking his head at his own foolishness.

What was it about people from the past that dragged one straight back to the place they'd been in the last time they'd been amongst them?

It hardly seemed fair.

At least they'd taken verbal note of his transformation, for what that was worth.

Or Ruby had, anyway.

He grimaced, making his way into the parlor.

Harriet French was reclining on a chaise in a striped dressing gown of vibrant marigold and black, holding a cool compress made up of a folded, damp towel to her head. He watched Mr. Harcourt through one eye as he spoke. Her long mane of spiraling, brassy hair was loose down her shoulders and catching along her arms and elbows, her thin sleeping shift visible in slivers through the cracks of the robe.

Oddly, Harcourt seemed utterly unaffected by this display,

more interested in the notes he was taking than the sprawl of feminine beauty slathered out in front of him.

Elias tensed, resisting the urge to snatch a coverlet from the nearest surface and drape it over her, head and all. "Good morning," he said, far more tersely than he intended.

"Oh," she said, wincing as though the syllable had hurt her. "Elias."

"Harriet," he returned, still clipped as thin as a freshly shorn sheep.

"Lord Selwyn," the barrister said, glancing up over the top of his rarely used spectacles. "We are discussing the arrangement of a staff. Perhaps this is of interest to you?"

"It is," he agreed, looking around and settling on a chair that would form an uneven triangle, bringing him nearer to the safe starchiness of Mr. Harcourt than Hattie's languid flesh. "I just had to answer the front door."

"How terrible for you," she murmured, flopping onto her back and dropping the cool compress over both of her eyes, sadly before she could clock the way he glared at her insolence.

"'The door'?" Mr. Harcourt repeated with a frown. "Have we visitors already? I have not prepared."

"It was just Jasper Townsend," said Elias with a lift of his shoulder. "Not anyone of note."

"Townsend," the barrister said, tapping the edge of his quill to his chin. "Shipyard boy?"

Elias nodded. "Here to see Malcolm."

"Well, that's fine, then," Harcourt decided. "I would've come to find you, but as the house belongs to Miss French, I assumed the staff details would go through her primary decision-making for the time being, given that we are looking at several weeks before nuptials can be executed."

"Three," Harriet muttered from behind her mask of pain. "Chimes and candy."

Elias glared at her again.

"One, two, three," she continued, oblivious. "It's green, you know."

"Do I have to marry her?" he snapped at the barrister, who ignored him, chuckling to himself.

"Not a dark green," Hattie continued, slurring a little. "Very soft, like mint rolled into marzipan."

"Yes, all right," Elias said impatiently. "Did you decide on which positions to fill?"

She nodded, making the wet towelette tumble down over her nose and onto her mouth before making a leap over her chin and onto her bosom.

Elias certainly did not watch its progress with keen, unwavering interest.

She had been in Russia this last year. He'd read about it in *The Chronicle.*

"British Beauty Translates for Tsar."

It hadn't named her, but he'd known, anyhow. He'd known it had been her. That Russian toast last night had only cemented his suspicion.

Had she said things like this to the tsar?

"Necessary woman," she said, holding up fingers as she spoke. "Cook. Maid-of-all-work. Three!"

"Butler?" he prompted, eyes on her other hand as she fumbled for the bottle. "Footmen? I need a valet."

"I s'pose," she said, immediately falling into a yawn.

Elias, hating himself, immediately yawned too.

"Oh, goodness," said Mr. Harcourt, yawning as well. "Well, that won't do. I'll just go fetch us some coffee from the dining room, shall I? And then we should discuss wedding particulars."

He stood before either could answer him, dropping his notes on the chair where he'd been sitting, and left so quickly that Elias had to wonder if he'd somehow chased the man out.

He looked back to Hattie, wondering if she felt the same, but she'd already splayed the damp compress back over her face and was smiling softly to herself, her fingers laced over her chest.

"Three," she muttered happily, under her breath.

Chapter Eight

IT TOOK MR. Harcourt an unseemly long time to pour a few cups of coffee. Hattie began to wonder if perhaps he'd gotten waylaid.

She lay there, hiding under her compress, even though her head had stopped throbbing some time ago, because it was sufficient shelter from the gaze of Elias Selwyn.

The Russian prince who'd gifted her this dressing gown had told her he'd chosen it for her because she reminded him of a tigress, but Hattie couldn't have felt less fearsome in that moment if she'd tried. If anything, the marigold and obsidian stripes likely made her look more like a crushed bumblebee than a prowling predator.

"Is there no cook already?" Elias asked suddenly, startling her. "Where did all that food in the dining room come from if there isn't one?"

"What?" she said, grappling for the compress and pulling it down over one eye to peep at him. "What are you asking?"

"You said we needed to hire a cook," he reminded her, watching her with a faintly bemused air and something that might have been a smile. Was he laughing at her dishevelment? "If we don't have one, who prepared breakfast?"

"Oh," she said, releasing a little sigh of relief at the fact that she knew the answer to his question. "Mr. Harcourt hired someone temporarily from town, but I believe that person made it clear that she is not available on a permanent basis."

"I see," he replied, leaning onto his elbow and rubbing his fingers over his mouth, like he was attempting not to laugh at her. "Harriet, are you still drunk?"

She considered it, frowning. "Yes, I might be. A little. You see, I have been drinking a distilled alcohol made of fermented potatoes for the last year or so back in Russia and I thought, well, I assumed, that a spot of ale would be nothing at all in comparison. But I think perhaps I misjudged the quantity, or perhaps I misjudged the amount one is able to imbibe of a drink that does not burn on the way down."

"Alas," he replied, his lips twitching. "A tragic mistake."

"Go ahead and laugh, Elias," she said sourly. "I know that you want to."

And so he did, though at least it was understated.

She glared, anyway.

"I am sorry," he said, holding his hands up in apology. "I have simply never seen you compromised in such a way before. You are usually so … so …"

"Dignified?" she suggested.

"Rigid," he decided, tittering again. "I don't mind it."

"Elias," she said again, sinking back onto the chaise and dropping the compress onto her scalp rather than her eyes. "I have always liked your name. Do you know why?"

"Because it has three syllables?" he guessed, those bright-blue eyes watching her attempt to find a comfortable position. "And three pleases you so very much?"

"Oh, it does, doesn't it?" she exclaimed, blinking. "But no. No, it is because of its shape. It is serpentine, isn't it? Smooth and equally bent on all sides."

"I don't know what that means, Harriet," he said, still sounding rather amused. "It isn't because I am minty and candied due to my syllables? 'Chimes,' you said?"

"You? No, never," she said, wrinkling her brow. "You are

nothing like three. No, it is the shape of the thing. Syllables are important too, of course, and the more you have, I suppose the more detailed the feeling of a word. Do you know which country has the most marvelous multi-syllabic names?"

"Russia?" he guessed, resigning himself to lean on his hand.

"Oh, Russia is a very good guess," she said, smiling to herself. "Did you know I've just come from Russia? I met a Prince Kontarovsky while I was there. He gave me this dressing gown. Kontarovsky. Isn't that lovely? It sounds like a bouncing ball."

"Does it?"

"It is the Greeks, however," she continued. "The Greeks have the most delicious names. Fiorentinos, like sap dripping in a spiral down a tree. Papadopoulos, like a child blowing bubbles from under a bath full of warm water. Konstantinidis, like a handful of marbles falling down a tall, wooden staircase. So much color and texture and flavor. I love it."

"I can see that you do," he answered, though his expression had changed. He almost looked displeased now. "A prince gave you negligee?"

"Oh, it doesn't mean the same thing that it does here," she said, waving her hand.

"I find that difficult to believe," he replied, straightening in the chair and running his eyes over the fabric of her robe. "I think the connotation of a gift like that is the same universally."

"What?" she said, blinking rapidly. "I meant the title. Prince is not … It is like a count or an earl, you see. An actual son of the tsar, or king, if you will, would actually be a grand duke in Russia. It is wonderfully confusing."

He was staring at her, a deep line between his dark brows.

She cleared her throat and ran her hands self-consciously over the fabric of the robe, which only seemed to draw his eyes back down to it again. "I have been to Greece, you know," she said, a little too shrill and rapid for her own tastes, but she got the words out all the same. "When Willa sent me on my Continental tour, that was the stop where I lost my chaperone to a swarthy

Corinthian with green eyes. She's still there. They have five children. I ought to have found another one after that, but I could never be fussed. None would have been as good and I was old enough by then, anyhow."

"Harriet," he said, flatly.

"I should write to her," Hattie continued. "Oh, Mr. Harcourt! You return."

The barrister was hovering in the doorway with a tray of coffee and its garnishes, mugs, and what appeared to be freshly cut fruit. "Shall I give you some privacy?" he asked, looking from Hattie to Elias and back again. "I wouldn't mind."

"Absolutely not!" she exclaimed. "A stimulant is supposed to be just the thing for a headache, you know! Thank you for fetching it."

"Your dressing gown isn't stimulating enough?" Elias asked under his breath, winning a narrow-eyed look from her.

Either Mr. Harcourt did not hear the comment, or he was choosing not to hear it. Hattie supposed it did not matter which.

"I was going to inquire," the barrister said, setting the tray down and seeing to his own cup, "if either of you are interested in looking into a special license. I only ask because if we go down the traditional route with banns being read, your wedding will by necessity fall on the same week as the funeral, which seems a little foreboding to me."

"Whyever does it?" Elias replied with a tight smile, sipping his coffee straight from the pot, without even a fleck of sugar. "Sounds appropriately auspicious to me."

"Would the banns be read here?" Hattie asked, tilting her head curiously. "I don't know if the parish considers us Brighton residents anymore. I have been abroad for some time, and Elias resides in … erm?"

He turned slowly to stare at her as she fumbled her way through the city's name. "Hunslow," he provided. "Isn't it wonderful how well we know each other?"

"Well, there will be plenty of time for that!" Mr. Harcourt

said briskly. "Though the matter of Hunslow does remind me that we need to address your commission, Lord Selwyn. I think the most sensible course of action is an initial request of stasis while we sort out whether you wish to sell or defer or seek some other remedy in light of the demands of your inheritance."

"I'm selling it," Elias said impatiently. "Why put off the inevitable? Initiate the process yourself if you like, Harcourt."

"I certainly can assist with that," Mr. Harcourt replied, as though it had been a friendly request. "As for the banns, due to the inherited property, it is legal if they are read locally, yes. Is that your desired direction? I suppose it would take just as long to write to the archbishop and await a response, anyhow."

Hattie managed to nod, still a little uncertain any of this was truly happening.

"Excellent," Mr. Harcourt replied, flashing her an encouraging smile. "Now, there is the matter of your quarters here in the Rest. Due to the fact that Willa had the baron's room converted to a library sometime after his death, there is but one functional bedroom in the master suite at present. As such, only one of you can move into the master suite until such a time as the nuptials are concluded, but we ought to open the rooms up and make any necessary changes in preparation for that as quickly as possible. As I said, there is a bedroom, but it is likely not in a state of good repair. I have the keys here in the baroness's particulars."

"'The master suite'?" they both echoed, at varied paces and octaves of horror, giving Mr. Harcourt pause as he reached for his folio.

"Well, yes," he replied, blinking through his spectacles. "That is where the lord and lady of the estate typically live, is it not?"

Hattie glanced at Elias and found him staring back at her with a look of wide-eyed disbelief, her lips pressed hard together.

"We have never even seen the inside of those rooms," she explained, feeling around for her compress as little tremor of warning rang through her temples again. "It was not allowed."

"Well, it is allowed now," Mr. Harcourt said, patiently but

with a clear note of confusion. "You can redecorate however you see fit."

Elias released a huffing sound that was not quite laughter, dry and incredulous. "Are you *certain* she is dead?"

"The law is," said the barrister, in a tone that said there would be no more discussion. "Here is the key. The two of you may decide how to proceed at your leisure."

He dropped the key, heavy and silver, on the tray with a clatter, where it made the bowl of berries shake and the coffee cups ripple, and went back to his folio without a care for the weight of what he'd just done.

Hattie and Elias stared at the key for a time, and then at each other.

She gave him what she hoped was a look that was pleading, though she could not account for why she did not open her mouth and plea with her words, the way a sensible woman ought.

Still, apparently it worked.

He flattened his mouth at her, his head ticking resignedly to the side, but did reach forward and clasp the cursed thing in his hand, taking it into his possession.

He had taken it. He had understood her.

Perhaps more remarkably, he had understood her and chosen mercy.

And now, despite being a little bit baffled, Hattie could breathe again.

"Onto the matter of a butler," Mr. Harcourt said, and then he continued on with their morning, as though that key had never appeared at all.

※

Chapter Nine

"ARE YOU LEAVING?" Elias asked, surprised as Mr. Harcourt appeared to be making his way to the front door with a valise. "Permanently?"

"I live on the other side of town, just past the Lanes," the barrister said, turning with a wry smile to the other man. "I would have gone home last night if the lot of you hadn't sneaked out. I'll be back frequently as we continue to untangle your aunt's knot, of course, and anytime you need me, but with the household evidently observing the Spanish tradition of *siesta* today, I thought perhaps I ought to go check in on my own home."

Elias had the grace to blush, scratching at his hair as he nodded. "Sorry about that, by the by."

"Don't be," Mr. Harcourt said. "I daresay it was a necessary release of tension for the lot of you. Grief is an odd thing, Lord Selwyn. We all navigate it how we must."

"Grief," Elias repeated. "Right."

"Oh, Mr. Harcourt!" came Monica Thresher's voice, dove soft and trilling. "You aren't leaving us? I wished to measure you for a new suit."

The barrister looked up, blinking rapidly at her earnest face, her pale hands clutched under her chin. "Me?" he said, baffled. "Haven't you got costumes to make for all your fellow wards?"

"Most of them," she said with a nod. "Rhys and Libba already have plenty of my creations. I'll need to measure you too, Lord Selwyn."

Elias stepped back, wrinkling his brow. "I don't have an act," he reminded her.

Shaking her head, she gave a soft giggle and released her clasped hands, revealing the measuring tape that was caught between her palms. "You are the showmaster now, are you not? The baron. You will require a fitting."

"Well," said Mr. Harcourt, sounding relieved. "It sounds as though you will be very busy."

"Nonsense," she replied, turning those soft, brown eyes from one man to the other. "Why are you both so resistant to the idea of a gift? Please allow me to do this. I can measure you both now if you wish."

Their protestations sounded in unison, tumbling over one another in such bumbling, awkward accord that it made her giggle again.

"Very well," she said. "I am just finishing up with Malcolm. Elias, why don't you at least join us to watch the process? It is not so very terrible."

"I was going to nap," he lied.

She studied him, her pale lashes blinking thrice. "Were you?"

He winced. "No."

"Well, I'll be off, then," Mr. Harcourt announced, grabbing his valise by the handle and turning on his heel. "I'll see you all very soon!"

Monica frowned as she watched him go, making Elias feel guilty enough that he had no choice but to slump after her back toward her hostage party with Malcolm Lennox.

He peeked into the parlor as they walked past it but saw that Hattie's languid position on the chaise had been taken up by Jasper Townsend, who was apparently participating in the afternoon *siesta* with the rest of the household, his hat over his face and his fingers laced over his steadily rising and falling chest.

Elias never had been able to nap midday.

Another shortfalling.

"You aren't tired from last night?" he asked curiously, watching Monica bustle down the halls. "I was told you were trying to fall asleep in the booth at the public house."

"I was simply enjoying the view of the ceiling," she said wryly. "And I do intend to rest, but it is hard to pin Malcolm at the best of times, and he was willing just now. I had to fetch my measuring tape."

"Malcolm's resistant?" Elias said with some surprise. "He seems to me a fellow who enjoys expanding his wardrobe."

"Oh, he is," she said with a titter, "as the debonair gambler and banking man. Not as the Marvelous Human Abacus."

"Ah," said Elias, feeling a little slapped by how that resonated. "That does make sense."

"Bah," said Monica. "One ought to be grateful for discovery. If Willa hadn't found me, I'd still be scrubbing stained particulars next to my mother's lean-to. Now she has her own laundry and I've seen the Continent. What's to complain about?"

He pressed his lips together, his cheeks warming at his own many, many complaints, and resolved not to complain himself through the next hour of pinning and prodding and pinching as he and Malcolm Lennox shared sympathetic glances between themselves, propped like mannequins in front of a set of dusty, old mirrors that Monica had not yet had time to wipe down.

Afterward, he did rather wish he could take a nap.

Instead, he found himself standing at the foot of the foyer stairs as the sun began to sink lower in the late-afternoon sky, his hand brushing the dusty banisters as he gazed up toward the master suite, pondering whether or not he should go have a peek into his future without Harriet in tow.

He knew that he should not. He had already decided not to do it.

But that didn't change how it likely looked to her when she found him there.

"Have you gone up?" she asked softly, startling him so much, he might have broken off part of the stair railing, the way he spun around.

She had changed, he saw, after her *siesta*. Her wealth of brassy, red-blonde hair was piled up on her head now, pinned into order, and she was wearing a diaphanous orange gown that glowed like an ember opposite the lowering sun.

It hit him right between the ribs, the way she glowed there, as though nothing at all were amiss. His eyes followed her fingers as she twisted a strand of her brassy hair over her knuckles, pulling her lip between her teeth as she gazed up the stairs. She looked just as worried as she had back in the parlor.

Oddly, knowing she was capable of anything other than total confidence and bizarre trains of thought was somehow reassuring to him.

He shook his head, following her gaze up the banister. "No," he bit off. "I only considered it. Hadn't quite worked up the nerve."

She nodded, running her thumbnail against the pads of her fingertips as her eyes tilted up to the darkened hall above. "If we are going to go up today," she said, "we ought to do it right now, before it gets any darker. What do you think, Elias?"

He swallowed, considering it. "Do you think it will get any less ominous tomorrow?"

She gave him a thin smile. "I do not."

"Well, then…" He shrugged and jerked his head toward the stairs to indicate that they should climb them.

"So," he said between footfalls on the creaking wood, "do you picture a serpent every time you say my name?"

Her lips gave a delicate twist, her eyes down watching her slippered feet take one step at a time. "Not a literal snake, no," she said, shaking her head. "It is more the shape of the word as it escapes into the air. I do not find you snake-like, Elias."

"No?" He reached the landing and fished the heavy, silver key out of his pocket, taking a deep breath as they turned to walk toward the master suite doors. "What do you find me like? Not three, either. Not candy and chimes."

"Definitely not candy and chimes," she agreed, still wearing that little look of amusement. "Nothing so fleeting or fluffy. I hear thunder sometimes. I taste salt. I smell the bonfire from the summer's end festival, from that day that you pushed me into the water, right before the rain started. I didn't know that was what it was. I didn't realize it was a memory until last night. Barren fields. I do remember now. And I am sorry."

"*You* are sorry?" he repeated, stopping dead in his tracks. "Why are *you* sorry?"

She grimaced, drawing that lip back between the clamp of her teeth. "It was … I was … silly. I was a silly child, and I said something unkind, even if I didn't mean to. It doesn't make it less unkind just because it was unintentional. I understand that now."

He paused, frowning. "I never thought you were being cruel," he said, guilt pricking up in his veins. "Just … relentless."

"'Relentless,'" she repeated, as though she didn't know the meaning of the word. Though, of course, she did. "I've never been described as such, to my knowledge. *Tenacious*, perhaps."

"That isn't what I meant," he said with a sigh, rubbing his hand over his face. "You were just quite a lot as a girl and I got overwhelmed on that day. I am sorry too."

"Oh," she said, blinking at him in clear surprise. "Well, if we are both sorry, then I suppose the only sensible thing to do is agree on mutual forgiveness."

He blinked. And then he laughed. "Sensible," he said, watching her through the half-shadows of the hallway. "Is that what you are now? Instead of relentless?"

She stared back at him, her narrow throat flexing as though she were trying to get the question down into her belly, to digest it before she could justify answering it. Apparently, it was not an agreeable meal, because she turned abruptly and pointed at the two heavy mahogany panels in front of them.

"This is the door," she announced, staring ahead blankly.

He turned and looked at them, frowning. "I know that, Harriet," he said, sharper than he ought to have. "Obviously."

He stepped past her, ignoring the scent she wore, something spiced and unusual, just like she was, and pushed the key into the lock, rotating it first to the left, which found no purchase, and then to the right.

The door swung open like it had been recently oiled and accustomed to use, shafts of sunlight dancing, swirling in the cavernous apartment of rooms that it revealed to them as both panels glided inward on their hinges.

Elias left the key in the door, taking a slow, deliberate step over the threshold with the same tentative and tense posture he'd use on the battlefield or hunting a boar. It wasn't that he half-expected Willa to jump out from behind a tapestry necessarily, only that it was impossible not to feel her presence here, in this place.

He paused only once, when he felt the warm grasp of both of Harriet French's hands encircle his bicep, her body clinging to his side as she followed him into the room. Oddly, it eased his own tension about the place.

He caught her scent again, the spiced notes lingering on the air and settling over the fabric of his jacket.

Most of the furniture had been covered and the room had a musty quality to it, despite having been occasionally cleaned over the years, due to the windows remaining shut for so long.

He looked around until his eyes fell on an old lantern sitting on the mantel of the fireplace, right next to a tinderbox, and gave a little sigh of relief.

"Do you think that still has any oil in it?" he asked Hattie, nodding toward the lantern.

She didn't answer immediately, her eyes drawn instead to the painting hung above the mantel. It was a family he did not recognize, a pale, bearded man and a smiling woman, both with a hand on either shoulder of their young daughter.

"That's Willa," Hattie said, sounding amazed. "As a little girl."

"No," said Elias, squinting in the dimming light. "She was never a child, surely."

The child did have an air about her, her chin lifted and dark eyes painted with a glint to them. Her hair was the correct shade of rich auburn and there were the tightly coiled curls.

But this was no noble house portrait. If Elias had to guess, the people in it were merchant class at most.

"Starling," he murmured to himself, glancing down at Hattie. "I've never met anyone else from her maiden line. Have you?"

Hattie shook her head. "No. But she told me once that she was born wealthy, not titled, so I always assumed she married into the peerage."

"Well, that's something to chew on," Elias said, frowning. "I could write to my parents and ask, though I couldn't guarantee they'd ever open the letter, much less answer it, unless I included some bank notes with the inquiry."

Hattie squeezed his arm, making him look down into her frowning face. "Is that true?"

He gave a short, humorless chuckle. "It doesn't matter. I was only jesting. Let me see if I can get that lantern lit."

He pressed his lips together at the cold band that seemed to glow around his arm when her hands slid away from his bicep, even though it had been his own doing, his own brisk removal of himself from her attempt at closeness.

He took up the tinderbox, listening to the way she turned and moved about the room as he attempted to find a spark. It gave his hands something to do. It gave his eyes something to watch. His mind something in which to lose itself.

Was he being serpentine, just now?

Was he living up to his name?

"Ah, there we go," he said, just a little too heartily as the flame sparked to life. "There's a bit of oil in the old girl after all."

He took up the lantern by the handle and turned to find Hattie peeking under sheets, flipping them halfway up as she went, as though to mark her progress in case she forgot her way back.

"There is a pianoforte," she told him, those amber eyes of hers fixed on the flame in his hand. "We need not keep it up here. I've no ear for music."

"No?" he said, raising his brows. "Isn't that just another language to you?"

She paused, her fist clenching around the sheet above an armchair, and grimaced. "Yes and no," she said. "I can read the sheet music easily enough. I can hear it, when it's spelled out, in the *solfège*, you know? Do-re-mi and so on. I am *hopeless* at recreating it. Not with an instrument, not with my voice. It vexes me so."

He didn't mean to laugh, but the titter escaped him before he could stop it, his free hand coming up to try to catch it before she could hear.

Those eyes of hers narrowed. "Oh, is that funny?"

"Yes," he admitted, attempting to sound apologetic. "It is … unexpected, anyway. I thought everything was easy for you. Is your singing voice very terrible?"

She flashed her teeth at him. "Yes," she said curtly. "I sound like a drowning hen."

"Harriet," he said with complete sincerity, "I should very much like to hear you sing someday."

She stared at him for a moment, clearly baffled by this, her lips forming around several potential opening words to say in response and then puffing them out into the air before they could take shape.

She was glowing just now, opposite the glare of sunset, her hair and dress set off like fire in profile, and she didn't even know it. He suspected she never knew it.

"What other languages do you struggle with?" he asked, his voice gone soft and deep. "Where else do you falter?"

"What?" she replied, a little choked.

He took a step closer, setting the lantern onto one of her upturned sheets. "Tell me," he entreated. "Please."

She shook her head, color rising in her face. "I don't know what you want me to say."

"You love words so much," he continued. "Aren't there any that you hate?"

"I …" She cut herself off, swallowing with some apparent effort. "I hate acronyms."

"'Acronyms,'" he repeated, unable to stop the smile tugging at the corners of his mouth. "Why?"

She made wrinkled up her nose. "They are lazy and trite. I hate them. There is no *why*."

"You just said why," he pointed out, smiling wider when her glower deepened.

"You said I struggle to communicate, despite my languages," she snapped, crossing her arms over her chest and hugging them close. "I … think that might be true sometimes. Like people have a secret silent language with no letters or grammar or punctuation, and it is the only one I will never have the opportunity to learn."

"'A silent language'?" he asked, wishing he could touch her just now, that he could test the temperature of the glowing side of her face against the one in shadow. "You mean adjustments in posture and expression and so on?"

She shook her head, shrugging, and gave her body an agitated shake. "I don't know. Perhaps. *You* have never struggled with that language, Elias. Even as a boy, you seemed to know when someone was cross or tired or about to tell a long, boring story before they ever said a word. How? You don't know, do you? I've asked others like you. They never know."

"Perhaps it is instinct," he suggested, watching the way she seemed to resonate with fury at this thing that was locked off to her. "Nothing more, and nothing all that special, if you have met so many who can do it."

She gave a huff. "If it weren't special, I would not covet it, I think," she said. "Or perhaps it is all the more galling that I cannot access something the world considers pedestrian."

"You think you don't communicate with your body, but you do," he told her. "You're doing it right now, vibrating with indignant rage, hugging yourself like a phantom mother comforting your child self."

She furrowed her brow, dropping her arms and looking down at herself. And then, frowning, she looked back up at him.

Her eyes traveled over his form, studying his hand resting on the lantern over the sheet, the crook of his elbow, the bend of his knee. She took a step closer, peering at his face, and shook her head. "If you are doing the same," she said, "I cannot translate it."

He smiled at her, offering his arm again as he took up the lantern. "I wish you'd told me this when we were children," he said. "I think perhaps it might have changed things between us."

"Why is that?" she asked, floating forward and accepting his elbow, even though she was clearly still disgruntled.

"Who can say, now?" he replied, rather than stating the obvious. "Perhaps it might have just given us the opportunity to teach one another something, instead of clashing as we did."

"Well," she said, tilting her head to the side. "I suppose I'm not completely hopeless at using my body in some forms of survival. After all, I did learn to swim. Rather abruptly, too, if you recall."

"Thank God for that," he replied with a chuckle watching the way her mouth curved into a shy little smile as they moved to exit the master suite. "Harriet French is many things, but let none forget that she was always a strong swimmer."

Part III

The Silent Language

Chapter Ten

H ATTIE HADN'T BEEN fitted for one of Monica's costumes in a decade, and yet somehow, standing on this little platform again had returned her to exactly the same dreamy, distracted state of mind in which she'd always found herself during this ritual.

Today, while things were pinned and tucked and measured, she drifted beyond the chatter of the other women as she'd always done, past Libba quoting the stack of newspapers she'd finally gotten in the post from London, past Ruby examining fabrics and staking claims on the prettiest ones, past Monica muttering about a pincushion she'd lost when she had been thirteen and was convinced was still hiding somewhere in this very room.

She was thinking about Elias Selwyn.

"If you want to learn this silent language you so covet," he had said to her as they'd left the master suite, some days ago, *"you may observe me at any time, make your guesses, and then ask me if your translations were correct. Perhaps you may find you can build the skill if it is not inherent."*

And so she had been. Watching, that is.

She had not yet gotten the courage to approach him with any hypothetical interpretations. She imagined she needed time to hone her skill first, anyhow.

It was odd. She had never felt abashed about having an accent in a new tongue or getting a turn of phrase grammatically incorrect whilst learning something new, even when her teacher was already fluent in English. It had always been a bit of fun.

But she knew she would be far too embarrassed to reveal her stumbles to Elias. She wanted to find her feet first.

He was the most intriguing to watch at dinner.

The way he held his utensils. The way he cut his food. The slow way he lifted things to his lips and the way he listened and tilted his head while he chewed and tasted things. He always ran his fingers over the little crystal spikes at the base of the wine-glasses before he took a sip of what was inside, and afterward, he stroked the stem or traced the circle of the base.

Why did he do that?

She could see him now, could see his lips on the rim of the crystal.

"Hattie!" Libba exclaimed. "Gracious, girl. Share your reverie with the class."

"I … Pardon?" Hattie said, sounding rather hoarse. "What?"

Libba was grinning at her over the top of a copy of London's *Morning Chronicle*, dated ten days past, while Ruby was frowning at the sketch Monica was referencing in her folio.

"That's for Hattie?" she asked tartly. "You've never made me anything like that."

"Well, it's about words," Monica said defensively, curling the page to hide it and hunching her shoulders. "And it's just a concept. Velvet is too heavy for summertime, anyhow. I was thinking perhaps suede."

"What is it?" Hattie asked, forcing herself to swallow, to amass some moisture in her throat.

"A duochrome medieval *bonbon*," Ruby snapped.

"It is a recreation," Monica corrected, before the other woman had even gotten the words out. "Of Jadwiga of Poland's famous split gown, royal blue and gold on one side, creamy ivory and orange on the other. She was a king."

"A … what?" Libba said, already flipping her paper back up over her face. "'Queen,' you meant to say."

Monica shook her head. "No, she styled herself king. I thought it the type of thing Hattie might play with. Do you speak any Polish, Hattie? I think you'd need to, if we made this?"

"A woman king?" Ruby said, her dark eyebrows climbing. "Have there been others?"

"Hatshepsut," Hattie murmured, leaning forward to peer at the sketch. "She was a pharaoh. She wore a fake gold beard."

"There, you see?" said Ruby. "Make Hattie wear the beard and give me the gown."

"Anne Boleyn was a marquess," Libba put in idly. "Christ, but I'm missing so much in London! It hasn't even been a month. Can you imagine what I'll miss if a whole year goes by?"

"What's happened?" Ruby demanded, immediately distracted. "Scandal?"

"Of course," said Libba with a sigh. "Someone broke the bollocks off a Biblical statue at my parish picnic and then got caught with the vicar's hand up her skirt. I should have been there!"

"Your parish?" Monica repeated, sounding amused. "Are you a churchgoer, Libba?"

Libba pulled a face. "Of course I am. The clergy are the best showmen in Europe. You get stuck with a single book of stories and try to keep a crowd engaged and entertained with retellings for the whole of your life, hm? Besides, you should see my vicar. He's delicious."

"Sounds like he's not going to be your vicar much longer, if that's in the paper," Monica pointed out.

Libba shrugged. "We shall see. He could always marry the statue gelder. Damn! I should have been there."

"Who got gelded, then?" Ruby asked, throwing herself on the sofa next to Libba. "Moses? Abraham?"

"It doesn't say," Libba noted, squinting at the gossip column. "Let's hope it was Lot."

"Not Lucifer?" Hattie asked curiously, unable to stop herself from imagining exactly *how* one might snap just the genitals off a marble statue.

"Never Lucifer," Libba said immediately, with Ruby echoing, "Absolutely not."

The two exchanged glances and broke into giggles, winning looks of confusion from both Monica and Hattie.

"Ah," said Libba, resting her head on Ruby's shoulder. "They've never seen a good Lucifer statue, obviously."

"Always so beautiful." Ruby sighed, shaping the general form of a man with her hands in front of her. "Always so well built."

And they collapsed into giggles again.

"There was a story," Libba said, wicking a tear from her eye, "of a statue of Lucifer that was too seductive, so the church hired the sculptor's brother to make another one, and unfortunately, the second one was even more devastating. What a pity!"

Ruby nodded, hiccupping. "I've seen them both. I would put them in my bedroom and apologize to God in the mornings."

"Well!" said Monica, pink and gaping. "Goodness!"

Hattie touched her cheeks, which felt rather pink as well. She was thinking of the feeling of Elias Selwyn's muscled bicep under the fine linen of his coat as they'd walked into the master suite. He wasn't made of marble. He could move. He was warm.

"Hattie!" Libba cried again, staring at what must have been a look of true distraction on her face.

"I could pick up enough Polish for the showcase, I think," Hattie immediately announced, clearing her throat and shaking her head to dispel thoughts of her husband-to-be. She told herself to instead focus on the upcoming performance she must give and sent her mind reaching out to feel the bumps over interconnected Slavic tongues. "Are there any local Poles about? Perhaps one might practice with me?"

"There are always foreigners about during the summer season," Monica answered, looking relieved to have turned back to the dress. "We can ask at the Cauldron. If not, the Travellers' caravan sometimes has people from the Continent in their retinue."

"Oh, that's true!" said Libba, her eyes sparkling. "We should all go see Miss Persephone and beg an audience. Rhys's hair will fall out and he'll have to do his showcase bald."

This time, all four women burst into giggles together.

ELIAS WAS LATE to dinner, leaving Hattie somewhat at a loss for how to occupy herself in the absence of her new course of study.

She found herself feeling a little restless, checking the archway that led to the dining room as often as she could without being conspicuous. Or at least, without being what she thought might come across as conspicuous.

As though to prove the point of her poor natural aptitude for silent communication, Malcolm immediately made note of it.

"I'm certain he's just running a bit late," he said, not unkindly, watching her as he stuck his fork into a green bean, one tine at a time. "I'm surprised you are so fussed."

She frowned at him. "You are very good at reading body language, aren't you?"

He gave her half a smile, a twinkle of self-satisfaction in his dark eyes. "I think so. It wouldn't be fun at the tables if I weren't."

She considered this, turning her chair a bit toward him and her plate and cup with it, putting her back to the entry as a means of resisting further inspection. "Tell me," she said, leaning close so they would not be overheard, "if you observed another gambler, touching their wineglass just so, how might you interpret it?"

Mal blinked at her, watching her stroke the crystal details at the base of the glass, then run her pinched fingers up and down the stem. He cleared his throat, coloring. "I … erm. Really shouldn't say."

"I'll say it," Rhys volunteered, getting an immediate snap of the head and glare from Malcolm.

Hattie gave a helpless little shake of the head, frustrating burning in her jaw. "I wish someone would," she confessed, dropping her hand away from the glass. "Why do people not just say what they are thinking at all times? I do."

"We know," said Rhys, reaching across the table and patting her hand. "We know."

"It is blue on one side, and white on the other," Ruby's voice suddenly exclaimed, shrill as she described the Jadwiga dress to Errol. "It was obviously made to be worn by me. Hattie favors fire colors, anyhow. I wear the jewel tones."

Hattie gave a small smile across the table at Rhys. "See? Ruby says what she's thinking too."

He chuckled, releasing her hand and swiping a bean off her plate to pop into his mouth. "Sometimes. She's sneaky, though."

"Agreed," said Malcolm. "She is inconsistent. Dangerous in a game."

"And don't you forget it," Ruby announced, clearly eavesdropping, even whilst ranting to her favorite open ear.

Errol chuckled into his napkin.

"Apologies," Elias's voice announced, bringing Hattie back up to sudden, perfect posture. "I got waylaid at the post office. Have I missed serving?"

"You've a plate," Libba said, gesturing with her fork to his place. "Might be a bit tepid."

Elias nodded in thanks, sighing and crossing the room, still in his riding boots and kit.

Hattie did not stare.

"Don't stare," Malcolm whispered unnecessarily.

She pressed her lips together. Because she was not.

"Did you sell your commission, then?" Rhys asked as Elias took his seat, dropping his cheek into his hand as the question left his mouth. "I feel like someone will take offense, but I suppose that's not how military types operate, is it?"

"Someone very well might," Elias said with a wince. "But yes, it's done now, or will be once the letters reach their destinations."

"And?" said Errol, perhaps just as curious, even if he wasn't lolling about on the table to demonstrate it. "How do you feel about it?"

Elias looked surprised, Hattie thought. His eyes widened, dark, slightly arched brows rising just a smidge. The corner of his lips ticked, almost like it struck him as funny to be asked.

He had not yet touched his wineglass.

"Relieved, I think?" he said, after considering it a moment. "Yes. I think I'm relieved. Which is odd because I liked my commission."

"Like parting ways with a lover who's run his course," Ruby suggested, blinking her big, glossy lashes.

"Erm," said Elias Selwyn. "Perhaps."

"Oho," Rhys said with a grin. "This one doesn't part with his lovers. He keeps them all in perpetuity."

Elias colored a bit, giving a stilted chuckle, and shook his head. "If that's what you want to believe," he managed, reaching out for the wine, his fingers just short of grasping the crystal, "I shan't dissuade it."

"Oh, well, perhaps you should," Monica suggested softly, making him pause, his hand hovering just short of its prize. "You are about to be married, after all."

"Ah," he said, retreating from the glass, seemingly oblivious to the pain it was causing Hattie that he would not just grasp the thing. "That is an astute point, Miss Thresher."

"You should only dissuade the things that are not true," Hattie said, her voice going louder with exasperation. "Why would you do otherwise?"

Malcolm sighed as Rhys began to giggle.

Elias was now staring at her, something very curious in those dark-blue eyes of his as she began to color.

"You must forgive us for our prying," Malcolm said, as diplomatic as a royal envoy. "You left the house so long ago, and we are all just trying to remember who you are."

"Or find out for the first time, as it were?" Elias suggested, tilting his head. "The disorientation is mutual, at the very least."

"It is easy to forget being a child," Hattie said softly, gazing at him across the candles and food. "You left just as we were growing into something new, so in a way, it really is like meeting for the first time again, isn't it?"

He glanced back at her, a smile tugging at the corners of his lips. "I certainly hope so," he said. "Miss French."

Libba cleared her throat. "Have you chosen a poem to read for the opening of the showcase yet, Elias?" she asked, louder than strictly necessary. "Willa always chose one about prodigiousness, but perhaps you've different tastes."

"I … What?" he said, blinking twice before he turned his eyes from Hattie to Libba. "No one has said anything about a poem."

"That's not true," she said, smirking. "I just did."

"Perhaps an elegy," Monica said thoughtfully, pressing the handle of her fork into her bottom lip. "Or something wistful."

"Are you wistful, Lord Selwyn?" Malcolm asked, in a tone that suggested he knew that Elias was not.

"If the occasion calls for it," Elias replied, archly enough that Malcolm looked impressed. "I shall have to ponder the matter."

"We should have told you," Monica said apologetically. "It is easy to forget you have not always been here with us, now that you are again."

He looked baffled and perhaps a little sheepish at what she'd said, giving her a slight nod and then finally, at long last and with the mercy of the angels, reaching out and taking up the damned wineglass.

Hattie exhaled, her shoulders drooping.

She watched with the oddest feeling of relief as he began his ritual with the glass, rotating it in his fingers, tracing the patterns, touching the stem. It felt like someone had finally fixed a clock that was just a little bit off.

"Do you like poetry, Miss French?" Elias asked her, over the rim of the wineglass. "As our resident linguaphile, you must have an opinion on it."

She paused, licking her lips, and reached for her own glass to moisten her throat, considering the question.

"Sometimes," she said. "When the poem is written in obvious reverence for the beats and sounds of a language. When it has rhythm or motion or clever double meaning. But often, I find it just meanders and sometimes is a little nonsensical."

"Abstract, you mean," Libba said, tilting her curly head to the side.

Hattie frowned. "No, I mean nonsensical. Simile pushed past the point of credulity. It isn't beautiful anymore when it's bizarre."

"And here I thought that's when it was at pinnacle," Rhys said, giving an exaggerated frown. "I don't mind the surreal. It's often a metaphor for something else, after all."

Hattie sighed. "So it is another instance of people saying something other than what they mean. Yes, I suppose that is why I don't like it."

At this juncture, the table erupted into several threads of conversation, dissecting this school of thought and the merits of abstraction in poetry and indeed, art in general.

Hattie crossed her arms and simply listened, for she had already said all there was to say on the matter.

Elias, however, said nothing at all.

He simply continued to make love to his wineglass and watch her as he did so. He did not say what he was thinking. Or what he meant. Or anything whatsoever.

And Hattie suspected that was deliberate.

For he was choosing to speak in the one language she had not yet mastered, instead.

※ ❧ ❧ ❧ ※

Chapter Eleven

ELIAS HAD BEEN intending to address something when he'd come home that night, but there was just something about entering a room filled to the brim with Willa's full menagerie that scrambled his tidy thoughts to scraps of rubbish.

Even if tonight's dinner had been verging on enjoyable, it had still addled him.

It wasn't until hours later, as he was securing the buttons on his pajamas and stifling a yawn, that he recalled what it was that he had wanted to discuss.

And damned if it wasn't important!

He grunted in frustration, glancing at his wet hair and general disarray in the tilted mirror that sat against his bedroom wall. He grimaced at the shadow of stubble on his jaw and the fact that he'd started the buttons at the wrong place and the top half of his pajama set was now askew.

It didn't matter.

She might still be awake.

He pushed his toes into his slippers as he grabbed the dressing gown off the bed poster, already moving to exit the room, annoyance battling impatience in his chest as he tried to pull the fabric over his arms without it billowing out around him like a diva's cape during her aria.

He got it into place as he rounded the corner out of the boys'

102

wing and made a turn toward the girls', fumbling for the sash and making a hasty, overly tight knot at his waist as he pivoted on his cushioned toes.

Less than a dozen steps from Hattie French's door, she emerged, looking a bit panicked herself, with a lantern in her hand that cast a dancing series of shadows onto her orange-and-black dressing gown. "Elias!" she exclaimed, blinking rapidly.

He halted, his feet crashing about in the absurd, fluffy embrace of his slippers, and immediately made a face at the robe she was wearing.

He would have to have that burned, he thought. Or donated to orphans, perhaps.

He'd get her a different one.

"I was about to come and speak to you," she said, lifting the lantern up by her face as though he'd need to watch her mouth make the words to understand them. "Are you all right?"

He made a face and nodded back toward her room, taking a few steps forward to usher her back into it rather than continue conversing out here in the hall, where any of the other little miracles of talent might emerge at any given moment.

He glanced over his shoulder to ensure that the hall was empty as she made her reluctant path back into her chamber and followed her in, pulling the door shut behind him.

"I thought of a poet," she said immediately, still holding that lantern up by her face like a ghoul. "But then I was not sure if it would offend you or not."

"What?" he snapped, crossing the room and reaching up to take that stupid lantern from her. He got as far as wrapping his fingers around the metal hoop at the top before he realized she wasn't going to just release it. "Harriet!"

She tilted her head up to meet his eye, blinking curiously. "There is an Australian poet," she said. "He was a friend of Willa's, a barrister aspiring to become one of Australia's first lauded poets, but …"

He paused, suddenly aware of their proximity, his shoulders

coming down softly as he urged the lantern down from her preferred, aloft position in the air. "'But'?"

She looked pinker than usual, her lips pressed together. "I changed my mind. It is a silly idea."

"Harriet," he said again, his voice going thin in exasperation.

She released the lantern into his grip, her fingers passing over his, and sighed. "His name is Barron Field."

He almost dropped the lantern. He blinked at her, an involuntary bluster of a laugh rising in his throat. "You are making that up."

She shook her head, definitely pinker than usual. "I am not," she said. "I am a terrible liar, you know."

"I didn't know," he answered, a second huff of laughter making its way up. "But it doesn't surprise me. Barron Field?"

"Well, you see, his mother's maiden name was Barron," she said quickly, that shrill rambling quality already starting in her voice.

"At ease," he said quickly, taking a step back and looking about for somewhere to put the lantern. "I needed to talk to you."

"You did?" she said. "With words?"

He paused, halfway to placing the lit lantern on her chest of drawers, and deliberately releasing the tension that had immediately shot into his shoulders and jaw at that bizarre question. "Yes, Harriet," he said slowly, clanking the thing into place and watching the flame jump. "With words. I do have some, you know."

"Oh," she said, making him sigh.

He ran both hands over his damp hair, knowing he was only mussing it further, and turned to look at her. "Are they all just going to stay here?" he said, before he could second-guess himself. "For the entire year?"

She blinked. "Who?"

"Your fellow prodigies," he snapped, gesturing at her door. "And all their minions. Already, Monica has three seamstresses helping her with the costumes and she hasn't even gone to see her new storefront yet. And I understand Libba is shipping in a full acting troupe from London?"

"Oh, yes," said Hattie, deflating, like she was somehow relieved that he was making sense. "But only Lem will stay in the house."

"Who the devil is Lem?" he demanded, trying to keep his voice down in the midst of exploding.

"A muscle," she said. "Don't worry. He doesn't talk very much."

"What?!"

"We'll need another chair at the dining room table," she realized, tilting her head to the side, "if we have both Lem and the occasional visit from Mr. Harcourt."

"So they do all intend to live here?" he pressed, a sight more panicked than he'd intended to be. "The whole year?"

She shook her head and wrinkled up that lovely brow. "I do not know. They are all staying in Brighton, but I suppose some might wish to seek external accommodations, even though I think that would be a silly and unnecessary expense. We could ask them."

"Ask? If people intend to take over our house?" he repeated, incredulous.

"Well, it is their house too," she said.

"No," he corrected. "Right now, it is yours, and when we marry, it is ours, but it is not theirs any more than my old dormitory bed at Eton is mine."

She gave a soft, thoughtful little blink, her mouth melting into a wistful smile. "Oh, that is funny," she said, reaching up to toy with the braid of bronze hair that was sitting on her shoulder. "I had a bed at the foundling home once. It must be another child's now."

He stared at her, a little needle of guilt tapping at his ribs. "You're saying they have nowhere else to go," he realized.

"What?" she said, frowning. "No, I was ... but there are all these beds, Elias. Why should we keep them empty? And two more when we move into the master suite."

"For the sake of peace?" he suggested, already knowing he'd lost. "No, no. I know you are right. Hell, Harcourt can have my room."

She tittered then, just a little thing, such a rare sound that it shot through him, right past that needling guilt and directly into the base of his gut, his eyes snapping up to watch her.

She covered her mouth, shaking her head and giggling again. "Do you think he would redecorate? I have always imagined he keeps a file cabinet next to his bed."

Elias couldn't stop himself from smiling at the image, shaking his head in half surrender to the absurdity of this encounter. "So when he rolls over in the morning, he can immediately reach inside?"

"Oh, all throughout the night," she replied, hiccupping with amusement. "He keeps a pad of paper and a fresh ink pot on top so he can wake in spurts and jot down docket amendments in the wee hours."

He laughed then, unintentionally and perhaps a little too loud for a man who did not want anyone knowing he was in here. He looked around, resolving to just allow the rest of the conversation to unfold however it might, and realized with a frown, "There are no chairs in here. Just that little vanity stool."

"Oh," she said, looking around as though she were just realizing it for the first time too. "You can sit with me on the bed. It is very comfortable."

As though to demonstrate, she fell backward onto the rumpled sheets, her dressing gown spooling out around her in a silken heap, and patted the space to her side.

His resolve flickered. Perhaps he ought to flee, after all.

"Do you want something to drink?" she asked, her eyes going wide as though she were a new bride receiving her first polite guest. "I have some port here somewhere. Oh! And the little crystal glasses. I can see if you do the same things."

"What?" he croaked as she pushed herself off the bed and went past him in a gust of that unusual, spiced perfume she wore, in search of said port and tiny glasses.

"Please sit," she said without turning around, already falling to her knees to dig in the little beverage cabinet next to her vanity table. "Oh, here they are! Bit dusty. I'll rinse them."

He was frozen in place, watching her kneeling on the rug in her negligee, bits of her curling brassy hair escaping her braid as she rummaged around inside that cabinet. "Perhaps I ought to go. You were sleeping."

She paused, glancing over her shoulder. "I wasn't," she reminded him. "I was coming to tell you about Barron Field. Ah! The port. Sit down!"

She pushed herself back to her feet in a single elegant motion, taking up the glasses between her fingers and the bottle of port in her other hand as she marched toward him in the direction of her washbasin.

He thought perhaps sitting was the safest option, just now, and did so. Rapidly.

He watched her, splashing the glasses and drying them against her silken sleeve, then uncorking the port and humming a tuneless meandering series of notes as she poured.

She really couldn't sing. And for some reason that was melting every muscle in his body.

Shit.

"Did you write to your parents?" she asked, turning back to him with all the effect of a bucket of ice water.

"What? No! Why would I do that?" he demanded, his spine coming up.

"About the Starlings," she reminded him, looking very curious about his sudden change in demeanor. "Here you are. I hope you like port. It is accidentally quite aged."

"Oh, right," he said, easing again with a little frown. "No, I didn't. Maybe Harcourt knows. They were friends."

"Maybe so," she agreed, holding her glass while staring at his with what appeared to be extremely intense expectation. "Go on, then."

"I … All right?" he said, lifting it to his lips and giving it a little sip.

She frowned. "No, I mean your ritual with the glass. Proceed."

"My what?" he said, helplessly as she made a little clicking sound with her tongue.

She set her own glass aside and reached out to push his fingers against the base of the little glass. "Like this," she said impatiently, her fingers soft and insistent over his. "Then the stem, like you do at dinner."

"I do what?" he managed, staring down at the glass like he'd never seen one before.

She huffed, leaning back, and watched him for a moment, her eyes flashing with indignation. "You're not doing it purposefully?"

"Doing *what*?!" he demanded, throwing the rest of the port into his mouth as a matter of necessity and swallowing it down.

"Testing me!" she burst out, throwing her hands up. "Teaching me the silent language!"

"The … oh!" he said, realization bursting over his skin and muddying the confusion that still lingeried just beneath. "At dinners?"

"At dinners!" she repeated, shrill again.

He couldn't help but gawk at her for a moment, gloriously furious, glowing with her own frustration. And then he began to laugh again.

Not intentionally.

But he couldn't help it.

"Elias Selwyn!" she shrieked, outrage glowing on her like a mantle.

It only made him laugh harder, dropping his face into his hands and shaking his head in apology as he tried to get his mirth under control.

"Fine!" she snapped, and he heard her take up her own port

and swallow it in a single gulp as he had. "I shan't learn it, then. That is fine. I never expected to, anyhow."

"Harriet," he managed, peeking up at her through his fingers, his ribs aching with how good it felt to release some of the tension that had been bottled up beneath them. "Please."

She glared at him. "You promised you would help me."

He drew in a deep breath and pushed it out as a sigh, dropping his hands and rubbing his lips together in an effort to quell the curve of amusement that still lingered there. "I did," he managed, as apologetically as possible. "And I meant it."

She huffed, crossing her arms. "You don't understand," she said, a marked pout in her tone. "I don't like not being good at things right away."

It took every ounce of fortitude in his body not to laugh again. Instead, he only pressed his lips together and gave a somber nod. "Right," he said. "Can't imagine what that must be like."

"You only do it when you are watching me," she said with a little sigh, shaking her curls. "I thought for certain you were attempting to impart a lesson."

"Well, now hold on," he said, raising his brows. "If I only do it when I'm watching you, then it likely is some form of communication, even if unintentional. Do you want to show me again?"

She considered it, her eyes glinting in the low light as she studied his face. "No," she decided. "I am embarrassed."

This time, he could not suppress the twisting beginnings of a smile, charmed despite himself though still doing his level best not to laugh and send her off into a snit again. "What were you going to tell me the other day?" he asked. "About tribes in Siberia? I cut you off and I shouldn't have."

She wrinkled her brow, as though she did not quite remember.

He did chuckle at that, but only in reaction to his own peevishness. "I was being a beast, if you recall, about the will," he reminded her, holding up the flat of his hand and brushing it against the tip of her nose just the way he had in his room that first day, when he'd wanted her to stop talking. "You wanted to come to some sort of accord about the marriage and you said something about Siberian tribes."

She blinked, giving a little shiver as he pulled his hand away, her eyes drifting down to look at her empty port glass. "Oh," she said, half-whispering. "That. It is nothing, really. Only that there is a tribe that often matches children they consider the most opposite when arranging marriages, because they think that opposing elements of temperament produce the strongest households and the most resilient children. I thought perhaps Willa was thinking along similar lines, with her decree."

"You think us complete opposites?" he pressed, raising his brows. "I also do not like failing to be good at things right away, you know."

"You don't?" she asked, sounding genuinely surprised.

He shook his head, letting another ripple of laughter escape him. "So how do you think it felt," he pressed, "sitting beside you in Latin lessons? Or beside Malcolm in arithmetic?"

"Well," she said, frowning. "I also had to sit next to Malcolm in arithmetic."

He paused, a little flash of surprise passing through him. "Oh," he said. "I suppose that is true. Did you hate it as much as I did?"

She grimaced, her teeth reflecting the low light. "Of course I did. Especially when it was algebra or logic problems. And he'd take such glee in answering very fast, before I could even wrap my head around the question."

"He would!" Elias exclaimed, eyes widening. "What a little peacock he was."

"Was," said Hattie with a shrug. "Is?"

And they both laughed this time, for a stolen, quiet moment.

"Ah," she said, shaking her head. "I suppose I did the same thing in language lessons, didn't I? And the more of us Willa took in, the more unbearable lessons must have been for you, one by one."

He gave her a wan smile and a shrug. "Must have been," he echoed. "Who can remember now?"

"But now you are the instructor," she reminded him, "and I the struggling pupil. You have the answers and I do not. Perhaps you may motivate yourself in teaching me as some sort of revenge, hm? Do I not deserve it?"

He narrowed his eyes. "You do, actually."

She smiled, lowering her lashes. "So what were you thinking? Watching me at dinner, holding your crystal wineglass?"

He straightened, breathing with intent, and angled himself toward her, their knees brushing on the edge of the mattress. It immediately distracted him, his eyes falling to the collision of his velvet robe and her tiger-striped silken one. "I can scarcely recall," he confessed, though, just now, he had an inkling.

"Oh," she whispered, raising her eyes back up to meet his, her tongue darting out to moisten her lips. "That is a shame."

"Forget the wineglass," he said, a bit throatier than he would have liked, nudging closer to her on the mattress. "What do you think my body is conveying? Right now?"

She was silent for a moment, though Elias was of the mind that she even *thought* a bit more loudly than was polite.

He dragged his eyes up to meet hers, trailing over all the details of the damned robe in the process, until there was nothing left in his view but the dark shadows and dancing lights around her irises, the color of amber stones in the dark.

She swallowed, her narrow throat flexing, and ran those eyes of hers over his face. "Perhaps I am too close," she said in barely a whisper, her little, pink tongue darting out to moisten her lips.

"You are not close enough," he returned without thinking, his hands itching to remove that robe now and be done with it forever.

"Elias," she said, her tongue rolling over the syllables in that serpentine shape she loved so well, her eyes fixed on his mouth. "If I were any closer, we would be touching."

"Indeed?" he said. "And is that not part of the silent language as well? Touch?"

"Is it?" she asked, just a breath on the air, so soft, he might have missed it. "I didn't know."

"Guess what I'm saying silently," he persisted, reaching up to touch one of those wayward curls that had worked its way loose just over her ear, wrapping his finger around it. "Go on."

"You want …" she managed, her breath catching when he touched her hair.

"Yes?" he said, his own gaze traveling over her face now, noting the delicate pulse in her throat, the shallowness of her breath, the color in her cheeks. "What do I want?"

"I don't …" she said as he leaned closer, his thumb tracing the line of her cheek.

"Yes, you do," he replied, soft and firm, just the way she'd tried to force his hands to speak to her on that little port glass. "You do."

He wondered if she would taste the way she smelled. Like a spiced dessert, forbidden and foreign and just a little bit incorrect. He could find out right now, he realized. He could answer an impulse that had hounded him for half of his life.

Or …

He pulled back, dropping his hand away, his heart roaring in his ears, and watched the blink of confusion, the scatter of gooseflesh that arose on her throat and collarbones and crept down to the tantalizing swell of her bosom.

"When you have a guess," he said softly, pushing himself to stand, "I look forward to hearing it."

"Elias?" she managed, evidently dumbfounded.

He stifled a false yawn, glancing over her head at the window by her washbasin. "We ought to get some sleep," he told her, relishing in this rare feeling, in her presence at least, of being good at something right away. Good at something that she was not.

And there was something else.

Something he could not quite name, but it was damned endearing in the locus of her pouting and fretting about the matter.

He grinned at her. "It is getting very late. I think I'll sleep well tonight."

And he turned to leave as quickly as he could, before he looked at her for a single moment more, rumpled and flushed and waiting for him on the edge of a warm bed.

He left before he could lose his resolve.

Chapter Twelve

B Y LUNCHEON THE next day, Hattie had written no fewer than
three full orations dedicated to one Elias Selwyn, Baron
Selwyn, denier of pleasures and purveyor of cruelty.

She had skipped breakfast, pacing about her room as she
muttered to herself, pulling tresses free from her braid as she
thought of all the things she wished to say to him after he'd left
her there last night, ablaze and flustered, without so much as a
peck on the cheek for her trouble.

What on earth was his aim, doing such a thing?

She'd have preferred another dip in the ocean!

When a rap sounded at her door, thinking it must have been
he who'd delivered such torment, she had stomped to it
immediately and wrenched it open, with all three of her opening
salvos colliding on the curl of her tongue, ready to be unleashed
like the cracks on a whip as soon as she got the damned hinges to
cooperate.

But it was not Elias on her threshold.

It was Ruby Little.

Who was also red-faced.

"Will you please," Ruby immediately exploded, pushing into
the room in a flurry of skirts and ichor, "tell your new *cook* that
this is my *home* as much as it is *yours*? And that when I *demand* she
hand over the jar of vanilla beans so that I may … I say, you

aren't dressed."

Hattie stared at Ruby, who now stood in the center of her room, and released the doorknob. "I'm not," she agreed as the door swung shut with a pitiful click behind her.

Ruby frowned, looking about the room until her eyes fell on the vanity. "Aha!" she said, marching over and snapping up the bottle of *eau de toilette* from its perch. "I knew you were almost out! How in the blazes am I to make more without the damned vanilla beans, Hattie? Make her give them to me!"

"There's vanilla in that?" Hattie asked, baffled.

"And cardamom and ginger and cinnamon and cloves," Ruby said, shaking the bottle at her like a magic wand. "And black tea! Make her give me the vanilla!"

"Ruby, I am not …" Hattie trailed off, dazed. "Dressed?"

Ruby was glaring, her eyes darting around the room as if looking for hidden vanilla stores. "Yes, why aren't you?" she said. "The cook said you are the lady of the house and I am a *guest. A guest*! In my own home!"

"I'll speak to her," Hattie promised, stepping quickly over to the bed to kick the port glasses beneath it. "She is new."

"Yes, well," Ruby said, deflating a bit, the glass vial sagging at her side, "I have not yet set up my laboratory and I need to get my scents in order before the showcase. I do not enjoy being treated like one of Monica's seamstresses."

"Oh, the seamstresses," said Hattie, blinking. "One of them is Polish, I believe?"

"How should I know?" Ruby snapped, stepping forward and pushing the vial into Hattie's palm. "Here. Use it sparingly until I can make more. God knows what else Cerberus will try to hide from me."

"Are you calling her a dog?" Hattie asked her retreating foster sister. "Or a demon?"

"Yes!" Ruby shouted, slamming the door behind her.

Hattie blinked.

Was this what it would be like, as baroness?

Perhaps Elias hadn't been wrong to express concern about all of the wards staying here for the full year.

She had been the first of Willa's wards. Or the second, if one were to count Elias, which Hattie never really had. He was her real, actual, legally bound family, after all, not a lucky talent in need of a patroness.

Seven.

She tapped her fingertips again with her thumbnail.

Eight.

He was the eighth. She still smelled smoke when the number rounded itself in the air upon thinking it, but the doom had gone. The feeling of trepidation had eased.

How could she have forgotten him? Why had she locked him so tightly away that his very existence had distressed her so?

Was it just about that nonsense on the pier? Or was it because he had left the house after it and she'd always known, deep down, that it had been her doing? That she had been the thing that had driven him away?

What if she drove the others away now too, as baroness?

She frowned, shaking her head.

She had been the first, but Libba was right: she had never been the authority amongst them. She had never wished to be. If anything, she had observed and been grateful for inclusion when it had come along.

And after Elias had gone … well …

She supposed she might have kept herself at a bit of a distance after he'd left, lest she drive another away again. She'd been the first to venture out into the world. Even as a child, she'd often watch the others play rather than participate.

She'd gotten close to Elias once, and he'd shoved her into the sea for the trouble, after all.

She sighed, shaking her head.

She was likely thinking in circles because she hadn't slept and because Elias had thrown her mind into disarray, because he'd chosen to teach via torment rather than titillation! Perhaps she ought to give him a stern talking-to about the merits of teaching with encouragement and reward rather than … well, whatever the devil he was doing to her.

Yes, it was Elias's fault she was all turned about this morning.

That was all it was.

In any event, she supposed her days of lounging about in her shift until noon were likely over, at least at Starling's Rest and for the duration of this very unusual year.

Perhaps forever.

She hoped not forever.

By the time she had dressed, dabbed a modest amount of perfume onto her throat and wrists, and commandeered the vanilla jar from the kitchens, however, Ruby had vanished, evidently gone down to the boardwalk with Monica and Errol to examine the new storefront and workshop.

"They invited me, you know," Rhys said sullenly from the dining room table, "but I don't like to walk past that chicanery shop en route."

"What?" said Hattie, whilst Malcolm attempted to shush her.

Thus commenced a twenty-minute rant about the many evils of Persephone Boswell and her curiosity cabinet.

And still there had been no sign of Elias.

If she hadn't been half-convinced that she'd arrive just as they were leaving, Hattie had a mind to go find her bonnet and make her way to the boardwalk herself, just to indulge in a bit of distraction. As it was, she didn't fancy feeling like a fool twice in one day.

She had never felt like this in Russia.

Or in Greece.

Or in Switzerland.

She kicked an empty rubbish bin purely by accident, but it did make her feel a little better. At least, it would have, if that hadn't been the exact moment that Elias Selwyn deigned to return.

"Problem?" he asked, already grinning at her victorious stance over the toppled basket.

She spun around, eyes already narrowed, to find him holding a stack of boxes, lingering in the entryway with a rosy flush to his cheeks and a windswept tousle to his dark hair. "Many!"

"Oh, 'many,'" he repeated, clicking his tongue with mock sympathy. "Do you wish to talk about it?"

"No!"

He smiled wider. "I don't believe you."

She drew herself up, her body rippling with fury, and took a stalking step toward him, pointing one finger in his direction. "You!" she hissed. "You appear so very smug after what you did … what you *didn't* …"

"'What I didn't …'?" he prompted, still flashing those even, white teeth.

She paused, her face radiating warmth as Libba and Malcolm passed in the hallway beyond the parlor, glancing curiously inside. It made her clamp her teeth together, her lips sealed against revealing too much, but her eyes had gone down to mere slits.

"You know very well," she said as softly as she could manage.

"I suppose I might," he replied jovially, looking fit to spring around the room like a satyr. He strode into the parlor, depositing the parcels from his arms onto the chaise, and took a step back, admiring the effect. "Here, I've brought you some things."

She froze, confusion puncturing the heat of her rage as her eyes fell on the boxes. "What things?"

"Wedding things," he said with a shrug. "Fabrics that Miss Thresher asked me to fetch, some silk flowers, and a dressing gown I saw in a shop window."

"'A … dressing gown'?" she repeated as she raised her eyes to meet his, blue and twinkling with abject self-satisfaction. "I have a dressing gown."

"Do you, indeed?" he said, as though he weren't perfectly well aware. "You might find that it has gone missing, in fact. Terrible shame. That happens in full houses."

"What?!" she exclaimed, turning to look over her shoulder, as though she might see the thief absconding at her rear. "I was just wearing it this morning. I shall go check."

She took a single step. Just one, toward the door, before she felt his hand on her wrist, anchoring her in place.

"Hattie," he said, low and warm in her ear. How had he gotten across the room so fast?

She stumbled, her shoulder and back falling against the solid wall of his chest as she turned in surprise to see the full presence of him there.

Had he just called her 'Hattie'? He always called her 'Harriet,' didn't he?

She turned, trying to keep him only in her periphery, the warmth of his breath on her neck and tickling her ear. "Elias?" she managed, though she sounded a bit strangled.

He smiled again, though this time, it did not look amused, his teeth glinting in the afternoon light. "You can't really expect me to let you keep an intimate gift from a Russian prince? Surely, my silent language has told you that much?"

Her jaw dropped, her breath catching in her chest. "It has told me no such thing!" she breathed, still unable to turn and face him directly. "'Intimate gift,' indeed! That prince was nearly eighty years old!"

"Oh, indeed?" He sounded surprised. Relieved, even? Pleased!

She ground her teeth. "And much more of a gentleman than you will ever be!"

"Well, I can't account for your tastes," he said with a shrug. "The point remains."

"Elias!" she gasped, turning then only because there was no other choice, and finding him somehow both intense and utterly at ease with what was passing between them. "Release me!"

"Fine," he said, shrugging and dropping his hand away, leaving a band of ice-cold air around her wrist in its place.

She frowned, somehow even angrier than she'd been a second ago as he backed away, raising his hands in a symbol of surrender and collapsing next to his damned parcels with his elbow propped atop them.

She snatched her wrist up against her chest, rubbing her own hand around it in an effort to restore the warmth he'd taken from her flesh. It was ineffective. She supposed he might just run hotter than she, as a matter of standard.

He watched her, his eyes lingering on her fingers as they rubbed the delicate bones and pale skin there, until she felt so conspicuous that she had no choice but to drop her hands uselessly at her sides.

It was at that moment that she realized she had not used any of the fine speeches she'd penned in her mind this morning, even in outline. She had not spoken a word of that finely wrought prose, and that was why he was sitting there so comfortably, without a single lash mark on his person to sting in reminder of the one tool she had against him.

She opened her mouth and then clamped it shut again at the way he started to smirk.

It was obviously too late now.

And that might have deflated her, on another day. It might have made it all worse.

Instead, she brightened.

"I've read you," she whispered, her eyes widening, her hands coming up to touch her lips. "Elias! I've read your silent language! Just now!"

He raised his dark brows, his smirk melting away. "Oh?"

She nodded, bouncing on the balls of her feet, and gave a little squeak of pleasure. "Yes! I … I was going to speak, and then I saw your posture and your face and I knew I oughtn't because I could feel your mindset! But you said no words! I did it, Elias!"

He was silent for a moment, his countenance shifting from sunlight to something a little darker, something that smelled of nearing rain. He dropped his arm off the parcels and draped both onto his knees, leaning toward her, eyes glittering. "That was not the first time," he told her firmly. "You knew very well what I was conveying last night."

She blinked, a smile tugging at the corners of her lips. "Oh, I suppose that might be true," she realized with awe. "Though I must have been wrong at that time, considering your actions directly following said interpretation. Yes, I think I was wrong then. But I am not wrong now."

He watched her again as another tick of the clock passed them, mirrored by a tick in his jaw, a little jumping muscle that conducted the music of silence that was swelling in the air.

"You called me 'Hattie' just now," she told him, allowing the smile to fully form on her face. "You never do that. You never have."

"What?" he snapped, fully frowning now. "I didn't."

She nodded. "You did. I assure you."

There was another beat of silence. Outside, the clock tower at the nearby church sounded the toll of the hour.

Hattie gave a happy, little sigh. "I did it," she said quietly, once more, to herself.

"I have things to do," Elias said abruptly, shoving himself to his feet.

"No, you don't," Hattie observed as he stalked past her and exited the room entirely, leaving her smiling countenance in his wake.

✦

Chapter Thirteen

I F IT WOULD not have announced his petulance to the world at large, Elias Selwyn would have taken dinner in his room.

As it was, he would not give her the satisfaction. Or himself, he supposed.

It wasn't exactly that he was displeased that she'd read him and read him well. It was just that she'd caught on so damned quickly. He thought he'd have at least one full day of enjoying the upper hand in their endless sparring.

Instead, he'd had about twelve hours.

And damned if he wasn't proud of her amidst the frustration.

Yes, pouting in his room over a solitary meal had held some appeal, but he was coming to enjoy these communal meals in a queer sort of way. The more time he spent with the wards, grown as they had into mostly adults, the less outside their sheen he felt. They squabbled and faltered and blustered like any other person.

And that was oddly comforting.

Besides, he had been taught once and over again in the cavalry that there are only two options in moments of combat: engagement and retreat. And one should only retreat if defeat is a certainty or as a strategic gambit.

Retreat, Elias knew, should never be a thing of indulgence.

Still, it burned him a little that he could not indulge.

And he liked lamb, he supposed. Tonight they were having lamb.

"Mint jelly is a vile thing," Ruby Little observed, jiggling a sample of it on the edge of a spoon. "Tell me, why do we explore the globe, corner markets in divine samples of all things sensory, and then put mint on lamb?"

"Why eat lamb at all?" Errol Cagney pondered, helping himself to more summer cauliflower, roasted to a caramelized golden brown. "Sweet *leanbhaí.*"

Ruby frowned at him. "Do not make me feel guilty. I only wished to lament the lack of cumin."

"Mint jelly," Elias echoed, glancing at Hattie, who was also looking at hers with a discontent wrinkle of her brow. "Three?"

She blinked, looking up at him with a flash of alarm. "What?"

"Three," he repeated, slower, a little glow of pettiness alight in his chest. "Isn't it?"

She blinked. Thrice. "Yes."

"Oh, excellent," said Rhys Caradoc. "Now there are two of them."

Elias grinned for the first time since that afternoon, but he did not take his eyes off Hattie, lingering and relishing in the deepening of her frown.

He supposed the others were observing them, but it was hard to care.

He wondered if she had torn her room apart yet, looking for that hideous tiger-striped dressing gown.

She wouldn't find it.

And the new one would suit her much better, anyhow.

He had taken his time choosing it. He had considered which colors might glow against her skin and hair. Which hues best suited brass and molten bronze.

He had settled on a glinting, garnet red in cool, liquid satin, with bell-shaped sleeves and a broad sash resembling an Eastern kimono. The boxes had vanished from the chaise in the parlor, but he did not know if she had opened them yet.

She was going to have to, he thought, if she wanted to wear anything other than a shift after changing out of her dress tonight.

Libba Lennox cleared her throat very loudly and made a show of clicking her knife against her plate as she cut into her lamb. She whispered a word under her breath that might have been, "Lewd."

He smiled to himself, dropping his eyes to his plate, and curated his own bite of food.

He'd have to buy Hattie a second dressing gown, he realized. For when the weather turned colder.

He wouldn't mind that task at all.

"Miss French!" came a panicked voice, the new head maid bursting into the dining room and startling them all into staring up at her. "My ... My lord? I don't know who to tell, but we've had an incident."

"Oh, thank God for that," Rhys muttered.

"What's happened?" Hattie asked, half out of her chair already. "What's the matter?"

"There's someone upstairs!" the girl exclaimed, her face sheet white. "We were cleaning out the master suite, as we were told, of course, and ... Well, someone's up there. Someone who's not us!"

"That's impossible," Malcolm Lennox said, frowning. "Unless ... Has anyone brought someone else into the house tonight?"

One by one, they shook their heads.

"My girls have gone home," Monica insisted.

"My people won't arrive for another day or two," Libba snapped. "Stop looking at me."

"Why do you think there's someone upstairs?" Errol asked, his voice soothing as he stood and ushered the young woman into his chair, moving to pour her a glass of wine. "What frightened you?"

"We heard ... well, whispers, my lord," she said, blinking her big eyes up at him with a softening in her face as she accepted the glass. "And rustling. Like people were hiding and afraid of being discovered. Spooked us all!"

"Hattie!" Elias snapped, only just realizing that she was on her way out of the room. "Where are you going?"

She startled, turning on her heel to stare at him. "There!" she said, shrill as you please. "You've done it again!"

He grimaced at her, pushing his chair back. "Going to fight them off with your bare hands?" he demanded. "You should let the men go up and check."

"What men?" Rhys demanded, frowning.

"It is my room," she reminded him, bunching her skirts into her hands and turning. "I am going."

"God in heaven," he muttered, flinging the chair away and scrambling after her as it clattered to the floor. "You are impossible!"

"Someone pass me the jelly?" Rhys's voice said behind them. "What? They're handling it."

Elias stomped after her, annoyed with how quickly she was moving, those burnished-peach skirts of hers swishing over the floors as she clipped away from him. He wasn't going to run. He wasn't going to chase after her like some lovesick swain.

"Hattie!" he boomed again, his jaw aching from how badly his teeth wished to smash into one another.

"I am Hattie to you now," she sang over her shoulder. "Harriet no more!"

"Harriet!" he corrected, grasping the banister and bounding up the stairs after her. "Slow down!"

She ignored him, marching past the piles of sheets the staff had removed from the suite, and the pianoforte that now sat in the hall.

The doors hung open, with two young women in maid uniforms retreating to the end of the hall observing them warily from the shadows. The rooms had been lit, even as the summer sun was still setting, likely in preparation for an evening of devoted cleaning.

The flamelight danced down the hall in a cacophony of combating shadows, likely doing nothing to alleviate the anxiety of the spooked cleaners.

"You may go rest," Hattie said to them without pausing, flicking her wrist like an empress well accustomed to giving orders. "I shall see to this!"

He wondered exactly what sort of trouble he would get in for running ahead and locking her out of her own rooms.

He stopped, holding a hand up to the two servants before they could flee. "Where exactly," he said through his teeth, "did you hear the sounds?"

"Near the bed, sir," one maid said. "Lord. My lord. Near the bed. On the side with the wardrobe."

"In the wardrobe," the other maid said. "Or under the bed?"

"Fine," he said. "You may go."

He gave a little sigh of relief as he turned and found Hattie in entirely the wrong portion of the suite, peeking under armchairs. He noted that she had taken up a fire poker, though he was unclear on if she intended to use it as a weapon or a probe.

Perhaps he could just lock the entire house up and put everyone in a nearby inn. Surely, no one would argue with that.

"Willa?" she called, making him freeze with his foot halfway through a step. "Is it you?"

"Harriet," he said, exasperated. "It is not Willa."

She frowned, turning to shoot him a look. "You don't know that."

Despite himself, it did put a chill up his back. "It isn't," he repeated as firmly as he could muster. "And you're in the wrong place. Give me that poker before you harm yourself."

"No," she said, hugging it to her body as she came up to standing and gave a sniff. "All the windows are open. What if someone came in through one?"

"Scaled up the painted brickwork with their fingernails, did they?" he said flatly. "Hattie."

"Harriet?" she repeated, mocking him.

He paused, taking a long, slow inhale through his nostrils and closing his eyes against the spark of impulse that rang through his hands at that. He gave his head a little shake and sighed, blinking his vision back into place and nodding toward the bedchamber. "Come on," he said. "The maids said it was over here."

She nodded, scooting across the floor with shuffling steps until she was standing in his shadow, following him to the place where the wraiths had sounded.

The bed had been stripped down to its tufted, eiderdown mattress, he saw, and a polish rag was hanging over the footboard, dust half removed along the heavy cedar bevels. He held his arm back to stop Hattie from coming any further and bent at the knees, attempting to peer under the bed to see if anything was lurking down there in the dark.

The light from the windows was casting a harsh shadow, unfortunately, and he couldn't make much out. Though he did note that it smelled much better in here with the surf in the air than it did with the must of seven years of sealed air.

"Well?" she whispered, huffing when he only shook his head.

He turned and looked at her, reaching out to take the poker from her hands, slowly, so as not to make her grip it harder. Mercifully, she relented, letting it slip free with nothing more than a frown and whimper in protest.

He reached the poker in his hand out toward the wardrobe towering over the corner, aiming the tip of the thing at the door, and then gave two quick taps to the wood.

The sound responded immediately.

Rustling, like naughty children hiding in a corner, whispering and panicking at being caught.

"Oh, Christ!" Hattie squeaked, slapping her hands over her mouth.

He frowned.

"Is someone there?" he asked, attempting to sound stern.

More rustling. More whispers.

He glanced back at Hattie and handed her the poker, which

she snatched with more enthusiasm than Elias felt strictly necessary. "Go stand by the door," he instructed.

He waited for her to retreat, Hattie standing between the foot of the bed and the door with the poker held like a bludgeon, before he put his hands on the wardrobe handles. He counted to three. Mint jelly three. And then he swung them open.

Bats.

She screamed.

He might have too, ducking his head down as no fewer than half a dozen of them exploded out of the tattered remains of Willa's clothing, screeching and flapping about the room in just as much of a panic as Elias and Hattie.

"Get down!" he boomed at Hattie as she attempted to swing the poker wildly in the air. "On the floor!"

She ignored him, screaming incoherently at the winged interlopers as she attempted and failed to smash them with iron.

He grabbed one of the only things available—a pillow sitting on the bare bed—and smacked one of the bats toward the windows, followed by another. They kept coming back, as though they were enjoying the game, though he was certain he had begun to beg them verbally to go. *Go and be free!*

He did not know how long it took. Certainly an hour. Or a second. Or both? But one bat, one genius, blessed bat, finally found the open window.

And it must have called to the others.

Because in just a few moments, they had gone.

They had gone.

And Hattie and Elias were left panting and wild-eyed in the midst of their wreckage.

She stared at him, poker still gripped in her hands, and he stared back, his heart thundering in his chest, blood rushing in a roar in his ears.

She dropped the poker, letting it clatter to the floor, her chest rising and falling as she sucked in ragged gulps of air.

He tossed the pillow aside.

He crossed the room.

And he grabbed her, dragging her to him as he sank a hand into her hair. He claimed that intelligent, little mouth of hers before it could get itself around a single taunting observational word and he did so with relish.

She hesitated for only a second, only half a breath, before her hands came up and wrapped around the lapels of his jacket, her back arching and pressing her body firmer against his as she returned the claim, a soft, little sigh of satisfaction escaping her throat as her lips moved.

He lost himself a little, his tongue flicking out to taste her, to test if he had been right about the sweet, spiced strangeness of her flavor and the complexity of that talented tongue. He curled his fingers in her hair, groaning into her mouth, his body gone feverish and taut with the answers.

Engage or retreat, something whispered in his mind. *Choose.*

He batted the thought away, sliding his other hand down the curve of her back, dragging her closer, pressing his hips against hers.

Engage or retreat, the voice said again.

And he sighed in frustration, pulling back just a touch, just a breath, and resting his forehead against hers.

"Elias," she whispered, her lips slick and warm against his, her fingers tripping over the lines of his chest through his clothes.

"The door is open," he reminded her, reluctant and damned. "There might be more bats."

"Oh," she said, licking the taste of him from her mouth. "All right."

He sighed, taking his time unwrapping himself from her, stroking the back of her neck as he untangled his hand from her hair. Stepping back as slowly as he could muster.

She did not look angry at the interruption, however.

She was wearing that little curving smile she got when she was thoughtful, those amber eyes tilted up at him as she observed every move he made.

"Elias," she said, almost a whisper. "What is my name?"

"Harriet," he answered, a little puzzled by the question.

She shook her head, the smile still in place.

"Hattie?" he corrected. A guess.

She showed her teeth then, the little curve of her mouth breaking into something more satisfied, and leaned forward on her toes to claim one more kiss from him, small and quick.

"My name is Harriet," she reminded him, sounding very much like the girl she'd once been, "but my people call me 'Hattie.'"

And then she spun on her heel and fled back out into the house proper.

Part IV

Rote, Rehearsal, and Repetition

Chapter Fourteen

IT SEEMED TO Hattie that things did not accelerate with proper urgency at Starling's Rest until they had crested the halfway mark between the reading of Willa's final wishes and their culmination. Though, of course, she had been frantic about it all since the very first.

In a sudden tide of activity, there was abruptly an absence of bodies within the Rest itself, with Rhys at his pavilion and Libba at her theater. Monica had taken her seamstresses and fabrics to her workshop while Ruby had opted to set up a small laboratory in Errol's greenhouse for the time being, insisting that she could not be bothered to go into town whilst preparing for something so imminent.

Even Mr. Harcourt had begun to appear again with startling regularity, often in conference with Malcolm about the termination of his contract at the bank in London and the commencement of his quarter share at Stockton & Holloway, which Hattie supposed must now become Stockton, Holloway, & Lennox, if things were equitable.

Apparently, Mr. Stockton was agreeable to this, but Mr. Holloway and son had reservations about putting a Black man on the awning.

Hattie was not concerned. Mr. Harcourt would set them straight.

She did wonder if Malcolm intended to take Jasper Townsend from his clerk's post at the East India Company and elevate him at this new post. She had not asked because she was uncertain if such a question would be uncouth.

She liked Jasper and would hate to offend him so shortly after resuming his acquaintance.

Then, of course, there was Elias.

He had also been much away as their wedding and the funeral drew closer.

"Do you want to hear the banns read?" he had asked her last night. "We only have one more Sunday to go."

She had declined, anxiety spiking in her chest at the thought that such a thing was being announced, week after week, just a few blocks down toward the sea.

She thought about it now, every time the church bells rang.

The master suite was almost ready. She was to move into it first. She had chosen drapery and linens, a new rug, and, naturally, a completely different standing wardrobe, which had never, insofar as she could be apprised, been host to any winged nesting.

The bats did not end in that first discovered cache, as it happened, and Errol had gone with his father to investigate the walls and route them back out into their natural habitat: which was to say, not the house.

Never the house.

After which, Errol, Mr. Cagney, Hattie, Elias, and all four of the maids had been forced to undergo a fully violating examination by Brighton's best surgeon in search of any tiny bite or puncture marks on their person, lest the bats have transferred to them the ultimate death sentence of rabidity.

"If you find it," Hattie had pointed out, "there is nothing to be done but experience woe. And then perish."

"Not so," Rhys had said from his observational perch in the corner. "The surgeon can muzzle you so you don't come after us before the perishing."

"I still shall," Hattie had replied with a sniff. "And I am faster than you."

"On foot, perhaps," Rhys had said ominously.

Luckily, no one had been marked for a horrible death, and all were cleared to resume their normal activities.

How bats had found their way into the upper floors with all the windows sealed remained a mystery, and Hattie was not certain she cared to ever solve it. She had no space in her mind opposite all the other things currently in residence, which did not exclusively refer to one Elias Selwyn, thank you very much.

It also extended to matters like what to do with that portrait of Willa's childhood family. And the discovery that in addition to half a dozen new costumes and who knew what else, that Monica Thresher had taken it upon herself to make Hattie a wedding dress.

"Ruby gave me the idea," she had said excitedly as she'd pulled the first assembly of the thing over Hattie's head for tailoring. "Flame colors, she said, and she was right! You are a flame. So I thought orange and gold for the dress itself and the piping will be blue and red. It will look spectacular!"

"Are you making a matching suit for Elias?" Hattie had asked, still dizzy from the costume fitting for the showcase, her gown fit for a king.

At which point, Monica had laughed for some time. "Of course not," she said. "No one looks at the groom."

"That is a thought, though," Ruby Little had put in, holding the Jadwiga costume up to herself in the mirror. "I've not made a scent for Elias yet. What do you think, Hattie? What smells spark in that strange, little mind of yours when you think of him?"

"None with vanilla," Hattie had remarked primly and then ignored the knowing glance that Monica and Ruby shared in response.

As for Elias himself, she had not truly spoken to him since that day in the master suite. The odd comment here and there, like the barb about going to hear the banns, had been exchanged.

There had been plenty of silent language to untangle from meal to meal. But there had been no private discourse, and as a matter of consequence, no further kissing or intimacy whatsoever.

She did not care. Not one whit.

And she did not think it mattered how well she liked the new red dressing gown, either. It was only that it was odd, how well it fit her. The other one, the one that had gone missing, had always been just a little too large above the waist, and a bit too tight about the hips.

This one fit like she had allowed Monica to pin it to her during creation.

It was not worth pondering that she liked the garment itself. Nor was the thrill that Elias had been moved to do something so spectacularly childish for her, specifically. No, not worth pondering at all.

Still, she had grabbed Ruby by the arm and told her in no uncertain terms, "Saltwater accidentally swallowed, bonfire smoke, and the smell of clouds heavy with rain they are about to unleash. Silver and gray and the rumble of far-off thunder, rolling ever nearer."

And Ruby, for once, had not mocked or needled her about it, but only nodded, wide-eyed. "Anything else?"

"Eight," Hattie had said, and then she'd sighed in frustration and fled to her next task.

If it had occurred to her to be so petulant in her ruminations on Elias's withholding of private discourse, she might have made hyperbolic notes on what could compel him to finally come to her, as he ought. And if, had she been so compelled, she had allowed her mind to flit toward hypothetical grandiosity, she might have thought that perhaps it would take a royal decree to simply make him behave sensibly. For once.

As it happened, one came.

And so did Elias.

"Harriet!" he called, stalking through the halls in his Hessian riding boots like an angry schoolmaster. "Did you write to the prince?!"

Hattie, in that moment, had been sitting with the Polish seamstress, practicing a volley of rhymes. "Me?" she said, truly confused. "No. At least not the English one."

"Harriet," he said again, slower and less patient as he brandished forth a letter. "I do not have the patience to address your retinue of princes just now. This was addressed to you, from *our* Prince Regent."

She stood, crossing the room, and took it from him, ensuring that their fingers brushed as she did so. "Oh," she said, flipping the thing over in her hands with a little sigh of annoyance. "He always sends this. Or he used to, anyhow, when we did the showcase as children. He attends."

"Oh, 'he *attends*,'" Elias said mockingly in what she thought was a very poor mimic of her voice. "What the devil am I supposed to do to prepare for it?"

"Shall I go?" the seamstress said, already halfway gone, using Hattie's nod as the final seal on her retreat.

"Look what you've done," Hattie said, frowning after the young woman. "I've only got a week left to practice, Elias!"

He was staring at her with an incredulous, simmering heat in his eyes, like he wanted to grip her by the shoulders and shake her. "Practice," he repeated. "Yes, perhaps that is something we ought to discuss? Are there rehearsals for this event? A schedule? Anything resembling structure?"

"Of course," said Hattie, frowning. "Libba does that, usually. She was ever the director."

"She hasn't said a word to me about it!" he said, throwing his hands up. "What is my role here?!"

Hattie narrowed her eyes. "She told you to find a poem. I was there, Elias. We discussed it."

"Oh, find a poem!" he exclaimed, sarcasm tipping each consonant. "Is that all?"

"Well, no ..."

He made a noise like a kicked cat, throwing his hands up and stomping around her to collapse on the chaise. His head dropped into his hands, all the while shaking as he muttered unintelligibly to himself and stared blankly ahead at a particular fiber of the carpet between his toes.

Hattie watched this, a little befuddled about why he was in such a state. "You are being very theatrical," she observed. "Are you often so?"

He blinked, like the carpet fiber were speaking to him, his fingers pressing into the flesh above his eyebrows.

"We will find you a poem," she decided. "Please do not resign to catatonia on the account of something so small. And I shall speak to Libba about rehearsals if it will soothe you."

"'Soothe' me," he repeated, almost dreamily, chuckling to himself like he'd gone mad. "You know," he said, glancing up, "I have oft wondered if any of you are actually sad that she is dead. I know she requested this bizarre celebration of a requiem, but … none of you are acting as though it were strange at all."

Hattie blinked, a little thump of pain landing between her breasts, and frowned at him. "Are *you* sad?"

He watched her for a moment, also frowning, and sighed, leaning back against the chaise, dropping his head into the shaft of sunlight from the window, and turned his eyes up to the ceiling. "Yes," he said. "I think I am. That's a little stupid, isn't it? I don't think she even liked me."

Hattie hesitated for a moment, uncertain what the right thing to say was, what the right language for this could be.

She found herself crossing the room without deciding she ought to and sinking into the chaise at his side. It was a surprise, she noted, how naturally her body moved in this way, and with intention, reached out to place her hand over his, dipping her fingers into the recesses between his knuckles.

"I cannot accept that she is actually dead," she whispered. "So it is hard to know what to feel. In her letter to me, she speaks of her body in the earth and a gravestone atop it, of my visiting her on a bench next to her resting place and speaking to her there.

But there is no body. She is not here. We do not know where she is or what happened."

"You think she is alive?" he asked, turning his head from where it was cradled against the top of the chaise and looking at her through the glare of sunlight. "She just stopped communicating with everyone seven years ago?"

Hattie shrugged, giving a little sigh. "Perhaps. She loved to travel and she was never particularly forthcoming about her motivations or aims. I would rather believe she has started anew somewhere sunny and foreign than consider that she wandered into tragedy alone, and far from home."

He gave a little smile, a short, reluctant chuckle escaping his chest. "Perhaps she married a villager on some remote island," he said, "and has a gaggle of loinclothed children to look after now."

"It would make keeping up with her letters very difficult," Hattie agreed, mirroring his little smile. "I stopped writing to her as often, you know. And so she stopped writing to me as well. If I hadn't done that, I might have noticed how long it had been since anyone had heard from her."

"Noticing wouldn't likely have changed anything," he told her. "And you were doing what she wished you to do. You were living your life, fulfilling your potential, and so on."

"Was I?" she said, considering it. "If that is what she wanted for us all, then why anchor us here again as her final wish? Perhaps we oughtn't have left in the first place."

He frowned, looking down at her slender fingers stroking the spaces between his knuckles. "Do you not wish to stay here?" he asked. "For the year to come? After that?"

"I don't wish to leave in any active way," she replied, turning the thought over in her head. "Do you?"

He shook his head slowly. "No. I thought I would. I thought I'd come here and listen to the will and get back to Hounslow as fast as my carriage would get me there. The year imposition sounded outrageous initially, but now … I don't know. I can't imagine going back."

"Neither can I," she agreed. "Even though it is my fault you left this place for so long, Elias, I am glad you have found your way home again."

He was silent for a moment, his brows drawing together as his gaze snapped up to meet hers. "It was not your fault I left."

"It was," she protested. "It is all right. I am not too delicate to know my faults. I said that awful thing to you that day and—"

"Hattie!" he said, sounding a little desperate somehow.

It did silence her.

He gave an odd, dry laugh, shaking his head. "I didn't leave because of what you said. I didn't even leave because of what I did, though that was absolutely humiliating enough that I wished to run as far and fast as I could from here and never look back. I was convinced that I couldn't belong here. It was no one's direct doing but my own."

"But you are the baron," she protested, shaking her head. "You are the *only* one who belongs here."

He shrugged, coloring a little. "It didn't seem that way to me then. Willa was forced to raise me. She didn't choose me. And she wouldn't have. I knew that and she did too."

Hattie tensed, frustration fluttering against the bones in her throat, flapping like wings. It was like the indignation she felt at how wrong he was had slowed the formation of her ability to correct him into coherent words, catching them halfway between the mud of thought and the flint of speech behind her tongue.

"She didn't dislike you, Elias," she finally managed to blurt out. "Not in the way you mean."

He laughed outright then, flipping his hand over under hers and dragging his fingertips against the palm of her hand. "No? In what way did she dislike me?"

"The way we often dislike a mirror," Hattie said seriously. "The day you finally convinced her to let you go away, I was outside the door, still wet from the pier. I was eavesdropping. And after, she stalked out and said to me, 'That boy is too much like me to ever listen to a word from my mouth.'"

"She didn't say that," he protested, a little hopeful, by Hattie's estimation.

She raised her eyebrows. "I am a terrible liar," she reminded him. "She also got angry at Ruby once and told her that one day, she would be grown and fate had a way of forcing you to contend with copies of your own youthful insufferableness. She got close to Ruby's face and said she could not wait to watch her raise a daughter."

"What did Ruby say?" he asked, his smile looking steadier now, more real.

"That she would simply never have a child," Hattie replied earnestly. "At which point Willa laughed and said such abstinence hadn't saved her from the trial of it, so why should it save Ruby, either?"

"Insufferableness," Elias repeated. "What a word."

"It is unwieldy," Hattie agreed. "But that's why I remember it, maybe. Ugly words stick in the mind."

He chuckled again, pressing his thumb against her palm. "I did ask Mr. Harcourt about Willa's family," he said. "After you reminded me. He didn't say much that was useful, just that she was an orphan by the time she married and came into the marriage with a hefty fortune."

"Perhaps her name was not even truly Starling, then," said Hattie, watching their entwined hands with a fascination that was bubbling somewhere at the juncture of her ribs, threatening to hiccup out of her mouth if she did not focus elsewhere. "It might be like my surname and Ruby's, given by a foundling home. A noun to describe or something from a list."

"A noun?" Elias said, looking surprised. "Your parents were not called French?"

She shook her head. "I do not think so, though I suppose anything is possible. They gave me that name because my first word was a French one. I'd learned from all the French maids and minders who flooded into Brighton when we were young, fleeing the unrest. And Ruby was always so tiny, so much smaller than the other girls her age, so she is called 'Little.' Some children were just given the color of their hair or the month they were delivered to the home."

He stared at her, those dark-blue eyes searching her face. "That seems rather callous," he said softly.

"Does it?" she responded. "I can't say it is any less sentimental than families called 'Cooper' or 'Fletcher' because some ancestor made barrels or arrows. Can you?"

He blinked, a flicker of something like awe passing over his face. "I suppose not," he admitted. "I do not even know what 'Selwyn' means."

"It means 'good friend,'" she said immediately. "From Old or Middle English. 'Sele' could also mean … hm, 'prosperous' or 'fortunate,' rather than 'good.' So it could also be 'lucky friend' or 'auspicious friend.'"

He made a little sound in his throat, half choke, half laugh. "Well," he said. "I'd say my father has lost the plot, but I know enough Coopers and Fletchers who don't make a damn thing out of wood, so perhaps that's unfair."

"You also need feathers," she said with a sparkle in her eye. "To fletch. Like, say, from a …"

"Starling?" he guessed, smiling now. "It is a bird."

"A common bird," she replied. "But shiny. Perhaps Errol will know more about them?"

"It seems unlikely it is not her real name," he mused. "An heiress would have legacy if she had money, surely?"

"I do not know," said Hattie. "I am only newly an heiress myself. And I have no legacy to speak of."

"Well, now," he said. "You said that convincingly, and it is a bald-faced lie. Perhaps you're more skilled at deception than you thought."

She laughed, her cheeks tingling with something between pleasure and bashfulness as he continued to tangle their fingers together. "I met someone else with my surname once," she told him, "but he spelled it with two *F*s. Ffrench. I was still a child, so I asked him if he was from France, a question to which he took serious offense."

"Two *Fs*," Elias said with amusement. "Welsh? They like their double letters."

She shook her head. "That was my second guess, at which point he got even more flustered. I will never forget the way he shouted, *'Galway, my dear!'*, as though his ancestors had overheard my error. And, to wit, I have never made that mistake again."

"Ah, well," he said, lifting her hand and pressing a soft kiss to the back of it. "How else do we ever learn?"

Chapter Fifteen

I T TOOK ALL of twenty minutes into the first showcase rehearsal for Elias to regret ever opening his fool mouth and requesting such a thing.

"Shoulders *back*, Elias," Libba snapped at him, slapping the intersection of his spine and ribs with her knuckles. "You're a baron, not a barmaid. This isn't the jacket he's wearing on the day, is it?"

"God, no," Monica said from her stool near a quartet of dress forms. "I can fix it, though, if he lets me."

"What's wrong with it?" he demanded, only to be ignored by both women as he looked helplessly down at the double-breasted linen jacket, which had looked, to him, perfectly serviceable this morning.

"Color's all wrong," Ruby told him from her chemist's stand a few feet away, dripping with sympathy. "Why would you wear brown?"

"Everyone wears brown," he insisted, ignoring that none of the wards were, just now, wearing it.

"Doesn't taper at the waist," Monica added. "Too baggy about the shoulders."

"It's such a shame, really," Ruby continued, arranging her glass vials and bottles on her little table in the sunlight. "You've such a scrumptious shape."

"All right," Errol Cagney said mildly. "Leave him."

"How's my form?" Rhys Caradoc asked, puffing his chest up and striking a knightly pose.

"Skinny," said Ruby without looking at him.

"Rangey," Libba corrected, tilting her head to the side.

"I wish I were either," Monica put in gently, patting her pleasantly plump hips. "You're beautiful, Rhys."

"Damn right, I am," he said. "And so are you, *chwaer*."

She grinned, tucking her wispy, blonde hair behind her ears, and shook her head. "The poem," she said. "Try again."

Elias groaned. "Where is Harriet?"

"Oh, he wants Hattie," said Libba with an exaggerated pout. "Isn't that sweet?"

"She'll be along," Rhys said, his eyes sparkling. "She doesn't need to rehearse the same way we do."

"She and Malcolm don't perform as such," Errol explained. "They haven't props or scripts. They have to wait for the audience to engage them."

"With numbers and letters," Ruby said, tapping her fingernails against the rims of her beakers. "One, two … Rhys! Give it back!"

"No, I need it!" he retorted, which immediately devolved into one chasing the other around the pavilion while Elias watched in helpless fascination.

"You don't have any siblings, do you, Selwyn?" Errol asked him, sidling up next to Libba to join in their observation of the chasing farce.

Elias shook his head, eyes following their progress. "No, my mother remarried after I was born and the two of them realized in fast order that children are too much of a fuss for their sensibilities. They didn't make the same mistake again," he said. "I don't think this is usual, even for siblings, all the same."

"Of course it is," said Libba with a sniff. "We're not siblings, anyhow. Not really. Well, Mal and I are, but not the others."

"No," Errol agreed, his eyes following Ruby's petite frame as it feinted and spun in her red skirts, knocking Rhys flat on his bottom. "No, we aren't."

"Get your own!" Ruby crowed, planting a dainty slippered foot on his chest and leaning down to pluck the beaker from his hand.

"You could've broken it!" Rhys whined.

"And it would have been worth it, honestly," Ruby replied, smirking as she let him up.

"You can't humiliate me in my own domain," he continued, leaping to his feet like a cat. "I own the stone you stand on!"

"Yes, yes," said Ruby, already walking back to her table. "Rhys bloody Caradoc, master of the gazebo."

"It's a *pavilion*," he intoned, following her just a little too closely to maximize his antagonism. "I need more scent, by the by."

"Are you going to pay for it this time?" Ruby asked, winning a sputtering scoff from Rhys.

"Oh, it is easy to forget how wonderful it is when we're together." Monica sighed wistfully, as though she were watching an idyllic family tableau. "I'm barely even sad about Berlin anymore."

Elias cleared his throat, attempting to find his slot in this odd woodwork puzzle. "Oh, right," he said politely. "You were making opera costumes, yes? What was the production?"

She blinked at him, smiling brightly. "*Dido and Aeneas*," she said. "Terribly sad. We were doing it in Rococo style. Quite a lot of pastel. You would look well in a nice powder blue, you know."

"Oh," he said.

"Ah, Christ," said Errol, suddenly hopping to action and striding off toward the street. "My pigs!"

"Oh, the pigs!" Ruby echoed in a far more excited tone of voice, dropping all of her vials to hurry after him. "The little one is mine! You promised!"

"What are you going to do with a pig?" Errol chuckled, turning to wait for her.

Rhys immediately swiped the beaker again and tucked it into his waistcoat.

Elias frowned, watching them greet the wagon. "'Pigs'?"

"They do tricks," Libba offered, patting him on the shoulder. "You'll see it soon. Now again, from the first stanza!"

He sighed, turning back to face her and wondering just how high she might have climbed in the cavalry, in a different world.

And he obeyed.

Oddly, the pigs ended up helping him. They seemed to enjoy the flow of rhyming verse and keeping them entranced was enough motivation to sufficiently ease him into repeating the verses over and over again until they were fully memorized.

It did not, however, stop him from thinking about his apparently deeply unflattering jacket. And when the afternoon grew very hot, he took it off and handed it to Monica.

"Oh," she said, clutching it to her chest. "To fix?"

"Or burn. Whichever," he said, shrugging as he rolled his sleeves to his elbows. "Feel free to come by my chambers at your leisure to assess the rest of my wardrobe."

"Truly?" she asked, as though he'd just baked her a sheet cake.

He grimaced. "Truly."

They watched as Libba's troupe arrived from their lodgings at the inn, flocking around her as she explained the program of hours she had created for the showcase to come, stepping over the pigs as though they were unsurprised to share the stage with the wriggling pink rivals while she spoke.

"I wish we had time to finish *Pyramus and Thisbe*, but alas." Libba sighed. "We will revert to our troupe's lauded variation on Ovid's *Pygmalion*, in highlight only. Where is Lem?"

"Sick," a woman with short, cropped hair said, raising her eyebrows. "He didn't like the boat."

Elias felt a bump against his shin and looked down to find a pig nudging him with its forehead, apparently in search of more poetry. He stared down at the creature for a moment before kneeling and giving it a scratch behind the ears.

"I wish we had somewhere to sit," he whispered to the pig, who immediately flopped onto its hind parts in a dutiful sitting position, startling Elias. "Well," he said, "look at you."

"She can shake your hand as well," Errol called from the other side of the pavilion. "And play dead. Her name is Peach."

Elias chuckled, extending his hand half in jest. "Pleasure to meet you, Peach."

To his utter shock, the pig slapped her cloven foot against his palm and guided the shaking motion.

"Christ," he muttered, cupping his hand over her head. "I'll never eat pork again."

That was how Hattie came upon him, arriving from his rear, having observed God-knew-how-much of his discourse with Peach the pig. Her shadow fell across his back, bringing the pig's attention up before Elias caught on, and he turned to find her looking down at him with half a bemused smile while he had one hand on the pig's head and the other wrapped around her hoof.

"Good afternoon," she said, kneeling down to peer at the pig. "A rival?"

"Yes," he said. "I'm terribly sorry. I'm in love."

She giggled, reaching out to touch the pig's flat nose. "Did you teach Elias the language of jests, little one? So quickly, too!"

"I could always jest," he said with a sniff. "I just chose not to."

"And the language of lies as well," she marveled, her eyes sparkling amber gold in the sunlight as she beheld him.

It was then that he realized he hadn't been lying at all.

He was in love.

Shit.

"Hattie! Malcolm!" Libba cried. "Come! I have to show you your places!"

Hattie smiled and stood, using his shoulder to help herself to her feet and giving him a little squeeze before she sashayed off to receive her orders, leaving that odd spiced sweetness lingering in the air in her wake.

"Shit," he said aloud, just to the pig.

The pig seemed to nod in agreement, glancing over its pink shoulder to watch Hattie as well and then looking back at Elias with an expression of pure sympathy.

"Do you want a dog bed?" Elias asked her. "Or do you prefer to sleep at the foot of my bed instead?"

He stood, looking about for Errol, and strode toward him, pleased to a degree that ought to have alarmed him when the pig turned and trotted after him in concert.

"I'm keeping this pig," he said to Errol. "She's mine now."

Errol chuckled. "All right. But she still has to perform at the showcase."

"So must we all." Elias sighed and turned to watch his bride-to-be as she glittered in the sun, shaking the hands of a motley assemblage of actors and vagabonds, clearly finding many among them who spoke tongues other than English. "So must we all."

"You'll have questions, I assume?" Errol pressed, following Elias's eyeline to Hattie with a knowing raise of his tawny brows. "About the pig, I mean."

"The pig," he said, still watching Hattie. "Right. Many. Her preferences and so on?"

"I'm happy to answer any question you have," Errol told him, giving him a clap on the shoulder. "Feel free to ask."

"I'll do that," Elias replied, "if any good questions ever occur to me."

And, he thought privately, if he couldn't get up the courage to ask the lady directly.

Chapter Sixteen

B Y THE THIRD rehearsal, the Starling brood had begun to draw a crowd of curious onlookers. It was typical, at least so far as Hattie remembered, from back when they'd performed under the Grand Pavilion with Willa at their head, and not worth fussing over, as the same people would likely turn out to see the full performance on showcase day.

Still, Rhys seemed to take issue with it.

Or with one onlooker in particular.

Hattie wouldn't have noticed her there at all if he hadn't spun so suddenly, lighting up like a taper at Michaelmas, his curls quivering with outrage. "No!" he had sung, pointing a damning finger into the crowd, aimed at a coif of stylish, golden-blonde hair in their midst, until the others parted to reveal Persephone Boswell. "This is a closed rehearsal! Begone!"

"'Closed'?" she repeated, drawing nearer with a smirk on her lips. "You've no walls. How can it be closed?"

"'Walls'?" Rhys repeated, leaping off his pedestal and knocking over several of his props in the process as he prowled toward her. "You know what has walls?"

"No," she said, raising her pale brows. "What?"

He grimaced, coming up short. "Our … erm … house?"

"Oh, devastating," Ruby murmured.

"My goodness," Libba said quickly, stepping to Rhys's side

with a hand to his shoulder. "Lovely to see you again, Seph."

"Miss Elizabeth!" Persephone said, turning her attention to Libba with a blinding smile. "How do?"

"It's 'Liberty' now, actually," Libba replied with a grin. "Come, let's talk … elsewhere."

Which won a groan of disappointment from the rest of the tourists amassed outside Rhys's pavilion.

"Oh, go grouse by the shore!" he snapped at them, until they began to reluctantly disperse. "Ingrates."

"I think perhaps we're done for today, anyhow?" Errol suggested, looking for all the world like a man trying to swallow his amusement. "I think we've got the gist now, anyway."

"Until the dress rehearsal," Monica put in. "We can do that at the house, I suppose."

"Which does have walls, you know," Malcolm said with a grin.

"Does it?" Ruby replied, already packing up her things. "Oh, Hattie, come here. I've something for you."

She withdrew a strip of linen, waiting for Hattie to draw close enough, and tipped a vial of pale-blue liquid over to dampen the edge of it. She waved it in the air for a moment, then turned and passed it under Hattie's nose.

Immediately, the world swam a bit. Hattie could feel her pupils flaring, her skin prickling with sensation at the gust of clashing scents that hit her all at once. Salt, smoke, rain.

"How?" she whispered, staring at the dancing motes of color in the sky. "Ruby, how?"

"Excellent," said Ruby, grinning like a cat. "And look at this."

She produced her hand, holding it open with a delicate wrought-metal charm in her palm, shaped like the number eight.

Hattie stared at it, still dazed.

"It will go on the vial," Ruby announced, closing her hand and pulling away all of her surprises, dumping them into the leather bag she'd brought with her. "I'll bottle it up tonight. You can give it as a wedding present if you wish, though of course, I demand credit."

"Of course," Hattie said, still a little stunned and resisting the urge to reach out and snatch the scent from Ruby. "Yes."

But Ruby was already gone.

It wasn't until later, watching the last of her things get moved out of her bedroom en route to the master suite, that she realized why it had affected her so. It was the maids pulling her linens loose and, in so doing, dislodging the two little port glasses, stained with dried-up wine, that had been hiding under her bed.

They'd rolled out, knocking against Hattie's feet, and with them, a flurry of memory had hit her in exactly the same register of color and scent as that wave of doused linen under the pavilion.

Elias here in her bed.

Elias digging his hands into her hair.

Elias's tongue in her mouth.

She shivered.

He hadn't kissed her again, had he?

Not like that.

Why hadn't he? Why not?

She had followed the maids closely, wanting to seal herself in the master suite the instant her things were deposited there so she could dig out the red dressing gown and hold it to her face. She wanted to wrap herself in it and ponder these questions.

She wanted to, but she could not.

She was forced to address other duties. The paintings. The pianoforte. The showcase. Dinner.

But the scent still clung to her, haunting her in wisps around her person.

And when he began his ritual with the crystal wineglass at dinner that night, it was all she could do not to throw her plate aside and crawl across the table to claim him.

"First night in the baroness's chambers, I hear?" Mal said to her, as though he could not tell she had gone half-rabid by his side.

Perhaps he was attempting to quell the madness.

She turned her head in a snap, trying to process what he'd said.

"I saw the painting you had covered and set aside," he continued, swirling his own wine, his dark eyes fixed on her. "Willa as a child. Intriguing."

"There are three paintings of her," Hattie said, more terse than she'd intended. "That one, the one with her late husband, and the one with us. I cannot find the last. Do you know where it is?"

Mal shook his head, his smooth brow wrinkling for once. "No. That is odd. Where it could it have gone?"

"I'd forgotten we sat for that," Ruby said, a little wistfully. "Elias, were you there for that? Or had you left already?"

Hattie's head swiveled back around to watch him, to observe his answer.

He gave a soft smile, setting his glass down with his long fingers lingering on the stem. "I wasn't here for the sitting," he said, "but she made me sit for the painter when I came home for Christmas so he could add me to the ensemble. I'm in it, but I wasn't really with you all. There but also not."

"Just like you always were, I suppose," Monica said softly. "But I'm glad you are there, even so."

He gave her a little chuckle, shaking his head. "I did it to myself, you know."

No one replied to that, though Hattie thought they all looked a little shocked that he had said it.

"I'm ready for dessert," she announced, startling most of them. "Something sweet, please!"

"You heard her," Rhys said, looking a little alarmed. "Get the baroness her sugar before she has an episode."

"Not the baroness yet," Elias pointed out, fingers sliding over that carved crystal, reflecting the red of his wine onto his knuckles as he observed her. "But soon."

Hattie managed not to make any noises of abject distress.

"Ah, my berries," Errol said with delight as the crumble was served. "You're all in for a treat. They were particularly plump and juicy this year."

At that, Hattie did moan. Just a little. And filled her spoon and her mouth to prevent any further outburst.

She did *not* watch Elias Selwyn eat his berry crumble or the way he smoothed out the dollop of clotted cream over the rich compote and buttery rolled oats. She did not document the curve of his smile as he lingered with the spoon over his lips before taking a bite, every time someone spoke to him.

She ate. And minded her business.

"Fittings tomorrow," Monica reminded them all as they'd dispersed. "Do *not* try to wriggle out of it. Rhys."

"Me?" he said, already clipping to a trot to get away from her.

"Rhys!" she said again, exasperated. "I know you modified that jacket! Come back here."

"Do you think she'll catch him?" Elias's voice, rich and soft, sliding over her skin like warm rain, asked at Hattie's ear.

She could feel him, the heat of his body, just a little too close, and closed her eyes for just a fraction of a breath, memorizing it. She shivered, turning to gaze up at him, so close, she could smell the sweetness of fruit and cream on his breath.

He paused, surprise flashing in those dark-blue eyes, as though he could see the desire in her face. His gaze flickered over her features, settling on her berry-stained lips. "Hattie," he said, a little hoarsely. "Stop it."

"I didn't do anything," she breathed, marveling at how the air seemed to spark and crackle between them. She wondered if it would shock her if she reached out to touch him just now. She turned her eyes up to lock on his. "Do you want to see the suite? Now that it is finished?"

He inhaled sharply, pressing his lips together. "Do you think that wise?"

"Yes," she said in barely a murmur. "Come."

He watched her for a moment, his hands flexing at his sides, and then released a gust of air, taking a hurried step back with a shake of his head and widening of his eyes. "God," he said. "You have to stop."

She frowned. "All right. I suppose you can see it after we're wed."

"That is when I'm supposed to," he said, running a hand through his hair. "See it."

She nodded, disappointment sagging in the heat that roared through her chest, dripping there like melting ice. "All right," she said again. "Good night, Elias."

She turned, her back to the suites where her bedroom had once been, and sucked in a crisp, little gust of air, steeling herself to spend her first night above. As mistress of this house.

She made it around the corner.

Six steps.

Maybe seven.

Almost eight.

And then she felt his hand encircle her arm, just above the elbow, pulling her around to face him as he backed her against the wall, the full warmth and power of his body looming over hers as he pressed all of that delicious, shimmering heat into her gown.

Her hands came up immediately, her fingers curling into that thick, dark hair, the heels of her hands sliding along the sharp angles of his jaw as his mouth fell onto hers, his tongue rolling into her mouth.

She whimpered into it, tasting him in turn, wrapping herself in the indulgence of it as the storm cracked and the rain unleashed in her senses. She felt her body arching, pulling him closer, willing him into every recess of her very flesh. She slid a leg between his, inviting him to pin her completely, to make her one with this wall to his heart's desire as his teeth raked over her lips.

"God, I want you," he breathed, his hands trailing down over her throat, whispering over the sides of her breasts as he anchored her waist into place.

Hearing it, hearing him say it nearly broke her. The beautiful chords of his voice, wrapping around those words while he loomed over her, tasting her, feeling her. She could have melted into a puddle on the spot if not for her grip on him, anchoring her on this plane.

"Have me," she begged. "Elias, please."

He groaned, his hands flexing on her, thumbs creeping up to trace the bottoms of her breasts, so close to crossing the line, to touching her in a way that could not be undone. He rocked his hips against hers, showing her in no uncertain terms that his want was real.

She gasped, her hands faltering, digging deeper into his hair as she dragged him closer, deepening the kiss, desperate for more of it. "Elias," she said again somehow.

"Hattie, we can't," he breathed, returning every kiss, making no move to release her. "Not yet."

"We can," she argued, letting her hands slide down his face, over his shoulders and the planes of his chest. "We should."

He made a helpless, primal sound, his hands quivering on her. "You want me to have you in Willa's bed?" he asked against her mouth. "Before we're married?"

She nodded, flicking her tongue against his lips.

It seemed to break some of his resolve, his hands coming up to cup her breasts, thumbs brushing over the lace that hid them from him as he gave another press of his hips against her. "We have to stop," he grumbled, raking his eyes over her like this, under his thrall. "Oh, Jesus God."

"Why?" she asked, burning from the inside. "Why do we have to stop?"

"Because I am going to devour you if we don't," he groaned, squeezing her breasts in his hands and licking his lips at the effect of it. "Jesus," he said again.

She let her fingers trail down to his hips, tracing the line of his waistband as her eyes flickered shut to enjoy the sensation of him touching her this way. She wanted to touch him too. To cross that threshold, to run her fingers over forbidden parts of him.

And he seemed to realize it too.

It was the only thing that appeared to actually bolster his resolve. His damned resolve.

He kissed her once more, very hard, his breathing labored and hot. "Patience," he said against her mouth.

"I don't have any patience," she said, helpless with want as he pulled away. "Elias, why?"

He took her hand with him, dragging her palm to his lips, his eyes sparkling with heat and desire. "Because," he said. "The torment is part of the pleasure. If nothing else, my Hattie, there has always been the sweetness of torment between us."

She sighed, dropping her full weight back against the wall and wrapping her arms around herself. "I do not wish for torment," she told him. "But if you do, I shall endeavor to provide it."

Elias blinked. "That's not what—"

It made her smile, a little thrill that spoke to the truth of his statement darting up her spine. "Good night, Elias," she said to him. "I hope your dreams provide all the suffering you crave."

Chapter Seventeen

I T BEGAN TO storm sometime in the night.

Elias thought it somehow appropriate, as though the unresolved tension, the utter unbearable heat, had spiraled out into the universe and cracked above them in the way that it had not here on the earth.

Every rumble of thunder, every flash of light, hit him like vindication. It allowed him to eventually sleep. And he was pleased to hear it still raging when he woke again, in the hours that must have been morning, even without the sun.

"So, the choice really comes down to the day before or the day after the funeral," Harcourt was saying to him, from his customary chair in the parlor, seemingly unbothered by his own wet boots or the flashing treachery outside. "It is an unseemly way to juxtapose a wedding, but here we are, anyhow."

"Those are the only days available?" Elias responded, frowning.

"Unless you want to wait another week," Mr. Harcourt replied, giving a dainty sip to his tea as the walls shook with the force of a thunderclap. "Do you?"

"I do not," said Elias.

"Perhaps we ought to call for Miss French and ask her opinion?" Mr. Harcourt suggested, raising his brows. "She is the bride, after all."

Elias lifted his own teacup, pressing it to his lips to hide his grin. "Harriet is indisposed this morning," he said. "She is not feeling quite herself."

In truth, she was sulking and had not come to breakfast, just like the morning after he'd shared port with her in her room. She was likely planning her revenge, her barbed reaction to his withholding of the pleasures they'd both wanted.

Why was that so unbelievably delightful to him?

He couldn't wait to see what she'd come up with.

"Are you certain?" Harcourt asked, his eyes flashing an unsettling silver blue from the next ripple of light. "I thought I saw her this morning, out in the greenhouse."

"What?" said Elias, frowning and dropping the teacup back to its saucer with a clatter. "The glass greenhouse? In this weather?"

"I might have been mistaken," Harcourt said quickly. "My eyes have been playing tricks on me today. I also thought I saw a pig in the foyer when I came in."

Elias sighed, pushing himself to his feet. "I will be right back."

Evidently, there were two ladies he needed to wrangle back to safety today. He must have left the bedroom door open.

He didn't think Peach was brave enough to scale the stairs on her own, small as she was, but evidently, he'd been mistaken. He thought he'd have to search for her and chase her down, like one of the fools at the harvest festival in the mud ring, but instead, the next boom of thunder sent her little, pink body barreling out of a shadowed corner and into his legs, her squealing voice ringing out in alarm.

"Oh, for God's sake," he muttered, leaning down to pick her up and holding her to his chest as he walked to the nearest window and peered out, frowning at the greenhouse while he stroked her head. "Is Hattie out there? Do you see her?"

Peach did not answer.

She did startle again, though, as the front doors slapped open, pushed to their limit by the gale of wind that followed them indoors and the duet of squealing feminine voices that followed.

Elias turned to see Ruby and Hattie, drenched to the very bone and flinging themselves against the wood in an effort to get the doors shut. He sighed, stepping forward to assist, only to watch them wrangle it in good order, using their backs in what appeared to be a choreographed two-step until the entryway was sealed again.

"The. Damned. Wind." Ruby panted, giggling a bit and pushing dark strands of sodden hair out of her face. "I had forgotten!"

"I hadn't," Hattie said softly, her eyes on Elias.

Ruby followed her gaze, smirking at him standing there, holding his quarry. "You stole my pig," she said, pushing away from the door and tossing her wet hair so that droplets showered both Elias and Peach, the latter of whom reveled in the speckling, waving her pink head back and forth as though in invitation for more. "I shan't forget that. I'm off to find towels, Hattie, my love."

"All right," said Hattie, not moving from her place against the door, a position that Elias could not help but find all too familiar in the wake of the previous evening.

"Harriet," he said softly, drawing a step closer as he took in the effect of her dress, plastered to her like a translucent second skin. "You should not have been outside in that."

"You," she managed, swallowing to clear the dryness in her throat, "are carrying a pig."

He frowned, looking down at Peach, who looked back up to him, guileless. "Yes."

Hattie was smiling when he returned to her gaze. Diamond-sharp droplets of water fell off the burnished copper of her wet hair, beading and gleaming down the column of her throat.

He wanted to lick the rainwater from the hollow between her collarbones.

"You know, you looked just like that," he said softly, taking her in from her water-logged slippers to the dripping curls of her tangled hair, "after I pushed you in the ocean."

She narrowed her eyes, her smile twisting into a smirk. "Did

I?"

He nodded slowly. "It was an awakening for me, in fact."

Her brows rose, spiky and flat against her pale face. "Oh, for me as well," she told him. "It awakened my ability to swim."

He felt himself grinning, flashing his teeth at her, sharp and hungry. "And can you still swim, little Harriet?"

"I suppose," she said, drawing her bottom lip between her teeth. "If someone tries to drown me."

He mirrored her glare, his own eyes narrowing as he took another step toward her. "Intriguing …"

"Ah, Miss French," came Julian Harcourt's twice-blasted voice, startling the poor pig again so badly that she twisted nearly free of Elias's embrace. "Oh! There *is* a pig!"

Elias cringed, managing to bend at the waist quickly enough to let her wriggle free, her hooves clattering on the tile as she fled back to the shadows.

"Well," Hattie observed, "she's had quite enough of you."

He tossed her another glare over his shoulder as he straightened.

Mr. Harcourt was standing politely, hands folded in front of him, averting his eyes from the sodden and very visible body of Harriet French.

"Ruby!" Elias boomed, spinning on his heel and poking his head out into the hall. "Where the devil are those towels?"

"Yes, yes, I'm coming!" she cried back, her footsteps echoing as she hurried in their direction. "Goodness. You think you're giving a pair some privacy!"

"Is that Mr. Harcourt?" came Monica's voice, her pale-blonde head appearing down the hall. "Send him down, will you? I've a jacket for him."

"Oh, God," muttered Harcourt, flushing.

Elias felt oddly smug about that, for some reason. "The barrister wishes to know if we want to be married the day before or the day after the funer… the showcase," he said briskly, turning his eyes back to Hattie. "What do you prefer, my dear?"

She gave him a lazy smile, her gaze lingering on his mouth. "Surely, you prefer to wait as long as possible, Lord Selwyn. Isn't that what you're always saying?"

"I've never said that," he returned, a note of warning in his tone at her wandering attentions.

"He enjoys delays," she said to Harcourt, who was still pointedly not looking at her. "The day after, I think."

"The day before it is," Elias snapped. "Before, Harcourt. You hear me?"

The barrister only sighed.

"Mr. Harcourt, if you please!" Monica called again from the hall, which, to Elias's surprise, had the immediate effect of making the man turn and slink off where he was bid.

"Before!" Elias called again, making Hattie giggle from her place at the door as she clutched a towel to her body, running it down her throat.

He spun to glower at her. "You! Go dry off before someone sees you like that."

"Perhaps I'll wear my new dressing gown," she cooed, floating past him as she went into the embrace of the house, leaving behind wet footprints in her wake.

He watched her go, his eyes fixed on the swinging detail of her soaked-through backside, until she faded from view, at which point he sighed and collapsed against the wall himself, pushing his fingers to his temples.

There was one blessed moment of silence before the doors slapped open again, and the exact same choreography that Ruby and Hattie had performed commenced, this time starring Rhys and Malcolm.

Elias only turned, head against the paneling, and watched this time.

"Why," he said, once the doors were closed, "is everyone outside in this weather?"

"Refreshing, isn't it?" Rhys shouted, as though he'd gone deaf from the gales of wind. "Oh! A towel!"

Malcolm made a disgusted noise as Rhys whipped Hattie's discarded towel from the ground and began to dry himself. "I'll just go get myself a new one," he said. "Baron."

"Lennox," said Elias, nodding as the other man passed him.

"You never call me 'Caradoc,'" Rhys observed, rubbing the towel over his hair. "Am I more of a first-name chap?"

Elias turned to give him an exhausted look, which made the other man giggle.

"Yes, I suppose I am," Rhys Caradoc decided.

"I was wondering, actually," Elias said, watching with a morbid sort of fascination as Rhys made a show of drying himself, "why Willa trained you to be an illusionist and not … Well, everyone else got a vocation."

"I do all right," said Rhys, wiggling his dark eyebrows with a chuckle. "She wanted me to be a surgeon, in fact. Something with precision. I just refused to cooperate with anything respectable."

"Ah," Elias said, nodding. "That makes sense."

"It does, doesn't it?" Rhys agreed, dropping the now-soaked towel back onto the tile floor with a plop and sauntering past him into the house. "Well, see you at dinner!"

He sighed, resuming his restorative wall lean as Peach emerged tentatively from her shadow and began to root at the towel, flopping over onto the thing as though it were warm and cozy and not cold and wet.

Elias wondered if she liked Rhys's scent. Or perhaps Hattie's.

"Oh, that scalawag," a maid exclaimed, marching into the foyer to retrieve the towel and hesitating when she saw the pig. "Oh. Pardon, my lord."

"No, it's all right," he said. "I'll move her."

"I'd box that Welsh lad's ears if he weren't so pretty," she said to the pig as Elias lifted her from the middle, her little cloven legs dangling as the maid whipped the towel off the floor. "Lucky for you, piglet, you're a pretty one too."

"You are," he agreed quietly to Peach, after the maid had gone.

He watched the door for a moment, wondering if anyone else was going to blow in from the outdoors.

Perhaps Willa herself, in fact.

And when no one did, he nodded, sighed, and took his pig back to his bedroom.

Chapter Eighteen

HARRIET FRENCH AWOKE on the eve of her wedding day in a raw panic.

Panic, as it happened, tasted like burnt toast and roasted tomato, smashed together in a rotten paste against her tongue. It was a nasty thing to awaken to, flooding her nose and mouth as she tore from sleep with an anguished gasp of anxiety.

Something, though she was not entirely certain *what* at first, was very wrong.

Images floated in her mind from the remnants of her nightmare, of wedding bells and the church aisle. What was it? What had she done that had disturbed her sleep so?

"The rings!" she croaked, flinging herself out of bed headfirst, hands to the rug and crawling out of her blankets like a demented acrobat. "I've forgotten to get the rings!"

It was, Hattie knew, an understatement.

She'd never even ordered the damned rings. Rings she had been planning ever since that afternoon in Elias's bedchamber, when he'd shown her the one Willa had left him. She had wanted engraved rings with something nicer than *mea culpa* to exchange after the wedding, a symbol that this was not going to be a marriage of fault and regret.

And she'd forgotten them! Entirely!

She could see them in her mind's eye. She had envisioned

them so clearly and in detail that she had thought they were bloody real! There they were, glinting just beyond the seal of her eyelids on an imaginary velvet cushion, nestled together in a perfect figure eight, glinting like liquid moonlight against the dark-blue fabric.

Imaginary.

It was imaginary.

She had stumbled down the stairs with one slipper on, her hair askew, running through possibilities in her mind.

Errol didn't wear rings.

Rhys wore too many, and they were all cheap.

Malcolm's were all far too expensive.

What was she going to do?!

"Saints in a stagecoach!" A maid gasped as she beheld her future baroness, hobbling past like a grotesque from a penny dreadful.

Hattie exploded into the dining room, where Libba and Monica were seated in polite discourse over toast that looked unburnt and juice from an orange, not a tomato.

"I've forgotten the rings," she cried, immediately slumping onto the floor with her head in her hands.

"Good morning to you too," said Libba, her fork still halfway to her mouth, as Monica let out a shrill cry of alarm and leapt up from her chair to usher Hattie into one of her own. "Beautiful dressing gown."

"What on Earth?" Malcolm voice demanded a few moments later, upon which event Hattie found herself pulled to her feet and ushered again to a new location.

Libba's room.

"No one will find you in here," Libba assured here while Monica continued to pat her head. "Did we leave a slipper behind?"

"Nooo," Hattie moaned, shaking her head. "It's in my bed-room!"

"Oh, all right," said Libba, flashing a widening of her eyes at

Monica. "I'll just go fetch Ruby."

"What are the rings actually for?" Monica asked gently, holding Hattie's face to her bosom like a brood mother. "Just love tokens? Those do not have to be ready on the day of the wedding."

"But," Hattie wailed, tears pooling in her eyes, "but *mea culpa.*"

"Yes, well, you're only human," Monica replied, clearly not understanding.

Hattie shook her head, hiccupping with the force of her despair.

"Oh, God," Ruby said as soon as she appeared. "I thought this would happen sooner."

The others exchanged glances that seemed to agree.

It did not improve Hattie's comport.

After much petting and murmuring, Hattie did manage to get herself into some semblance of calm. She found that at some point, tea had been pressed into her hands, and, judging from the bitter film in her mouth, she had consumed some and done so without the cushion of sugar or cream.

"What about costume rings?" Libba suggested, hugging the poster at the foot of her bed like it might have ideas as well. "That would do the job for the day."

Hattie shook her head. "It won't."

"Oh, it would. Come now," said Ruby, tutting. "Did Elias even know you had put it upon yourself to undertake this task? Is he even aware you had planned for such a thing?"

It was the only thing that punctured Hattie's grief.

"Oh," she said, blinking through her tears. "Oh, I suppose not."

"Correct," said Ruby, sounding more relieved than smug. "Hattie, have you even spoken to the man about these rings?"

"I ... No," said Hattie, blinking furiously.

She had been sure. So sure, when she'd woken.

The dream she'd had ...

Ruby sighed, patting her on the shoulder. "That's what I thought. I say, where did you get that robe? Who keeps putting Hattie in jewel tones when we have always known those are mine to wear?"

"What if we find a way to ask him what he thinks about the idea, as a gesture *after* your wedding, without giving the game away?" Libba suggested. "I'll tell Mal to do it when the boys kidnap him tonight. Would that ease your mind, love?"

"'Kid...'" Hattie hiccupped. "'Nap'?"

"They're taking him for drinks at the Coin and Cauldron," Monica explained, still soothing along Hattie's scalp with her fingers. "Against his will, most likely."

"Should we join them there?" Ruby pondered, tilting her head to the side. "Or shall we create our own festivities?"

"'Festiv...'" Hattie began, only to be immediately shushed by three cooing voices.

"It will be all right," Monica assured her, and though Hattie wanted to argue, she also still had the hiccups.

"I have champagne for tonight," Ruby volunteered. "I thought perhaps it might be time to finally show us the mysterious master suite. We may indulge our vices and our curiosities all at once, hm?"

"'Curio...'" Hattie began, only to be shushed and smothered again, this time with another splash of tea and a warm pastry on her lap.

"I have always wanted to see those rooms," Libba said wistfully, in the tiny wedge of silence that followed. "I think Willa would bless the endeavor, us gathering there to giggle over Elias's thigh muscles in his riding breeches. It is decided."

"Is that all right, Hattie?" Monica asked, stroking her hand over Hattie's tangled hair. "Champagne in the master suite while we prepare your bridal things?"

"Bridal?" Hattie said. "Yes." And she hiccupped one more time, for luck.

ELIAS WAS NOT entirely certain how he'd come to be at the Coin and Cauldron. Only that he had other things he very much needed to be doing instead.

And yet here he was, seated at a rustic wooden table with a tiny, squat glass of nondescript, murky liquid in front of him, and a firm voice in an Irish brogue telling him in no uncertain terms to swallow, not sip.

"It's not a pleasant drink," Errol elaborated. "But an effective one."

"What is it, exactly?" Malcolm asked, examining his own little glass.

"Swill," said Rhys, taking a third gulp from his row of them. "Aren't you listening? To the groom!"

"Yes, but what's in i—*Rhys!*" Malcolm sputtered as Rhys tipped Malcom's glass forcefully into his mouth. "Christ! It burns!"

"It burns!" Errol agreed, lifting his glass as though it were a toast.

"It burns," repeated Elias, lifting his own and tipping it back into his mouth, come what may.

It did burn.

"That's exactly the face you made when you were told to marry Hattie," Rhys observed. "You don't seem quite as opposed to it these days."

"You don't, at that," Malcolm agreed, looking a bit green about the gills as he slapped a flat hand over the top of his glass. "No more for me. I'll have something civilized, thank you very much."

"Killsport," Errol said with a grin, raising two fingers to signal for the barman. "Wine, I presume?"

"Anything but that," Malcolm said, mostly with his bottom row of teeth.

The diversion in topic at least prevented Elias from having to acknowledge their observations about his match or impending matrimony, though he did suspect that was the reason for this outing.

"I'll have his, then," Rhys said, swiping the empty glass from under Mal's hand and shaking it at Errol for a top up. "I don't mind the burn."

"I will also take the wine," Elias said, once the barman had reached them, though the warmth spreading in his chest did whisper that the swill wasn't such a terrible experience, once it got past the tongue and throat.

Still, he thought it best he did not appear at the altar in the morning with his head half off.

"So, Lord Selwyn, are you prepared for the gauntlet that is married life?" Malcolm asked, raising his eyebrows. "Did you prepare shackles and repast, as is customary?"

"'Shackles and repast'?" Elias repeated. "We have a wedding breakfast ready, but I didn't seek out manacles."

"Shame," said Rhys, shrugging.

"I did get her a ring," Elias said, after considering it. "Is that shackle-like enough? I even have one for myself, provided by the late baroness. All it needed was a polish and a bit of hammering and it's ready to wear."

"Willa gave you a ring?" Rhys asked, his curls bouncing up from a fervent concentration on building a pyramid out of empty tiny glasses. "My letter didn't have any presents in it. Did your lot?"

"What did your letter have in it?" Mal asked, cutting his eyes to the other man. "A feather and a clue?"

"Wouldn't you love to know?" Rhys sassed back, wrinkling his nose.

"It would be kind," Errol mused, "providing Rhys with his first clue."

"Oh, ho ho," Rhys parroted back in a bored monotone. "Hand me those glasses."

And then, to Elias's astonishment, both men did so, watching with clear interest as Rhys completed his transparent ziggurat with a little whoop of victory.

"Right," said Mal, looking summarily impressed.

"Do you have them?" Errol put in, leaning onto his elbow to nudge one of the glasses a touch to the left, bringing the corners more into line. "The rings, I mean?"

Elias frowned, nodding and reaching into his jacket pocket and withdrawing a little velvet pouch.

He had been returning from the jeweler's when they'd accosted him, halfway back to the house, after all.

"Oh, shiny things," Rhys said, plucking the pouch from Elias's fingers before either of the others could and fishing the woman's ring out of it before tossing the bag to Mal with disinterest. He held the elegant little band up to the light, peering up at the cracked amber, broken into two halfmoon pieces over a circle-cut garnet. "Pretty!"

"It is pretty," Errol agreed, leaning closer. "It is very suitable to Hattie."

"Yes," said Elias, still frowning. "I thought so as well."

"*Mea culpa,*" said Malcolm.

"Yes, we know," Rhys mumbled, still entranced by the jewels.

"No, you glittering insect," Mal said, slapping Rhys on the knee and jutting out the man's ring. "It's the inscription. Look."

"In a love token?" Errol said, already pouring more swill into four new little glasses, evidently disinterested in both Malcolm and Elias having said they wanted no more. "That seems an odd thing for it to say."

"This was Willa's?" Rhys asked, holding the two rings together like an eclipsed sun against the candle in the middle of the table. "The late Lord Selwyn's ring, perhaps?"

Elias shook his head. "No. He did wear a ring, but it was silver, apparently. I don't know whose it is. Certainly a man's, though, at that size and style."

"She didn't explain?" Errol said, sounding truly affronted as he pushed the glasses out in three different directions with seemingly effortless aim, not spilling a single drop in the process. "That doesn't sound like Willa."

Elias hesitated, his jaw feeling oddly warm as he cleared his throat and reached for his glass, his lips pressed together. In all honesty, in the madness that had been the last several weeks of his life, he had genuinely forgotten about that letter. Forgotten it entirely.

"Oh, good God," Malcolm said, a grin spreading over his face. "You haven't read the letter, have you? You've just been carrying around this cursed ring with no context for the last month."

Rhys gaped at him. "And you're going to wear it as a love token? What if she left it to you so you'd throw it in the sea? What if it's got her soul inside it? You going to wear that to bed tomorrow night?"

"Rhys," said Errol mildly as he drank his swill. "Stop."

"Well, I'm not wrong!" Rhys exclaimed, turning his eyes frantically on Errol. "Just because you're the most boring man alive it doesn't make the rest of the universe any less haunted."

"So it turns out his limit is eleven shots," Malcolm observed, taking his own drink back and then dropping his chin into the curl of his hand, propped up on the table by the elbow. "Who knew?"

"I'll have twelve more and still dance you under the table, banker boy," Rhys shot back. "Don't forget it was me who protected you from that banshee when we were boys."

Mal paled immediately, straightening in his chair. "Shut up, Rhys."

"Do banshees come this far south?" Elias asked, desperate for a breath of levity.

"We weren't here," Rhys replied solemnly. "We were in Edinburgh."

"Enough!" said Mal, somehow fading from ashen to plum in the space of a few seconds. "There was no banshee."

"There wasn't," agreed Errol. "It was a boggart."

"Where's my wine?!" Mal exclaimed, launching himself up from the table and stalking off, leaving both of the other men chortling to themselves while Elias watched in helpless discomfort.

Rhys slid the velvet bag from its discarded place on the table to his little glass palace and carefully put the rings back inside. "Here," he said to Elias. "Take these back before my baser impulses get the better of me."

"And I find them in the wedding cake tomorrow?" Elias guessed, feeling oddly pleased with the grin it got from the other man.

"No," said Rhys. "The food returns are only for Mal. I'd have to come up with something new for you. If you recall, I used to steal your desserts, and those all got eaten. They were true thefts."

"No true thefts tonight, if you please," Errol requested.

"Only abductions?" Elias retorted, raising his brows.

It got a slow grin out of Errol too. "Only abductions," he agreed. "Welcome to the family, at long last."

"Thank you for having me," Elias answered, clicking his glass against the other man's, "despite my tardy arrival."

Part V
Names

Chapter Nineteen

"WELL, THAT'S BAD luck," Libba said, frowning out the church window as dark clouds gathered in the sky for the third day in a row. "It had better not rain tomorrow too."

"It won't," said Hattie from the vanity table, her hair half styled. "And it isn't bad luck."

"It isn't?" Monica asked curiously from her position by the dress, which she was still fussing with at this late hour. "Rain on a wedding morning?"

"Rhys would know," Ruby said, dropping the newest ringlet with a flap of her hand, as though her fingers had been singed against its perfect coil and then immediately moving onto the next strand. "But it's all nonsense, anyhow."

"It isn't nonsense," Hattie said placidly. "It just isn't bad luck. Elias has always moved in tandem with the rain. I expected to wed beneath it."

"Oh," said Libba, blinking rapidly. "All right, then."

A roll of thunder sounded immediately in the wake of her words, making Hattie smile at herself in the mirror.

"A flame in the storm," Ruby mused, glancing at the dress. "You just need a bit of salt in your pocket and you'll match the scent I made."

"I haven't given it to him yet," said Hattie. "The charm, the number eight, the way you tied it to the top, makes it fall sideways. It looks like a symbol rather than a number."

"Yes," said Ruby wryly. "How unfortunate."

The quarter hour sounded next, chiming against the thunder like a songbird answering a war horse.

"Hurry up," Monica said. "She needs to be in the sanctuary by ten."

"At the pulpit, on the gallows," Libba intoned, pressing prayer hands over her chest. "Meeting her fate."

"Stop that," Ruby hissed. "You're giving me shivers. Is your entire troupe attending today?"

"Of course," said Libba with a tilt of her head. "You think that lot ever passes up an opportunity to dress up or eat free cake?"

"My seamstresses are coming too," said Monica, shaking out the skirt one final time and watching with narrowed eyes to make sure it fluttered correctly in the air. "And Miss Boswell."

"And the household staff," Hattie said.

"And Mr. Harcourt," Monica added in a soft, dreamy tone. "He's going to wear the jacket I made him."

"Ohh," Libba and Ruby chanted, in mocking, simpering voices until Monica was as red as a berry.

Despite it all, they did manage to get Hattie dressed on time, and all of her hair into pins, which fell softly against her bare nape when she left the dressing room in her new, flame-born dress and dark-blue slippers.

"He has the rings?" she said, one last time to Libba, who rolled her eyes and nodded curtly, likely resisting the urge to shove her for good measure.

"Yes. You're both bizarre enough to be well matched. He has them. For the love of God."

"Libba!" Monica hissed, glancing nervously at an overly realistic depiction of Jesus, carved into wood and hanging over the vestry, whose expression seemed fairly offended by the outburst as well.

"Errol!" Ruby echoed in something that managed to both be a whisper and a shout. "The bouquet!"

"Right!" came Errol's voice from seemingly the air.

He appeared a moment later with a bundle of bright-orange stargazer lilies, dotted throughout with bluebells, and proffered it to Hattie. "I wrapped them this morning," he said. "You look beautiful. Good luck."

And then they were all gone.

All of them.

And she was alone at the doors.

She swallowed, lifting the flowers to her nose and breathing them in as the thunder rumbled again outside.

It always storms in the summer, she thought. Flowers and sun, puddles and wind. They were all the things that made Brighton what it was, even beyond the shingles of the beach.

The flowers smelled like a duet to Hattie. Like pairs. Like two.

Like a wedding.

And then the music began.

She had expected an organ, deep and thrumming like a kitchen hearth, but to her surprise, the tune that spiraled out through the doors as they were pulled open on either side by Libba's actors was in the tinkling, feather-light strains of a harp.

It seemed to touch her face and hair. Seemed to beckon her down the aisle in the voice of Joseph Haydn's timeless composition.

Light glowed throughout the domed room, flashing in the windows as her steps were illuminated down the aisle toward her future.

Toward Elias.

And he turned to watch her arrive, a small, crooked smile sitting on his face, like the storm pleased him as well.

When she reached him, passing through the narrow route of all the people from her home, he held his hands out to her and helped her onto the altar, his eyes sliding over the details of her wedding gown.

"I hope you brought an umbrella," she whispered, unable to

think of anything else to say when one greeted her groom at the threshold of forever.

"I didn't," he said apologetically. "*Mea culpa.*"

It made her smile, an ease settling over her shoulders as the vicar pulled himself up to full height, cracked open his book, and began to recite the opening words to the marriage rite, silencing the harp in the process.

Hattie thought it odd that she could not quite parse the words and their meanings as he spoke. She heard them. She repeated the bits she was meant to and must have understood them because her tongue followed their sounds.

But it was perhaps the first time in her life that she said words and did not listen to them as she did so.

And it was because she could not look away from Elias Selwyn.

She could see his name spelled in the air between them. Could feel the shapes of the syllables as warm and soft as his hands holding her own.

Wasn't that funny? To keep those words and not the others.

And to not feel any of them as she spoke until at the very end, when she said, "I do."

And then they spoke the silent language because Elias kissed her. He kissed her in front of all of them, and they cheered as he did so.

It was not like their other kisses.

It was not burning and desperate and dizzying. This was sweet and gentle and somehow refreshing, like a little splash of water on the face after one has concentrated too hard for too long on one thing.

When they broke apart, Hattie blinked, and it was as though she could see and hear the world again, as she always had.

And the world was smiling.

It was smiling for one more blissful moment, one more roll of the thunder and flash of light, before it had to come apart again.

"Congratulations, Lady Selwyn," Elias said in her ear, his

hand sliding along hers as his fingers laced through her own.

Before she could respond, the doors were thrown open again, and the storm blew in.

Not the raindrops. Not the light or the sound.

But two people she had not seen in many years. People she'd met the day of the funeral and the burn, a lifetime ago.

Elias tensed immediately next to her, a curse leaving his mouth in a sharp, little whisper.

His mother and stepfather had come.

And their arrival dissipated the rain, the showering pattern ending with an abrupt, howling emptiness.

"Elias!" his mother cried, openly horrified. "Tell us we aren't too late."

"'Too late'?" Elias repeated, deceptively soft, as though his entire body hadn't tightened against Hattie's side like a copper coil under too much weight. "To congratulate me?"

"Boy, tell us you did not just wed a scullery maid!" his stepfather said, bristling to his full height. "You are a Selwyn! You are the Selwyn name, for God's sake!"

They were a handsome pair. A little grayer than she remembered them. He was Wallace and she was Catriona. She remembered the spelling of the name on a letter she'd seen once. With more vowels than sounds. How odd it must have been, she reflected, to have married a man and then his cousin. Did she ever get them confused?

"Ugh, and it's the simple one as well," his mother said with a wrinkle of her nose. "At least it isn't … well …" she said, casting a glance at Libba and Malcolm with a meaningful raise of her thin, black brows.

"Mr. and Mrs. Selwyn," Mr. Harcourt said, popping up from the middle of the pews like a daisy, hair just as white and disposition just as sunny yellow. "What a pleasant surprise. You've unfortunately interrupted the end of the ceremony. Would you care to come and chat with me while we await the procession?"

Wallace Selwyn gave a humorless, bombastic laugh. "Harcourt. Been enjoying sitting on our allowance this last month? You greedy toad."

Harcourt was still wearing a forced smile, beginning to wedge his way through the crowd to get to the couple.

Elias still had not moved.

"'Greedy'?" Elias repeated, so softly, only Hattie could hear him, could hear the way his voice trembled.

"I bet you've been paying the Widow Starling in good time, haven't you?" Wallace was continuing to say as Harcourt stumbled out onto the aisle runner and made a pleading little gesture with his hands clasped together.

"We can discuss this outside," he said again urgently.

"Are you going to drag us out, Harcourt?" Mr. Selwyn demanded.

"Be reasonable, sir," Harcourt said desperately.

Elias's mother sighed, taking a step backward. "Elias, wrangle your servants, if you please!"

Elias only blinked.

"Is this how you treat the mother of the groom?" The stepfather barked. "Elias! What is this? Have some pride!"

"'Pride'?" Elias managed, still too quietly to be heard by anyone but his new wife.

"Just outside, if you could," Harcourt said one last time, with what sounded like his final thimble of resolve.

"Why don't we take you back to the Rest?" Monica said, her hair glinting golden in the sunlight as she also stood. "Ruby and I? And you can have a seat of honor for the breakfast?"

"Well," said Wallace Selwyn, eyes flicking in quick assessment over Monica's form. "At least he didn't marry the fat one."

Hattie blinked. She blinked and she missed the crack of bone to flesh.

It seemed to her only that she was watching a verbal horror tableau one second, and in the next, Harcourt had flattened the late baron's cousin and bloodied his nose for good measure,

Elias's mother was screaming, and somehow half of Brighton was swarming into the aisle to meet them.

Chapter Twenty

ELIAS FOUND HIMSELF seated in the pews of a mostly empty church, some moments later, without much clarity on how he'd come to be there or what had passed in the time between now and when he had been standing in the aisle next to Hattie.

"Ruby and Errol took the guests to the Rest," Hattie was saying to him, squeezing into the little space between his body and the armrest at the end of the pew and putting her newly bejeweled hand above his own. He had given her this gift quickly, and in the aftermath of the unpleasantness, but still, it was a thing of beauty. Still, her heart fluttered to see it. "We offered to see your parents to the nearest clinic, but they insisted on traveling on their own directly to the constabulary. Presumably they intend to file a complaint against Mr. Harcourt."

Elias moved then, his head snapping over to look at the barrister, whose hand was currently being dabbed with a wet cloth by Monica.

Julian Harcourt's pale eyes raised and met Elias's and he gave a twist of his lips and a shrug. "Let them," he said. "I know a judge or two."

"Miss Thresher," Elias said, surprised to hear his own voice, and more surprised still to feel himself standing, pulling away from Harriet. "Monica. I am so very, very sorry for what my stepfather said."

Monica paused, the cloth, gone pink with Harcourt's knuckle scrapes, hovering above the knuckles themselves, and glanced up at him. "Me?" she said, sounding surprised. "I think maybe I got the least of it, Elias. Besides, I *am* the fat one. No secret in that."

"Miss Thresher," both Harcourt and Elias said in immediate, alarmed voices, winning a shake of the head and a giggle from her.

"I am well with it," she said. "Why should it be an insult?"

"They called me 'the simple one,'" Hattie said, looking amused by it from her place in the pew. "It does beg the question of how they measure intellect."

"Hattie," Elias said, the name tearing from his throat in a ragged whisper. "I did not know they would do that."

She blinked at him, eyes golden in the post-storm rays of sunlight. "Of course you didn't," she said, as though he'd just informed her that he didn't have wings and could not fly. "No one thinks you did."

"You will, however, likely be the one who has to get rid of them," Malcolm said, leaning against the church doors with his arms crossed over his chest. "Or whatever solution you decide is most appropriate. They aren't likely to listen to anyone else."

"Certainly not us," said Libba.

"I'm a little offended that they insulted everyone directly except me," Rhys noted, squinting out the window. "They got their shots in at Ruby and Errol on the way out. The lightskirt and the farmhand, apparently."

"They didn't actually name us," Malcolm pointed out, touching his sister's shoulder.

"They didn't have to," Rhys said. "We know what they meant."

"The Black ones," Libba provided, raising her brows.

"No," said Rhys with a curl of his lip. "The posh one and the pantomime."

Mal laughed, a short chuckle that seemed to ease his shoulders. "Yes, that's what they meant, Lib."

"Go on, then, Baron," Rhys said, turning to Elias with something behind that customary sparkle that looked like sympathy. "What's their shorthand for me? The thieving one? The skinny one? The beauty?"

"The eternal optimist?" Malcolm muttered.

Elias stared at them for a moment, his mind still stuck in the mire of before. "The Welsh one," he heard himself saying. "Usually."

"The …" Rhys repeated, his voice going up an octave in outrage. "'The *Welsh one*'?! That's it?!"

"Oh, you've angered him," Monica said with a little frown. "Rhys, it's all right."

"'The Welsh one'!" he repeated, waving his hands at Monica like the jiggle of his fingers would punctuate the point. "That *is* an insult. Oh, well done, you sneaky snakes. They know just where to strike to cause maximum pain."

Elias agreed with that. But he could not say so.

Instead, he turned to Harcourt and said, "Who is the Widow Starling?" And when the man looked up to him with a pained expression, he added, "You told me Willa was an orphan."

"She was," Harcourt said. "Lord Selwyn, you know very well that the widow they spoke of is Willa's aunt."

"I … do not know that," Elias managed, his brow furrowing.

Harcourt's eyes fell briefly to Elias's hands, flicking over his new ring. "Elias," said Harcourt, slowly. "It was in the letter."

"Oh, for God's sake, Selwyn!" Malcolm said, exasperated. "You still haven't read it?"

"And he's wearing that ring, anyway," Rhys said with a low whistle. "Brave."

"Well, we can't go fetch it right now," said Hattie, standing and walking toward Elias as she spoke. "Mr. Harcourt, perhaps you can summarize the information for us, in the name of brevity?"

"I …" Harcourt said, wincing as Monica dabbed a particularly jagged cut. "I am not certain that is wise. There are decisions outlined in that letter that Lord Selwyn was to make of his own private accord."

"I think they just became a sight less private, Harcourt," Malcolm pointed out with a raise of his brows.

Harcourt sighed heavily. "It is up to Elias," he said. "If he gives me leave, I will do as you ask."

Elias was staring at him, his mouth dry and immobile, unsure he was even comprehending what was being asked of him.

Hattie slid her hands over his arm, gripping him lightly but firmly enough to pull him back to earth.

"Yes," he managed. "Yes, you have my leave."

Harcourt nodded, looking very tired all of a sudden. "Very well. As you all know, the Selwyn land and the Starling house are, or were until today, I suppose, independent pieces of property. When your uncle died, and you became baron, your parents attempted to take the house from Willa as part of your inheritance. She had anticipated the attempt and prepared legally for it ahead of their arrival on the day of the funeral."

"They were going to try to evict her on the day of the funeral?" Rhys said, his face twisted up in disgust. "Jesus."

"They failed, obviously," said Harcourt with a shrug. "But seeing as young Elias here was already packed, Willa used the opportunity to bring him under her custody. She pointed out that she could oversee his tutelage and education as baron if he learned his own lands from standing upon them, even though he would not inherit her house until the time of her death."

"Or ever," Libba muttered.

"Yes, well," said Harcourt with a frown, "that hadn't happened yet. Hattie hadn't happened yet. Much less the rest of the wards.

"Your parents agreed to leave you with Willa in exchange for continuing to maintain the allowance they had been issued by the late baron, including the amount that would have been presumed for your care. She agreed to be rid of them and was forced to maintain that allowance to prevent their interference with you at various continued points in your life after that day."

"What?" Elias snapped. "Like what?"

"Like pulling you out of Eton," said Harcourt, though it sounded like it pained him. "Or Oxford. Like forbidding your military service or appearing in Society at events that were important to you."

Something in his chest wedged loose and shattered against his ribs. His insides felt cavernous and cold. "I see. And this allowance was paid out of the lands funding that I inherited, I take it?"

"Yes," Mr. Harcourt said. "And so was the living costs she sent to her elderly aunt in the Midlands. Neither has been paid out since the death certificate was signed because Willa was very clear that it would be your active choice if you wished to maintain them, and that silence should be taken not as a rejection, but a refusal to begin a new series of debts to those to whom you owe nothing."

"Release the aunt's funds immediately," he said. "As to the rest, I will make a decision bearing my conversation with the necessary parties."

"Elias," said Hattie, frowning. "You don't have to."

He looked down at her, glowing in her orange gown, and felt the full press of sadness against his chest. "I do," he said, holding up the ring for good measure.

She knew what it said, after all.

And she knew what it meant.

✦

Chapter Twenty-One

IT TOOK MOST of the afternoon, but Elias managed to wrangle things into some semblance of order.

In all honesty, it was familiar to him. Almost military in its requirements. And as such, it restored him to something bordering a state of calm, despite the fact that his wedding day had been utterly ruined.

Engage or retreat. Those were the options he thought he would always have. And instead, in a moment of utter and pressing necessity, he hadn't chosen either.

He had just stood there.

It was unforgivable.

Elias had found them at the constabulary, screaming at a baffled deputy while his stepfather's bloody nose crusted and flaked in his beard, and had stepped between the tirade and the young man with an air of exhausted resignation.

"Stop," he had said, unable to think of anything else. "Stop at once."

Shockingly, they had not.

It had taken a threat to get to that point.

"If you wish to stay in an inn tonight instead of making the journey back to your home at once, you will cease this immediately," he had snapped. "Or you will pay for it yourselves."

That had, at least, punctured the volume.

It had taken a bit more time and cajoling to get them out of the constable's offices and down the road into accommodations, though they complained the entire time.

Elias had not spoken much throughout it.

It occurred to him as they walked that he had not spoken much in their presence at all, ever.

Perhaps that explained his fluency in what Hattie called the silent language. Perhaps it was not a talent at all, but only a scar.

That would just figure, wouldn't it?

"How much?" he said to them, once the door was closed and they were seated in the finest room the inn had to offer. "How much for you to run along and never come back?"

"Well, that's a fine way to speak to your parents!" his stepfather had boomed, shedding more flecks of blood as he bristled. "She who bore you and gave you that name! It's only for us that you're wearing such a fine office this morning, *Baron* Selwyn."

"Indeed it's true," his mother had said with a sniff. "If you had only been a girl, it would have been your stepfather who had inherited instead. Isn't that right, Wallace? Isn't that true?"

"Just so, my dear, just so," said his stepfather, squeezing his mother's shoulder. "We should have held the barony, regardless. We would have raised you correctly. We would have prevented this spectacle the dowager orchestrated."

Elias only stared. For a long moment, he simply stared.

"Is that what this is about?" he finally asked, after he'd managed to digest this latest outburst. "You resent that you had a son?"

"Of course not," his stepfather said, flinging himself out of the chair and marching toward the basin in what appeared to be a very tardy impulse to tidy himself. "A man needs heirs. And you're a good boy. I just wish you'd been mine own and come along later is all."

"Yes, precisely. It is only that we were premature," his mother added with a grimace. "And evidently poor guidance."

"In that we can agree," Elias said flatly. "How much?"

"A place in that house to start," his mother said immediately.

"No."

She blinked at him, giving a short, shrill little laugh. "No, indeed? How dare you?"

"No," said Elias again, clenching his jaw. "You will go back to Rottingdean and stay there."

"Oh, we haven't lived in Rottingdean in five years," his stepfather grumbled. "Shows how much you care."

"Yes, I suppose it does," Elias said, leaning back against the door because he could no longer stand on his own accord. "How much?"

"Just restore what we were given before, I suppose," his mother said with a sniff and a sigh. "Though that is terribly cruel, given your good fortune. Even Willa Starling cared for an elderly aunt for the whole of her cursed life, and only an aunt by marriage at that. Some common barmaid of a girl now living in luxury on Selwyn coin in her dotage. If you do not honor us, you should at least honor your beloved patroness."

"I do," he said through his teeth. "And in so doing, I refuse to continue to humor the two of you more than absolutely necessary. You extorted her for all of my life and I am only just now learning of it."

"'Extorted,'" tutted his stepfather. "Such language."

"Oh, do you wish to speak about language?" Elias said, raising his brows, a flash of heat fanning in his chest. "Perhaps we should start with how you spoke to and about my wife?"

"'Wife,'" his mother echoed in a venomous whisper. "The scullery maid?"

"The *baroness*," Elias corrected, turning his mother's face red. "Something you will never be."

"She was always such an odd little bird," said his stepfather, using a comb to get his beard clean with a click of his tongue. "Your children might be odd too, you know. Touched and vacant, commenting on the oddest non-sequitur things in polite company. Terribly embarrassing."

"Hattie is not embarrassing. She is brilliant," Elias snapped. "She has been feted by the crowned heads of Europe. Who fetes you?"

"Oh, please," said his mother with a roll of her eyes. "Is that what she told you?"

"In just the last week, she has received wedding gifts from the Tsar and Tsarina of Russia, two Italian dukes, and a Swedish princess," Elias told them, raising his brows. "Not to mention the personal note I intercepted from our own prince regent."

Both his parents froze for a moment at that, his stepfather's dark-blue eyes narrowing.

Elias had those eyes. Selwyn eyes.

"Nonsense," his stepfather said, gruffly. "You are making things up. You always were a liar, boy."

Elias smiled then. It was an odd thing, an unexpected feeling as it spread over his face. "You think so?" he said. "Perhaps you ought to attend the funeral tomorrow if you don't believe me, and meet His Royal Highness yourself. It would do you good, I think."

"Meeting the prince?" his mother said, clearly intrigued. "Of course it would."

"No," said Elias. "Seeing a well-attended funeral for a woman who gave instead of took. It might make you both reflect on your own mortality."

His stepfather bowed up, his chest puffing out as he opened his mouth to rebut, but Elias only held up a hand.

"Come or don't," he said. "But if you interfere at all, it will be the last we speak of any allowance. The same applies to any attempt to punish Mr. Harcourt. I require him if I am to release any funds at all to you, after all."

"Oh," said his mother, crossing her arms. "Anything else, my lord?"

Elias turned his smile onto her, sharp and without amusement. "Yes," he said. "You will apologize to the baroness, or any consideration of an allowance is moot. And to Miss Thresher,

Father. Do you understand?"

"I ... I ..." Wallace Selwyn began to bumble.

"Do not answer me now," said Elias. "I haven't any more time to dawdle today. Think it over. If you can."

And, before they could ruin this little blip of satisfaction he'd managed to find in the wreckage of his wedding day, he turned on his heel and saw himself out.

He strode home, a manic thrill bordering hysteria fluttering in his chest, and turned his face to the humid rays of wet sunlight in the air. He walked quickly, breathing in the smell of surf and taking comfort in the trill of tourist voices from down on the docks.

Life is continuing on, he thought. Even with a storm in the height of the Brighton rush. Even with a melee on his wedding aisle.

Now, all he had to do was read that blasted letter and he could be done with this for today. He could put it away until tomorrow.

He could be a groom again for at least the last few hours of the day, surely?

Elias walked right through the front door and into the house without encountering a single soul. He supposed they were all gathered in the ballroom for the festivities still. He could hear music faintly echoing throughout the house.

A small, private smile found its way over his lips as he turned in the opposite direction and made his way toward his bedroom. He'd find the letter there, give it a quick read, and then go have a slice of his wedding cake if there was any left.

Honestly, Elias didn't even much care for cake, truth be told, but it was the principle of the thing.

He sighed and pushed his door open, only to freeze on the threshold, sagging at the visual reminder that he was not thinking clearly.

There was nothing left in here. Only a tidy bed stripped down to its sheets and furniture dusted and polished, empty of all the things previously held within.

Of course.

His things had been moved to the master suite today.

Which meant the letter too.

He crossed the room carefully, almost as though he were picking his way over the ghosts of his memories, scattered across the empty floor, and sank onto the side of the bed, giving one more sigh for good measure.

He shook his head and chuckled a little at the absurdity of it.

"There you are," called Hattie's voice, soft and relieved from his doorway.

He looked up, surprised to find her there, still in her wedding dress. The blue cording under her breasts glowed like the center of a flame in the low afternoon light. "Hattie."

She smiled. "Elias."

"Come sit with me?" he asked, tilting his head toward the tightly tucked white sheets around his childhood mattress. "I was just saying goodbye."

She pressed the door shut behind her as she came forward, taking the spot next to him. "It isn't goodbye," she said. "You are only down the hall and up a flight of stairs."

"True enough," he said with a chuckle, leaning against the bedpost to consider her, beautiful and his, sitting on this bed. "The boy who moved into this room would never believe this is how I would leave it."

She raised her brassy brows. "Oh? And how is that?"

"With you willingly sitting upon it with me," he said, grinning. "Looking like that. Wearing my token and my name."

"Fascinating," she said, tilting her head to the side. "How do you think he would react, if you could find and tell him what to expect?"

"A range of complicated emotions, I'd wager," Elias replied with a laugh. "Not all of them pleasant."

"Hm," she said, her lips twisting. "And how does this Elias feel about it?"

"A range of complicated emotions," he replied, a little softer. "Not all of them polite."

She flushed a little, her lashes flickering, and kicked off her dark-blue slippers, climbing further into the bed and letting him watch as she stretched out onto the pillows, her orange-and-gold skirts splayed out around her as she gazed up at the ceiling, languishing and stretching like a cat. "Ah," she said. "I am so very ready to retire today. Are you?"

"Yes," he said, not moving a muscle, save to watch all the delicious, little ways she moved as she settled into repose. "Retire from everyone's company but yours."

"Do you want to go to the master suite?" she asked, giving him a knowing little smirk. "Or do you like seeing me here, in this bed?"

"I like seeing you here very much," he confessed, reaching out to stroke the silky line of her ankle through its stocking. "I think this is the part that would confuse young Elias the most because whether he liked it or not, he pictured it many, many times."

"Ah, yes," she said softly, letting him push her skirt higher, his fingers tracing over the curve of her calf under the silk, the delicate little crux behind her knee. "You had an awakening, you said."

"I did," he confirmed, licking his lips as he pulled the ribbon free at the garter and began to roll the stocking down, baring her pale flesh to him. "When you came out of the ocean that day, I could see more of you than I'd bargained for. I was still furious with you but … also …"

"'Also' …?" she pressed, lifting her now-bare leg and draping it onto his lap, her foot pressed into his arousal as he released a hissing breath and took up her other leg, firmer with his grip this time, his eyes snapping to hers.

He jerked the ribbon free on this leg, raking the stocking down her leg as she smirked at him from her back, the arch of her foot sliding meaningfully against his cock. "Hattie," he said, with the only resolve he had left, the only warning he could muster.

"Elias," she replied, almost singsong. "There's nothing else under that skirt, you know."

"I know," he rasped, running his thumb along her naughtier ankle before pulling it away so that he could crawl into the bed above her, his fingers dragging along the sides of that glorious, fiery skirt as he pulled it farther up, along the curve of her thighs. "There never was, was there?"

She shook her head, her eyes on his lips. "Indeed not. Imagine what you might have been getting away with, all this time."

He groaned, falling onto her mouth with a desperate need, catching the spiced sweetness of her tongue against his as he rolled his hips against her, testing the promise of what he'd wanted for such a very long time. He slid his hands up along her waist, his thumbs brushing over her breasts through the dress, tugging down the fabric along her arms, hungry to reveal what he could of her but unwilling to let her up to do it properly.

She slid one of those bare legs around his, drawing him closer, and the world spun, light flickering and flashing behind his eyes as he tasted her deeper, demanded more from her, filled his hands with her breasts until her nipples were taut and straining against the fabric that hid them from him.

He kissed down the column of her throat, nipping and tasting her, burying his face in the swell of her bosom as he ground himself between her thighs.

He did not know why he was waiting, only that the waiting itself was just as delicious as the promise of taking her fully. That perhaps he had been truthful when he'd told her the torment was part of the pleasure.

She slid her fingers through his hair, gripping him firmly as he tasted her, rocking back against him like the madness was catching.

"I want you," she murmured. *"Je te veux,* Elias. *Pozhaluysta."*

It ripped something from his throat, his mind going white with heat. He reared up to hold her face, his thumb tracing her cheek as he claimed her mouth again. "Ask with your body," he said against her lips. "Like I taught you."

Her eyes slid open, blazing and golden against his as her hands ran down his back. She hooked her fingers into the waistband of his trousers, urging them down, her fingernails trailing underneath them, squeezing into the flesh hidden below as she arched her back into him.

"*Nu*," she breathed, watching him fumble for the ties at his navel with satisfaction as she filled her hands with his backside. "*Lige nu.*"

"Hattie," he groaned, certain he was going to collapse before he could claim her.

"Ah," she said as the fabric loosened, using first her hands to push the barrier away and then her feet, and legs, pulling his trousers down the length of his body with a serpentine coherence of limbs and movements. "*Muy bien.*"

"God," he muttered, filling his fists with her skirts, fighting the world around him as he dragged air into his lungs and collapsed forward again, sinking his teeth gently into the soft flesh at her clavicle as he used his hand to guide himself against her. "Oh, God."

He pushed into her, at long last. He took her. He filled her.

She was his.

And he could barely stand it.

He wanted to revel in this, to linger in it and gloat, to fuck her slowly and watch her come undone underneath him. And perhaps he would, someday. But just now, he couldn't. He couldn't.

He lost all powers of language, of elegance, of civilized strategy. He gripped her to him like she was the only thing keeping him alive, his hands clinging to her, filling with her hair and her skin, his mouth dragging against her lips and her throat and her breasts as he lost himself in the roll and snap of his hips against hers.

She wasn't speaking anymore, either. Instead, she simply

clung, her hands gripping and clawing, pulling at the clothes on his back as she met him thrust for thrust, her voice reduced to nothing but whimpers and gasps, mingled with the most delectable little cries of pleasure.

Her legs locked around his, pushing her bare feet into his calves and rocked back against him with such force that he went momentarily blind, just keeping her beneath him, just holding her to him and trying to contain the way it felt.

She sank her hands into his hair and pulled his mouth down to hers as she reached her apex, crying out against his tongue as she trembled and shook, inviting him to continue taking, to continue indulging in what he had wanted for so very, very long.

And that was all he could bear. It was the final blow against what remained between Elias the man and the animal beneath it all.

He held her by the hips and pumped himself into her, losing himself completely. He clashed with her, much as he always had, though this time, there was satisfaction in it. This time, it was right. And he did not stop until he broke, filling her with the proof of his desire and returning the taste of climax to her mouth the way she had done to his. He coiled, he tensed, and, miraculously, somehow, and at long last, he found release.

He released and he fell.

And Harriet French, the eternal thorn in his side, caught him in her arms when he landed.

Chapter Twenty-Two

HATTIE DOZED FOR a time, long enough that the sun had begun to sink down below the crest of the hill that held the house up and change the color of the room around them. She woke still wrapped around Elias, their legs tangled and his weight still eased onto the side of her body, his head resting on her shoulder.

She felt him holding her hand, the one that now had a beautiful ring upon it, turning and examining her fingers and knuckles and palm and heel, unaware that her eyes were blinking open again, until she gave a little chuckle, a smile spreading over her lips.

He glanced up at her, those eyes so very blue in the low light, and sheepishly smiled back. "There's no scar," he said, running his thumb along the line of her hand, where she had burned herself in the moment before they'd first met. "It's strange; I could've sworn there was one."

"There was, for many years," she said sleepily, stifling a little yawn. "It faded eventually."

"'Faded,'" he repeated thoughtfully. "Then it was never a scar in the first place. Just a very slow-healing wound."

"I suppose not," she said, her hand curling up to tangle in his hair. "You are right. A scar would have stayed forever."

"Not a scar," he said with a soft smile. "Not a scald."

"Well, it wasn't a scald," she said, laughing again, this time enough that her chest shook and shook him with it. "I thought the cook was going to strangle me."

"So did I," he said, marveling and bringing the hand up to kiss the place where the burn had once been. "I was amazed that you didn't look more afraid. Resentful, even. How dare a girl be braver than I? A new baron."

"How dare, indeed," she said, stroking those dark, silky locks, her fingernails trailing along the back of his neck until his eyes fluttered shut with a sigh. "I was afraid. I'm just often bad at showing it."

"There's power in that deficiency," he told her without opening his eyes. "I assure you."

"Yes, well…" she said with a snort. "It seemed to always infuriate you that I couldn't emote properly. Perhaps I *am* simple."

That got his eyes open again, his hand coming up to stop her ministrations and a frown tugging at his lips. "You are not simple," he said, pushing himself up onto his elbow to loom over her. "You are remarkable."

"One can be both," she said teasingly.

"And yet you are not," he replied, a little firmer than Hattie thought strictly necessary, but that had always been his way, hadn't it?

"Hm," she said, reaching up to trace the line of his face with her fingernails. "I sent your pig away for the night, by the by. I couldn't reckon with the idea of traumatizing that sweet creature with a forced audience to our consummation, but now I realize it was unnecessary. She would have remained innocent, sequestered in the master suite while we were depraved here, a floor below."

He watched her for a moment, those dark-blue eyes flicking back and forth over her face. "Who said we aren't going to defile the master suite as well?" he asked, raising his brows. "It is still early."

"It *is* still early," she agreed, glancing at the setting sun. "Isn't it?"

He sighed, leaning into the palm of her hand and nodding. "Yes. And I would wager our absence has been noted. And commented upon. And perhaps rendered in pantomime."

"The posh one and the pantomime," Hattie echoed, giggling, though in doing so, she remembered the context in which those words were spoken. "How … erm …"

"How did I fare against my parents?" he asked, his lips twisting in dry amusement as he sighed and pushed himself back to sitting. "As well as can be expected, I suppose. They shan't be incarcerating Mr. Harcourt tonight, in any event."

"Well," she said, scooting backward and pulling herself up as well. "That is something."

He shot her a look and she flattened her mouth in response, which did, at least, have the effect of making them both laugh.

She shook her head, reaching down to tug her bodice back into place, which took some doing, as it had become rather twisted and bunched after the abuse it had endured. She had to reach inside to reposition her stays and her body within so that the fabric would lie as intended and when she glanced up again, Elias was watching her with an intensity that immediately made her regret preparing to leave this room at all.

"Your stockings," he said, his voice gone a bit hoarse as he held up the two slips of silk. "Shall I put them back on you?"

"Do you think that wise?" she asked, a mild note of hope in her voice that it wasn't, and that he would do it, anyway.

He gave her a slow, predatory smile, his face half in shadow from the setting sun, teeth gleaming from the final flashes of light. "No."

She sighed at the sound of voices in the hall, her head turning toward the door with a furrowing of her brows. "No," she agreed, frowning.

"Hattie!" came Libba's voice, carrying down the hall as though she'd used a cone to amplify it, though Hattie knew very well she had not. "Are you down here?"

"Yes!" she called, scrambling to her feet in a panic and snatching the stockings from Elias's playful grip. "I'm coming!"

"Well …" he said, making her whirl around and slap her hand to his mouth, which grinned again, behind the skin of her palm.

"Hush," she said, stuffing the stockings into his pocket and shoving her bare feet back into her slippers. "Follow in a few moments. I don't fancy the commentary."

"You don't?" he asked, muffled and taunting.

She narrowed her eyes at him. "I don't."

She pulled her hand away and kissed him once more, harder than she really needed to, and gave him a light smack on the cheek at the way he was laughing before spinning and fleeing the room to intercept Libba before she could come any farther down the hall.

"Ah, there you are," said Libba, crossing her arms. "I can't believe you vanished like that. He'll be back when he's back. He's handling it."

"Yes, yes," said Hattie, taking the other woman's arm and steering her toward the ballroom. "You're right. I just get anxious, you know."

"Yes, I know," Libba said, her eyes narrowing with suspicion as she glanced over her shoulder back toward the bedroom. "Hattie …"

"Is there any cake left?" Hattie asked, knowing she was going shrill. "I wanted to save him a slice."

"Of course there's not." Libba was still trying to see behind Hattie but did give up once they had turned the corner, much to Hattie's relief.

It did not mean, of course, that Libba wouldn't bring it up later.

"Is that the pianoforte?" Hattie asked, marveling. "Who is playing?"

"Oh," said Libba, brightening. "It's Mr. Harcourt. Monica is beside herself over it."

"He's playing with his injured hand?"

"Mm, I think perhaps *because* of his injured hand," Libba said cryptically, turning Hattie back into the festivities with a cheer of welcome.

Her absence, she was forced to acknowledge, had indeed been noted.

"Still no sign of Elias?" Malcolm asked, trotting up to them in cadence with the march his best friend was currently coaxing out of the old instrument in the central ballroom. "He's been gone a bit long, hasn't he?"

"Oh, I'd say so," Libba said, cutting her eyes to Hattie, who immediately flushed.

"He'll be along shortly, I'm certain," she said, flushing further as Mal's eyes fell to her bare feet with a raise of his arched brows. "What did I miss?!" she asked, louder, which did at least get his attention back up to her face.

"Oh, not much," he said. "Some dancing. Miss Boswell danced an extremely contrary-looking waltz with Rhys. It was marvelous."

"And odd," Libba said, shaking her head. "They are so odd."

"Well, that's all right," Hattie replied, still mired in her own panic. "Sometimes things are just a bit odd and that's the way of it."

Mal and Libba both stared at her for quite a while after that, until, with great mercy, Elias appeared at the ballroom doors.

Then everyone cheered for him instead while Hattie curled her bare toes against her slippers and prayed for the evening to speed along with no further uncomfortable observations.

"Well?" said Mal as Elias arrived at her side, the warmth of his hand sliding along the small of her back. "Did you read it?"

"What?" said Elias. "Oh, the letter."

Mal's face crumpled in like a wad of discarded paper. "Yes, the letter!"

"I haven't had a moment," Elias said soothingly. "I was dealing with my parents and the constabulary. I will read it, Lennox. I promise."

"I read mine," Hattie said, still a bit frantic to say anything that might diffuse suspicion.

It made both Lennoxes stare at her again, which was the opposite of what she had intended.

"Yes?" said Libba. "And what did it say?"

"Oh," said Hattie, blinking. "Many things."

Mal sighed loudly.

"Do you want to dance?" Elias asked her, amusement clear in his tone, though the offer was pure benevolence. "Do you dance, Miss French?"

"I am not Miss French," she said without thinking.

"No," he agreed, grinning. "You are not. Who are you now?"

She paused, an odd bashfulness rising in her throat. "I am Lady Selwyn," she said, smaller and quieter than she'd been before.

"Oh, for God's sake." Mal threw his hands up and stalked away.

"And will you dance with me, Lady Selwyn?" Elias asked again, smooth and low, while Libba watched with great interest.

Hattie nodded. "Yes," she said. "Yes, I will."

And he led her away, into the spinning chaos of music and motion, languages she trusted him to speak, because she never had.

Chapter Twenty-Three

AFTER THE THIRD incident where Hattie was certain her stockings were about to be discovered in Elias's pocket, she made the decision that he should retire early, under the guise of preparing the marital chamber for their wedding night.

It was the only thing that would calm her nerves and it did seem to also please and placate the guests who were still assembled, well after dark, as well as signal to them that it was time for the party to conclude.

She suspected fairly strongly that her secret was less of a secret than a personally held bugaboo at this stage, with most of her fellow wards tossing her knowing looks at various points throughout the evening.

When she'd danced with Rhys, he'd scuffed the top of her foot with his boot and then grinned as he apologized for damaging her stocking, which he knew very well she was not wearing.

In any event, it was with relief that she stood near the doors of the Rest and shook the hands of departing well-wishers, many of whom delivered gifts to her as they departed.

"It is a puzzle for two," Persephone Boswell explained, tilting the conjoined wooden cubes one way and then another as she pressed them into Hattie's hands. "It can only be solved in tandem with a partner."

"And she couldn't sell it otherwise," Rhys commented tartly.

She winked at Hattie, her Traveller's lilt becoming more pronounced as she agreed. "And I couldn't sell it otherwise."

There were several handmade gifts from Libba's actors, including a variety of prose and theatrical compositions about the wedding itself, hastily scrawled in the corner of the ballroom in what appeared to have become a makeshift poetry station devoted to either the incident with Elias's parents or the general beauty of the ceremony.

The oddest gift, by far, was from Libba's large, muscled bodyguard, the man Hattie had met that day in the jail. He approached her as the troupe was filing out of the house and handed her a waxy, yellow lemon, exactly the size of her hand.

"Lemuel," he said, his voice deep and soothing as she marveled at the fruit in her grasp. "You asked me if that was my name. What does it mean?"

"'Child of God,' I believe," she said, blinking up at him.

He nodded. "Well, I am not the child of parents. 'Lem' is not short for 'Lemuel.' It is short for 'Lemon Boy.'"

She blinked, which got a smile out of him.

A truly lovely smile, truth be told, one that transformed his stoic visage into something quite dashing.

"I sold lemons on the wharf in London as a lad," he explained. "'Lemon Boy' became 'Lem.' I was a foundling, like you."

"Oh," she said. "They called me French because my first word was *coucou*. It means '*greetings*,' but in a very childish way."

He nodded. "I like Lemuel more. I think I will have it. So you take the lemon as a trade."

She opened her mouth, uncertain how to reply, but he just reached out and patted her shoulder like she were a fond, little child in his path and said, "Congratulations, Baroness," before he vanished down the hall, toward the guest chambers.

Hattie carried the lemon and the puzzle box with her as she trailed up the stairs, a little dazed still from the exchange. She walked through the doors of the master suite and past the little salon leading to the bedchamber, inhaling the scent of lavender soap on the air as she went.

They had not yet decided whether or not to reoutfit the library back into a secondary chamber. Too much else had been happening; too much else had been taking priority. Hattie, in this moment, hoped they never mentioned it again. One chamber was perfectly well for this marriage.

She found Elias already bathed, toweling off his wet hair and wrapped in a velvet dressing gown, with water still steaming in a copper tub next to the recently doused hearth on the far wall.

"It's still warm," he said unnecessarily, rubbing the towel back and forth over his glossy, black hair as rivulets of scented water trickled down the lines of his throat. "Have you brought me a snack?"

"What?" she said, glancing down at the lemon in her hand. "Oh. No. It is not for eating."

"No?" he questioned, dropping onto the corner of the bed with a curious raise of his brows. "What is it for, then?"

She frowned. "I haven't decided yet. I will tell you when I do."

He watched her for a second, an odd, little smile playing about his lips. "I look forward to when you do," he said after a moment. "What's the other thing?"

She held it out to him, crossing the room a few steps so that he could take it from her hand. "A puzzle," she said. "Built to be solved by two people in tandem."

He examined it with interest, turning it this way and that. "Hattie," he said seriously, fiddling with a loose rectangle wedged into the darker block. "We are going to solve this puzzle. Not tonight, but we will."

"If you say so," she said, a little surprised at his enthusiasm. "I can't promise I will be any help."

He flashed her a boyish grin, a curl of wet hair falling over his brow as he looked up at her over the top of the puzzle. "I just need your hands, love."

She looked down at them, spreading her fingers apart and turning them over to examine her palms. "Then you will have them." She nodded.

He chuckled, setting the toy aside and beckoning her closer. "Let me help you out of that dress before the water gets cold," he offered. "I promise I will actually let you bathe before I try anything untoward."

"Watching me bathe isn't untoward?" she asked, crossing the final few steps over to him, anyway, and turning as he stood to help her with the fastenings at the back of her gown.

"Allow me to rephrase," he said, lips brushing her hair as he breathed her in. "I promise I will let you bathe before I am lecherous with my hands, rather than my eyes."

"Hm," she said as the dress loosened and fell down around her shoulders, revealing the chemise and stays underneath. "If you must."

"I must," he told her, though he did not take any particular care to avoid caressing her as he unlaced her stays and peeled them off her body.

She tossed him a half-hooded look over her shoulder, crossing to the tub as she pulled a few pins from her hair to secure the loose bits overhead and tested the temperature with her toe. "We should not stay up very late," she said without turning. "We do have the showcase tomorrow, after all."

"Yes, I recall," he said from his place on the bed. "I chose the day before, didn't I?"

She smiled, withdrawing her foot and gathering her chemise up around her thighs. "You did," she said as she pulled it off overhead, listening for his intake of breath at the fully revealed visual of her naked backside.

She stepped into the water quickly, then, oddly shy about the whole thing, and sank down to sitting before he could get a good look at her, losing a few curls to the watery pull of the bath in the process and feeling them sag and cling to her neck.

She sighed, her eyes sliding shut, and let the temperature

embrace her for a moment.

"Did you find your gift?" she asked, without opening them again. "It was on your pillow."

"Oh, you've chosen which side is mine already?" he teased. "A bottle. With an infinity symbol upon it."

Her eyes opened, a quick popping sensation that brought he world flooding back into her visual focus. "An eight," she corrected, glancing over at him.

He was tilting the bottle curiously, flicking the charm with his thumbnail.

"Perhaps both," he said with a shrug, though that made her eyes narrow. "Is it cologne?"

She nodded. "Ruby made it, at my instruction. It is you, bottled."

"Is it, indeed?" he said, clearly intrigued. He pulled the stopper away and waved it under his nose while she watched, her breath held. "It is … smoky and … hm."

"Storm," she said. "And salt."

His teeth flashed, his eyes glancing up to meet hers. "That is how you see me? She couldn't bottle 'snake'?"

"I already told you," Hattie said impatiently. "I do not picture a literal snake. It is the—"

"Yes, yes," he said with a chuckle, tipping the bottle over onto his fingertip and dabbing some of the liquid at his throat and over his heart, his finger parting his dressing gown and revealing the intriguing shape of his chest and the dark coils of hair beneath the velvet. "The shape of my name. I recall."

"Then why do you pretend you do not?" she returned, trying to keep her eyes on his face and not his bare chest—his very, very distracting bare chest.

His smile widening, he tipped the bottle again, this time for his pulse behind his wrists. "Because it annoys you so," he replied. "Aren't you going to lather yourself for my pleasure?"

"No," she said, glaring. "I'm going to do it for my cleanliness."

"C'est blanc bonnet et bonnet blanc," he said with a shrug, which only irked her more.

"Sometimes something is one thing," she insisted. "Not many. It is an eight."

"Fine," he said with a sigh, re-stoppering the bottle and setting it on the bedside table. "It is an eight. *Mea culpa.*"

"Oh!" she said, splashing her hand against the water in a pique, which he clearly enjoyed very much.

She snatched up the washcloth and a petal of lavender soap and began to work the lather into the cloth, torn between begrudging amusement and the urge to throttle him. "Did you read the letter?" she snapped, glancing up at him as she began to soap her arms. "At long last?"

His smile slipped and he sighed. "No! Must I?"

She smirked. "You must. You may read it to me while I bathe, if you like."

"I don't like," he declared. "Where is it?"

She nodded toward the same bedside table where he'd just placed the cologne. "There. Once you do it, Elias, it will be done."

He grimaced at her. "Yes, I understand how verb tense works."

It was her turn to grin, wide and brilliant. "That is wonderful to hear."

He pursed his lips, his eyes narrowing at her. "Well played," he conceded, and then he turned to dig out the envelope with a resigned sigh.

He took his time unfolding it, raising the flame on the lantern next to him and scooting closer so he could read Willa's tight, narrow text clearly.

"'To my Elias, the most resistant of my wards,'" he began, hesitating with a dry chuckle. "She's not wrong."

Hattie's smile softened and she turned, draping her arms over the lip of the tub and resting her chin on her wrists to listen.

"'My father once told me that one should speak to business

first before devoting time to sentiment. He claimed that it was both pragmatic and sincere, and so I am honoring that in this letter to you because you have always reminded me of him, and because, I think, he was right,'" Elias read. "'So, first and foremost, let us address the reading of my will, which I presume you have now heard and are summarily raging about in some dark corner of the estate, either privately or at the expense of poor Hattie or poor Julian.

"'I would tell you to stop and consider, but I know you will not read this letter until after a time in which you have done both, and so I shan't. Only know that it is for your own good and I believe this marriage will make you happy, if you let it. All I have ever wanted, Elias, is to make you happy. And I am sorry that I never did.'"

He paused, frowning, and glanced at Hattie, the letter crumpling in his lap. "I don't know if I can do this," he said.

She nodded, tossing the rag to the side and splashing the soap off her arms, and rose from the water immediately, dragging a towel quickly down her form and wrapping herself in the red dressing gown, all the while moving across the room toward him.

He sighed, wincing as she pulled the letter from his hands and took the seat next to him, tilting it toward the light.

"'I could not be your mother because you already had one,'" Hattie said softly, her eyes moving over the words. "'But perhaps I was something else that you needed. I hope I was. When you came to live with me, you did so under the agreement that the monies generated by the baronial lands would be by and large submitted to the discretion of your parents' spending. At the time, I had only begun to build out the farmlands and investment properties along the grounds and agreed because I thought it best for you.

"'You will find, when you go over the expenses with Mr. Harcourt, that they generate quite a lot more income these days than your parents are aware of. Please do not tell them. That is your money, Elias, and you will need it to continue to thrive in your barony. You may continue their allowance as an exchange for their absence, the details of which are enclosed in the estate documents. Or you may not. It is your choice.

"'I also have provided a stipend to my father's brother's widow in the Midlands for some years. She was instrumental to my family's success as merchants in her youth, and it is her rightful inheritance. I am asking you to continue to provide for her, but if you do not, know that she is a canny woman and has not spent unwisely in the years that she has received my provision.

"'You are not obligated to vocally agree or disagree with these terms. You may remain silent, and Mr. Harcourt will take it as a signal to cease payments without judgment or rebuke. Your life is yours now, Elias, and I trust you will do well with it.'"

He made a little sound, a catching in his throat that brought her eyes up.

"Elias?"

He shook his head, reaching out to grip her knee as he pushed the spill of a tear from his cheek. "Keep reading," he begged. "Please."

She put her hand over his but obeyed, her heart aching beneath the silk he'd wrapped it in. "'In this envelope you will find a ring. It was my father's most-prized possession. He is wearing it in the portrait in my bedroom. There is a story behind it and it will explain to you many of the decisions I've made here in my most final words.

"'My parents met as children, both the children of farmers in the Midlands many years ago. The story, as I remember it, was that my father had finally been entrusted, at the ripe old age of twelve, to oversee the egg delivery to the market and was carrying several stacked crates along the high street on his way to his family's stall. My mother, meanwhile, was late to her first lesson with the village seamstress and was running at a tear down the adjacent avenue. He couldn't see where he was going and she was moving too fast to stop. So, you can guess what happened.

"'Despite the inauspicious beginnings, the two became fast

friends and eventually fell in love. The story of how they met would always arise a similar, good-natured argument about whose fault the collision was, but not in the way you might think. They would both claim fault because their thinking was that whoever was responsible was ultimately the one who brought them together, and thus the orchestrator of their ultimate happiness and fate.

"'When they wed, my mother gifted him this bauble, gold and fine and inscribed with *Mea Culpa*. My fault. It was how they said, *'I love you.'* I want you to have this ring because I want you to have that legacy. I want you to know that sometimes love comes at us with broken eggs and late lessons and that is well, even so.'"

Hattie stopped there, for a moment. Awe clashed with something a little heavier in her chest. She gazed over the letter at Elias, who was staring back at her, his cheeks now damp with tears he couldn't push away.

He gave a little laugh, a thing of wonder, and looked down at their clasped hands, where the ring embraced his finger.

"*Mea culpa*," he said, his voice thin and astounded.

"Yes," she said, setting the letter aside and cupping his cheek with her hand. She used her thumb to brush away the tears there and leaned forward to kiss him, tasting the salt on his lips. "*Mea culpa*."

She did not know if he meant it the way she did.

She did not need to know that, just now.

She just needed to let him hold her like this, as the lantern flickered down, and the letter sat beside them.

And at last they knew things that they hadn't before.

Part VI

Punctuation

Chapter Twenty-Four

ELIAS WOKE BEFORE the lantern had fully extinguished, surprised to find they had both fallen asleep above the blankets and in their dressing gowns.

Hattie's arms were wound around him, one hand tucked under the lapel of his robe and the other wrapped in the sash around his waist. He tilted his head down to watch her, breathing softly with the occasional, tiny snore escaping through her parted lips and pointy, little nose. Her face was buried so deeply into the pillow they were sharing that he was certain she was going to wake with creases down her cheek.

Why did that make him ache so inside?

He moved as slowly as he could, untangling her with soft and precise gentleness. He did not wish to wake her, and yet still, he watched her face with a kind of reserved hope that her eyes might slide open and her mouth might bend into a smile to find him trying to escape their tangle, here in the dead of the dark.

Instead, she made a little smacking sound and rolled to the side, pulling her knees up to her chest as the long, belled sleeves of the red dressing gown pooled out around her like a blanket.

He smiled, stifling the urge to chuckle, and slid from the mattress. He took up the letter, which had been discarded in a spray of sheets at the foot of the bed, and then flipped the coverlet up to encase her, tiny as she'd become, balled up like that on the far side of their new room.

She'd had the bed moved. She'd had everything moved, actually.

The room was still outfitted with most of the same furniture it had had on the day they'd exorcised the bats, but with the bed against a different wall and a new wardrobe opposite it, it seemed to Elias a new space entirely.

That was probably wise, he thought, taking up the sputtering lantern and moving it over to the table next to the tub and the fireplace, where a pair of armchairs had been situated.

It was their room now, after all.

Not Willa's.

Not anymore.

He settled into the cushions and carefully set aside the sheets that Hattie had already read aloud. The two at the top.

There were two more underneath.

The first continued Willa's story, explaining how her parents and her uncle and aunt had started a small trade network that had slowly grown into an empire.

"'By the time I met your uncle, my mother had long been gone,'" she had written, "'and my father was ailing. I was angry and contrary and likely impossible, and he still seemed enchanted with me, anyhow. I will always wonder at that. At the time, I told myself it was because he was a destitute noble, a beggar prince in need of an heiress to restore him to his former glory. But I know now that this was not true. He was more than that, just like you are.'"

Elias frowned, closing his eyes and trying to recall his uncle. He could remember slivers of things, brief impressions. A booming laugh. Twinkling, blue eyes. The way he would always sneak a coin into Elias's pocket and hold his finger over his lips with a meaningful glance toward the other adults.

He had died of a weak heart, something Willa had explained that he had contended with since he had been a boy.

"He knew he was a temporary husband," she said. "But he

was determined to be an eternal partner. And he cared for you very much, my boy. Very, very much."

He could hear her voice as he read, suddenly. He could hear her as clearly as though she were standing next to him, hand to his shoulder, reading aloud in the quiet night air. "'Hattie is my heir, but you were always his. And that is how I knew that the two of you must be together, for you are all of me and my father, and Hattie, bless her, has always reminded me of my late husband. Do you see it too?'"

He released a little breath, glancing up at the bed, at the coils of copper and bronze on his pillows.

He imagined Hattie sneaking a coin into a little boy's pocket, and his ribs quaked.

It was easy to see. Easy to conjure.

She had remembered the color of the late baron's ring, he realized. Perhaps she had seen his uncle in detail because they had been kindred, even back then. Even when she had been nothing but an orphan girl scrubbing dishes in the kitchens as he'd lived the final days of his life.

"Are you distressed, Elias?" Willa had asked him, the day of the funeral, when he had been staring down at Hattie for the first time.

And he had shaken his head.

Had it been a lie? Had he been lying back then?

He smiled to himself, shaking his head. Maybe 'distress' was the wrong word for everything he had felt the first time he'd seen her, defiant and gravy spattered, and cursing in terms half the world could understand.

He drew in a deep breath, turning to the last page.

He had avoided this for such a long time. It was funny, wasn't it? That now he was sad to see the end of it.

"'I suppose by now, you've been told about the poem and your new role at the showcase. I imagine you did not enjoy that revelation very much, but you did always wish to participate, did you not? And now is your chance,'" her voice said in his head as his eyes moved over the words, his lips twisting in amusement. "'Do not let Libba choose something horribly maudlin, please. She will, if you do not stop her.'"

He paused, pressing his lips together.

The poem they had chosen for tomorrow *was* rather sad. And he had memorized the damned thing, too.

> *The boast of heraldry, the pomp of pow'r,*
> *And all that beauty, all that wealth e'er gave,*
> *Awaits alike th' inevitable hour.*
> *The paths of glory lead but to the grave.*

He winced.

Was it too late to find something else?

After all, she *had* escaped the grave in a way, hadn't she? She hadn't died so much as she had vanished without a trace.

He bit his lip, pushing himself to his feet and carefully lifting the lantern, which was truly in its death rattles now, moving carefully toward the door. He had seen some books in the salon. Perhaps there was some poetry amongst them.

It did not escape him that he was leaving behind that last page of the letter, still half-unread. He stood there, staring down at it, torn between saving a few of her words, still unspoken, until such a time as he might need them, and knowing that he had to finish this task.

If nothing else, those final lines might contain something that would get him throttled by Malcolm if he did not read them tonight.

Still, they could wait a moment.

They could wait for him to refresh the lantern oil and browse the books in the salon.

Malcolm would never know.

He moved through the shadows as carefully as he could. And, despite leaving her words behind him on the hearthside table, he thought Willa must have approved of this detour.

Because he immediately found what he sought amongst those bundles and book spines, full of treasured literature and personal correspondences. He found them despite the hour, like a beacon in the dead of the night.

Chapter Twenty-Five

HATTIE DID NOT awaken so much as she *flew* from slumber into a state of alarm.

"Elias?!" she cried, coming straight up in the bed with her hands clutched in the blankets on either side of her. "What time is it?!"

But Elias was not there.

And the sun appeared to be fully present in the sky.

She had not been downstairs, and therefore she had not been present for Libba's customary ritual of rude awakening for showcase day. She had not heard the chimes or the drum or the shouting.

Oh, God, there was no clock in here!

This flavor of panic was *not* the cold paste of burnt toast and smashed, fire-roasted tomato. No, no. That was for things yet undone, not things currently in progress.

This tasted unbearably sweet, so sweet, it ached in the cheekbones and jaw. Like milk syrup and figs and yellow cake as well, all mushed together in an unbearable ball of saccharine assault.

"Elias!" she croaked again, confused at how she had come to be contained in a pocket of blankets, her feet trapped in a makeshift pouch as she flailed out of her cushioned and feathered prison. "Are we late?!"

She finally got herself free, flinging the blankets up and at the window so hard, the curtains trembled. Out of the bed and into her slippers, Hattie moved frantically, rearranging her robe as she moved out into the salon, where she found her husband, asleep in an armchair, surrounded by books and … and illustrations? Little sketches and doodles on stiff card stock, some with notes scribbled on them, each next to the envelope it had come in.

What the devil had he been about?!

"Elias!" she said, gripping his shoulder as he startled out of his own reverie. "The showcase!"

"What?" he barked, his palms slapping up over his eyes to rub the sleep away. "Who?"

"Oh, we need a clock!" she moaned. "I will go see how bad it is! Do not move!"

She got two steps from the door and made an impatient little sigh, flapping her hands as she turned back to him. "No, do move! Move!"

And he did, scrambling to his feet as she rushed out into the halls.

She caught herself on the banister, looking down at Errol and Ruby, fully dressed and in conversation below her, and shouted down to them, waving her arm. "What time is it?! I overslept!"

"Good," said Ruby, raking her eyes over Hattie's disheveled form.

"You've an hour yet," Errol told her, much more kindly, which was all she needed to hear.

She spun and flung herself back into the rooms with the announcement, finding Elias bent over a basin, mouth full of tooth powder.

"Oh, my hair! There's no time," she muttered, hands in claws as she stalked to the wardrobe and flung it open. "The dress! Elias, do you know how to lace a corset? Goodness, but we need a staff!"

He mumbled something in reply, which she took as assent.

"They'll go ahead of us, now that they know we're running late," she muttered, pulling his new suit free and tossing it on the bed next to her gown. "I can braid my hair. Braid it into a crown. That will do. Yes, that will do."

"Hattie," he said, trying to soothe her, his hand outstretched.

"No!" she squeaked, ducking under it to address the basin herself. "Get dressed!"

He sighed, looking suspiciously amused by it all, and nodded.

She scrubbed her mouth out, unable to fully rid herself of the flavor of sweet tardy panic, and splashed her face three times in an effort to erase any sign at all of extra sleep. Close to the mirror, she made a point of blinking her eyes as wide as they'd go in a semblance of alertness, though she was not entirely convinced by the reflection.

And it was no fault of hers at all that the mirror caught the reflection of Elias Selwyn removing his dressing gown.

She froze, unable to move or even think for a moment as the mirror framed him from his hips to his throat, the full expanse of his broad, sculpted chest revealed to her as the velvet was peeled away. There was more of that lovely, coiling black hair, so glossy and soft across his heart and trailing down to … to …

Hattie coughed, shaking her head, and reared back from the mirror.

She could hear him rustling about with fabric but could not turn. Could not look. Her face was ablaze with it.

She looked down at her own body in the red dressing gown and decided to move as well. To focus on the task at hand.

A clean chemise emerged from the chest of drawers and she shook it out hastily before sliding the satin belt free of its knot and letting it fall away from her shoulders.

She turned her head slightly to the side as she pulled the chemise on, aware that the rustling on his side of the room had stopped. Aware and curious.

Was he watching too?

She couldn't taste the panic anymore, strangely.

She tasted something else entirely. Smoke and salt, she thought, as the soft muslin tumbled down around her thighs.

She shook her hair out, pulling the few remaining pins from her night of sleep out and tossing them next to the basin. And she glanced in the mirror again.

This time, she could see his face. His chest was still bare, a loose pair of trousers pulled up over his hips, still open at the waist.

He *was* watching. With what appeared to be great interest.

She shivered, her body erupting in gooseflesh as her eyes slid down the exposed planes of his body again, rendered in reflection.

They were late. They couldn't.

They shouldn't.

She dragged her eyes up once more to his and felt herself falter at the heat she found there. And still, she might have maintained course, if he had not moved. Had not walked around the corner of the bed and very deliberately taken a seat on the edge.

She let out a distressed little sound, her hands sliding off the basin as she spun around to face him, without the barrier of quicksilver and fog. She faced him directly, warm flesh rising and falling as he breathed, eyes glowing hot, legs wide on the edge of the mattress, and she could not be expected not to move, in the face of that.

He leaned back, his arms bare and extended, muscles moving under the skin in the shafts of early light that came in through the disturbed curtains, and braced himself against the mattress, watching her silently.

It was the final blow to her devotion to punctuality.

She crossed the room in four long strides, climbing onto him without preamble as his arm caught around her waist, dragging her tightly into his lap. His free hand bunched in the hem of her chemise, his head tilting back in her own grasp so that she could claim that mouth of his, desperate and hungry, her tongue pushing in to taste what had been lingering on the edge of her senses since catching sight of him a moment ago.

"Off," he rasped against her mouth, tugging at the chemise.

"Off."

She pushed herself onto her knees, her back arching as she let him slide the chemise up over her body and over her head, her hair tumbling down over her bare shoulders as he flung it away. She clawed down the open waistband of his trousers, raking pink lines into his hips as he lifted them to assist her, kicking away his own fabric in the process before pulling her firmly back into the seat she had claimed with such urgency.

He pressed his mouth onto her throat, reaching down to guide himself into her, to connect them in the way they needed to be connected. His teeth grazed the delicate flesh of her neck as she dug her fingers into his hair, moving her hips as soon as he had found her entrance and sliding down the length of him, filling herself completely.

"Elias," she breathed, pushing her knees against his hips, gasping at the perfection of it, her hands slipping down over those bare, sculpted shoulders and grazing over the dusting of hair over his heart as she began to move.

He groaned, kissing her throat once more before leaning back against the bed again, his eyes roving over her like he was going to memorize every patch of skin on her body, his lip caught between his even, white teeth. His hand was big and warm on her hip, following her movements as he struggled for breath, his hips bucking up against hers every now and then, though he appeared to be trying very hard to stay still.

He watched, those dark-blue eyes of his half-hooded, and he studied her, his gaze roaming over her face, her throat, her breasts, until he could not stand it anymore and reared back up to sink his hand into her hair and pull her mouth down onto his again.

He tightened his grip on her hip as he kissed her, pinning her down astride him as he rolled his hips up in slow, agonizing movements that stole her breath, her body trembling in his grip.

"Oh," she managed, her eyes slipping shut as he continued to move this way, cresting under her like ocean waves breaking on the shingled beach outside.

It built in her like a storm. Like *his* storm.

His mouth was hot and traveling down her throat, over her breasts, tasting the peaks of her nipples, and still, he was anchoring her there, holding her hips tight against his own as he pulsed upward, their breath catching in matching volleys.

She came apart with very little warning, cracking like thunder had cracked during their wedding vows, bright and loud and spearing through her body with a rumble of release.

He met her there, he chose it, clinging to her and following her over the edge into oblivion, until those urgent, desperate thrusts slowed and evened, their grips on one another softening but persevering all the same.

And they breathed together, ragged and then slower, sharing the air between their mouths as they rested their foreheads together, still joined as the final tremors of their pleasure echoed through their bodies.

Dizzy and still somehow not quite sated, she ran her hand over his throat and along the back of his neck, twining in the ends of his hair.

"We will definitely be late now," she murmured, warm in his ear.

She felt him grin, felt the shape of it against her shoulder as his fingers traced over the bare lines of her back.

"I know," he said. *"Mea culpa."*

❦

Chapter Twenty-Six

ELIAS WAS IN a far more buoyant mood than he could have anticipated on the morning of a funerary rite.

Oddly, he did not feel it inappropriate in the least. In fact, he imagined Willa would have approved most heartily, though perhaps not with a fully detailed accounting as to why.

He had laced his bride into her king's regalia with aptitude, if not full devotion to timeliness, stealing kisses along her neck and spine where he could, despite her half-hearted protests and swatting.

He had even braided her hair, having become quite accustomed to the pattern required in his military days, though she saw to the pinning of it around her lovely head in the shape of a crown.

His own costume was more of a colorful variation on his usual clothing than anything outlandish, and once strapped fully into it and regarding himself in a mirror, he did not think he would retire it following the festivities.

While the orange cravat and goldenrod waistcoat were a bit louder than he would have chosen for himself, Monica had not been wrong about his suitability to a powder-blue fabric as the primary color of the piece itself.

Though, of course, his eyes might have only been shining so very well from the activities of the morning, rather than the complements of textile.

He gathered the poetry book he had chosen last night, Willa's letter, and a handful of the keepsake cards he'd unearthed to his chest as they made haste toward the door, though he could not resist stalling the former Miss French one final time, pushing his weight against the jamb and demanding one final kiss before they must emerge out into the world at large.

She gave it, but she also bit him in the process.

He liked that more than he was willing to reflect upon just now, with so much ahead for the day.

Luckily, Rhys was running late as well, and they were able to share a carriage to the pavilion, crammed into the seats with a variety of his props, including a fencing sword, half a dozen pilfered beakers, and several fabric-wrapped cubes.

It was the cubes on which Hattie was fixated as they went, her eyes narrowing as she beheld one that was a soft marigold color, punctuated with black stripes.

"Rhys," she said, very slowly, "is that my dressing gown?"

Rhys glanced at the box, and then at Elias, who immediately shook his head and widened his eyes for emphasis.

"No," said Rhys, unconvincingly and with a queasy smile. "Not anymore, anyway."

She drew in a hissing breath, her body thrumming out like a primed longbow. "If you *think*—"

"Oh, we're here!" Elias announced, reaching across her and scrambling for the carriage door hinge before the wheels had even stopped turning. "We made good time, didn't we?"

"We did, indeed. We did, indeed," Rhys chirped, kicking the door open and rolling out bodily while the carriage was still crunching to a halt. "I'll send someone for the props!"

Hattie was staring after him, chest heaving, eyes in glittering tiny slits. And it took only a moment for realization to hit her as her head began to pivot from her chaotic fellow ward to her guilty-as-sin husband, watching her warily from the cushion next to her.

"We have to alight!" Elias said. "I have to open the proceedings!"

"Elias!" she breathed, but he was already stepping over her and stumbling backward out onto the pebbled terrain.

He held his arms up to her, holding his face frozen in what he hoped was an acceptably innocent expression, until she sighed, shook her head, and accepted the aid.

"This is not over," she said to him. "That was an imperial gift!"

"It still is," Elias said weakly, only to get shoved and have her stalk away, hips swinging and blue-and-gold, orange-and-white skirts swinging like a particularly irate macaw as she marched off to the pavilion.

Rhys reappeared a breath later, though Elias could not account for where the devil he would have been hiding in this flat, open terrain.

"Good show," he said. "You hold the blade."

And he did because there was little else to do in the moment, and he needed to go back into the carriage, anyway, to retrieve his literature.

"There you bloody are!" Liberty cried, shoving several titled and well-monied people out of her way as she stalked toward the carriage. "Rhys, your corner is *empty*. Go fill it!"

"Aye, sir," he said sarcastically, spinning around Elias with the three cubes and sword stacked in a precarious tower in his arms as he trotted away, top hat gleaming in the sun.

"At least it isn't raining," she muttered, tossing a suspicious glance at Elias as though he might summon some rain, just to spite her. "We are starting soon. Go see Errol. Your pig is distressed."

"Oh, but I need to—" he began, but she had already vanished, her toga-like white gown fluttering out around her like a pair of wings as she flew to her next quarry.

"Right." Elias looked around for Errol and his menagerie.

He made it as far as the temporary fencing before Malcolm

intercepted him, stepping into his path so suddenly that Elias nearly smacked right into the other man, even dressed as he was in scarlet and eye-watering royal blue.

"Selwyn!" Mal exclaimed, gripping his shoulders to stop him short. "Did you read it?"

"Yes, I read it!" Elias shouted back, stumbling back into his footing. "Christ!"

"And?!" Mal demanded, eyes wild.

"And it says what Harcourt said it would," he replied. "Shall I have a copy drafted for you?"

Malcolm's eyes narrowed, just a hair. "If you would," he replied, snidely. "Very kind."

"Ruby, do not touch that pig!" Monica voice cried from across the pavilion. "You will ruin your dress!"

"Oh, but it needs me," Ruby cried back, already half-bent over Peach's eager form.

"I've got her," Elias said, pushing past Malcolm and stepping over the fence. "I'm here."

"Bah," said Ruby, frowning and drawing herself back up, metallic gown glinting silver and emerald green in the sun. "Brigand."

It took all of five minutes for Peach to be happily snorting again in Elias's arms and for Libba to appear once again in a cloud of fury and order, waving her hands as she summoned the remainder of the wards around them, half in and half out of the pigpen.

"Rhys was late," she began.

"I beg your pardon!" he replied, his top hat half off as he attempted to flip the brim properly.

"We'll swap the order of presentation," Libba continued over him. "First Elias with the elegy and then …"

"Oh, I needed to tell you—" Elias began, only to be silenced as well with a stiff hand held immediately in the air as she barreled past him.

"Then the pigs, as Rhys isn't ready," she said, nodding at

Errol, who nodded calmly back. "Then we will break for the interactive displays, pigs, translations, cup game, and scents while canapes are served and my troupe assembles our stage for the *Pygmalion* excerpt. We'll reopen on the play section and then move directly into Hattie's demonstration and Mal's panel."

"Are you canceling me entirely?" Rhys demanded.

"*Then*," Libba continued, her voice going up an octave, "another break for punch and onward to Rhys and then Monica."

"I can't perform opposite Monica," Rhys whined, frowning. "That's not fair."

"I'll be gentle, lamb," Monica said softly. "We ought to have planned something together."

"'Ought to' doesn't help us now," Libba snapped. "We'll finish with Ruby's sparkles, as planned."

"'As planned,'" Ruby echoed, still looking longingly at the pig. "Of course."

"Are the portraits ready?" Hattie asked softly, reaching toward Libba but not actually touching her. "By the podium?"

Libba paused, glancing over her shoulder, and gave a crisp nod. "Yes. And the prince's retinue will likely arrive shortly. Several people took it upon themselves to be early, in fact, including the honorable Mr. and Mrs. Selwyn. Elias?"

"Handled," Elias said, bending down to perch Peach back on the ground. "They won't cause trouble."

"Hm," said Libba, frowning. "Anything else?"

"Did anyone else think they saw—" Malcolm began, only to be immediately shushed by both Errol and Rhys.

The women looked on curiously as he pressed his lips together, clearly cowed out of saying what he had intended.

"Whom?" Libba demanded, curtly.

Mal shook his head. "Nothing. It was stupid."

Hattie met Elias's eyes over their shoulders and shrugged.

And without a single further word, the entire contingent of wards split apart like a dropped rock, each piece going in its determined direction, whilst Elias stood in the center, confused that he had missed the cue.

"What are you thinking?" Rhys hissed to Malcolm as they passed him. "Fool."

"Oh, *I'm* the fool?" Mal snapped back.

"Elias, come along!" Libba called from halfway down the path to the podium. "You are required!"

He sighed and nodded, trotting after her, still gripping the book and papers to his side. He had spoken in public many times, especially during his time in the cavalry, but this felt significantly odder than any address he'd ever delivered before.

Still, he listened as Libba told him where the important folk were sitting and waited for Lem to unveil the two portraits of Willa that Hattie had sent ahead for this event, each perched on an easel next to the stage.

Willa as a child with her parents. Willa as a bride with her husband.

They had never found the third portrait, of Willa as a mother with her wards.

He glanced up once his papers were arranged as needed and nodded at Libba, taking a bracing breath.

She quieted the crowd somehow.

Elias was not certain how.

She did not wave her arms or shout or flap a flag around.

Everyone just silenced themselves because Liberty Lennox had decided they ought to, and they all turned to him, expectantly.

He almost laughed at how eerie and alarming it was.

"Good afternoon," he said, raising his hand. "I do not know many of you assembled here today, but I am Elias Selwyn, Baron Selwyn, and I am here to open the festivities to honor the life of my Aunt Willa, the longtime dowager baroness, and the mind behind the prodigies of Brighton Beach."

He cleared his throat, casting a nervous glance at Libba before he shattered their carefully rehearsed script. "We had prepared an elegy for today's opening," he said with a wry smile and a shrug. "But last night, I read the final letter my aunt wrote to me, and she asked me in no uncertain terms *to please not be so damned maudlin.*"

There was a ripple of laughter, a drawing closer of parasols and top hats as the crowd began to thicken.

He could feel Libba's glare but did not dare meet it.

He laughed, shaking his head. "I spent all night in her library," he said. "My aunt loved to correspond with people in far-flung lands. She had a fascination for everything alien and queer and unknown to her. Every book on her bookshelf was littered through with correspondence from friends she had made and figures she had written in the varied corners of the globe. Many included, at her request, artistic interpretations of their homes and notes about the things they loved.

"I have brought some today, which I will display later, for open viewing, as a testament to her passion for living.

"But I have also decided to honor her final wish and shrug off the impulse to give a maudlin farewell, no matter how sad I might personally feel about her absence. Here amongst the keepsake cards with art of places like Marakesh and Melbourne and the Mississippi River, I found a poem about just such a queer creature as those for which Willa always had a fondness, and to me, it seemed the right thing to read to welcome this final farewell to her legacy."

He could see Hattie out of the corner of his eye, a swish of white and blue as she drew nearer, her hair glinting like molten bronze on her head.

"When we were children, Willa took us to see a collection of exotic creatures," Elias said, chuckling a little in memory. "And then she told us the most unusual creatures in the menagerie that day were us children, not the lemurs and tigers and kangaroos. Still. She had spent a great deal of time admiring the kangaroos."

"We all did," Ruby called, winning another little laugh from the assemblage.

Elias took a breath and opened the book in front of him,

flashing a grin at the crowd. "This is not a completed poem. It is a draft, shared with my aunt in friendship and happiness, sent to her after she had already vanished and left unopened in her quarters until I discovered it there. I do hope that someday, this work is published. I hope that someday it is completed and shared with the world at large, for it spoke to me in a way that reminded me strongly of my aunt. And I think it will speak to you too. *Kangaroo*," he recited. "By Barron Field."

And he lost himself a little, as he read.

She had made the squirrel fragile;
She had made the bounding hart;
But a third so strong and agile
Was beyond ev'n Nature's art;
So she join'd the former two
In thee, Kangaroo!
To describe thee, it is hard:
Converse of the camélopard,
Which beginneth camel-wise,
But endeth of the panther size,
Thy fore half, it would appear,
Had belong'd to some "small deer,"
Such as liveth in a tree;
By thy hinder, thou should'st be
A large animal of chace,
Bounding o'er the forest's space;—
Join'd by some divine mistake,
None but Nature's hand can make—
Nature, in her wisdom's play,
On Creation's holiday.

He only looked up again to check that he was still here, to look into the faces of the audience, pressing ever nearer, baffled as they might have been.

> *Thou can'st not be amended: no;*
> *Be as thou art; thou best art so.*
> *When sooty swans are once more rare,*
> *And duck-moles the Museum's care,*
> *Be still the glory of this land,*
> *Happiest Work of finest Hand!*

There was applause. If not for the applause, Elias might not have realized that he had come to the end. He looked up, dazed and teary eyed, and so unexpectedly full of joy that he thought he might burst.

And then he saw her too, for just a moment, against the surf and sky.

He saw her as clearly as he saw anyone else that day.

And then she was gone.

H ATTIE HAD WISHED to greet Elias the instant he had stepped from the platform and shower him with praise and gratitude.

She was, however, intercepted by the royal valet, who had been sent to retrieve Elias for an audience.

It occurred to Hattie that she might point out, at an advantageous moment in the future, that she was no longer the only one with princes as intimates. It was a thought that made her smile as she watched him be led to the dais where the prince was seated.

"That was just lovely," came Monica's voice, punctuated with a sniffle. "Perfect, I'd say. Though I imagine Libba will be steaming."

"She will cool," said Hattie, turning to the other woman with a smile.

Behind them, Errol was preparing his pigs and their props for a grand display.

"No grange," Hattie observed, nodding toward him. "He is distressed about that."

"Well," said Monica, "I never understood the appeal of giant vegetables, anyhow."

"Yes, they are better small and crisp," Hattie agreed. "But the flowers were always nice."

"There is always next year," said Monica, her pale brows

raising.

Hattie blinked at her, warmth in her chest. "Yes," she said. "There is always next year."

For a time, they stood side by side and watched the beginning of the pig act, though by now, they had seen it many times. The little porcine performers balanced on balls and acted on command. One was a high jumper among them that could leap directly into Errol's arms, which delighted the crowd.

"Have the Selwyns found you yet?" Monica asked her, after a while. "Your new parents-in-law?"

Hattie turned, surprised. "No. Are they here?"

Monica nodded. "The stepfather approached me to apologize if I took his observation at the wedding as an insult," she said, with a twist of her lips. "Not quite an apology, though I think he saw it as one. He then went onto tell me how fond he is of jiggly women."

"Oh, Christ," said Hattie, horrified. "Do not tell Elias."

Monica snorted, shaking her head. "I shan't. He then went on to say that he only would have decried a match between us because of Elias's childhood shape and the worry that we would produce a brood of soft boys combined together, unsuitable for Selwyn heirs."

Hattie tilted her head to the side, staring at Monica for a long while. She blinked and cleared her throat, shaking the visual from her head. "Perhaps tell Mr. Harcourt instead," she decided. "I should like to see what he thinks about this scenario, jiggle and sons alike."

Monica giggled, clearly startled by this suggestion, and bustled away, hiding her pink cheeks under her fingers while Hattie grinned after her departing form.

Unfortunately, the loss of crowd companion did, in fact, open her up to being approached by the Selwyns, who sidled into the spot Monica had vacated with alarming immediacy.

"Miss French!" the man boomed, already red-faced from the summer heat and sporting two shiny, purple bruises under each eye. His nose was puffy and had a line of talc sitting over the scab that ran horizontal across the bridge.

"She is *Lady Selwyn* now, Wallace," his wife said, fanning herself in agitation. "Good afternoon, dear. We've come to say *good afternoon.*"

Hattie did not sigh. "Good afternoon," she replied.

"What an unusual gown, my dear," her mother-in-law said, taking a step back and stepping to the blue side first, and then to the white-and-orange side. "It is two gowns in one, I daresay!"

"It is a replica," Hattie said, looking down at the skirt and shaking it out. "Of a medieval king's gown. Jadwiga of Poland."

"A king's gown, you say?" Mr. Selwyn repeated, blustering out a chuckle. "Bit light in the feet, was he?"

"*She*," said Hattie, blinking. "She was a king."

Mr. Selwyn stared at her a moment, his forehead muscles twitching in obvious confusion. "Oh," he finally decided, glancing at his wife with eyebrows that suggested they would discuss it later. "If you say so, Baroness."

Hattie forced a smile. "I must go and prepare. Thank you for greeting me."

"Wait, no!" Catriona Selwyn said, her hand shooting out to grab Hattie by the wrist. "We must … clear the air. After that unfortunate business at the wedding, you understand."

"Indeed?" Hattie said, staring down at her wrist with such pointed interest that the other woman immediately dropped her hold.

"Indeed," said Mrs. Selwyn, wincing. "We … have only one son, you understand. It was a blow to find out through gossip that he was to wed. We had no say in it, no inclusion. We were wounded. And we behaved badly. Without thinking."

Mr. Selwyn made a noise in his throat but did not otherwise comment.

"I wish we hadn't," Mrs. Selwyn said, looking exhausted by the effort it took to say those words, her face drawn and her eyes sagging at the corners. "In fact, I thought perhaps when we got back home, I might write to you, my dear."

"'Write to me'?" Hattie repeated, baffled.

"She likes the idea of her correspondence being tucked between letters from tsars and dukes," Mr. Selwyn said with an indulgent little chuckle that made Hattie want to break his nose again.

Mrs. Selwyn immediately reddened. "Well, all right, Wallace, that's quite enough. I only thought that a woman ought to get to know she whom her only son chose to marry."

"Oh, I think you will find me quite simple," Hattie said with a bright smile at their slack-jawed reactions to her words. "To get to know, of course. Please excuse me. I look forward to writing you!"

She walked away still grinning, her cheeks hurting from her delight at her own wordplay.

"So they are his siblings?" one fine lady was whispering to another. "He married one of them."

"No, no, they were the dowager baroness's wards," the other said back, clicking her tongue. "Honestly, this is what happens when you never summer in Brighton."

"But they're all … Well, they're quite *vocational* for a baroness's brood, are they not?" the other woman huffed.

"Starling's Rest is the domain of the *demimonde*, my dear," her friend replied with a shrug. "Enjoy it while the sun burns hot."

Demimonde, Hattie thought.

Half world.

Like the kangaroo in the poem.

She giggled to herself and made her way to Rhys's corner, flicking the back of his ear before he could hear her coming and reveling in his outraged spin of surprise.

"Whatever is left of my dressing gown," she said before he could speak, "you will deliver to Monica. And she will make something permanent and ostentatious that will live in a visible corner of the Rest and haunt you and my badly behaved husband until you too are being feted into the afterlife under this pavilion.

Do you understand me, Rhys?"

He blinked, his eyes burning emerald green in the sun. "You know," he said with a few blinks of his heavily lashed and kohled eyes, "for once, I actually do."

"I will have that box, too," she decided. "As penance."

"Not my box!" he cried, hands flying protectively out to shield said box and his half dozen stolen beakers from her greedy gaze.

Hattie only laughed and turned back to see if her husband had completed his royal duties. She wandered back to the podium to inspect the keepsake cards he had laid out, each from a different and strange corner of the world.

There were seven of them, she realized with amusement.

He ought to have brought eight.

Eight was far more correct.

She wanted to stay and read them all, to turn them over in her hands, but she was not the only curious onlooker, and given that the art cards would return to their bedroom with them tonight, she knew she needed to make way for the others, while they still had the chance.

Libba's troupe had moved to begin setting up the props for their play snippet in the center of the pavilion while canapes appeared on trays from the household staff, dotted throughout the crowd.

That meant interactive displays were next.

It was all so familiar that it was hard to really accept that it had been a decade since the last time they'd done this.

"I got you a biscuit," Elias's voice said, appearing at her elbow with a hazelnut confection in his hand and a smile on his face. "Last one."

She turned, reaching up to brush some of the wayward strands of his dark hair back into place. "Those are my favorites," she told him.

"Yes, I remember," he replied smugly. "What do they taste like to you?"

"Hm," she said, taking the offering and biting into it. She chewed slowly, her eyes sliding to the side as she considered it. "They taste like contentment."

He twinkled at her, swiping a bit of the hazelnut paste with his finger and dropping it onto his tongue. "What?" he said at her little gasp of outrage. "I want to taste contentment."

She narrowed her eyes but did not argue, her heart fluttering pleasantly in her chest at this cheek. "What did the prince say?"

"Oh, the usual things," Elias said with a shrug. "Condolences and congratulations and so on. It was a lot of words and not a lot of meaning."

"How is that possible?" Hattie demanded, frowning. "I can never get a single syllable out without meaning something, you know."

"I know," he replied—so fondly, she blushed.

She cleared her throat, shifting her weight from one foot to the other. "Your parents came to speak to me."

"Oh?" he said, raising his eyebrows. "An apology?"

"Their closest approximation, I think," she said. "I don't know where they got to."

She turned, her shoulder leaning against his chest as they surveyed the crowd in tandem and settled, at the same time, on the impression of Wallace Selwyn, just now crouched on the ground on his hands and knees, chortling like a child, as Errol's jumping pig made a running leap toward his back and cleared him in a single bound.

Mrs. Selwyn was standing nearby, covering her face in what appeared to be shame.

"Well," said Elias, sounding a little stunned. "All right."

"Oh," said Hattie, glancing at the scents table and Ruby situating herself with a silver blindfold in her hands. "I am supposed to go stop any guests from waving anything particularly vile under Ruby's nose. There's always one or two who try."

"Should I ask?" Elias said, wrinkling his own nose.

"No," said Hattie, grimacing. "It is astounding what people

will put in their pockets in the hopes of shocking others. Oh, I suppose Lemuel is going to do it."

"Lemuel?" Elias repeated as Lem's large frame stalked across the pavilion in his sultan costume, coming to stand before the table with crossed arms and a respectful nod to Ruby. "I thought 'Lem' was short for 'Lem.'"

"Not anymore," said Hattie. "Do you think Errol can grow a lemon tree in our bedroom?"

"What?!"

She broke into a broad smile, lacing her hands through his and squeezing. "Find us a good seat for the theatrical excerpt," she instructed. "I have to play the five tongues game."

"Wait," he said, gripping her hand before she could spin away and tugging her back to him. "I want to play."

She fell against his chest with a surprised squeak, her fingers brushing hazelnut crumbs onto his waistcoat, and gazed up at him, uncertain if she was being teased. "You do?"

"I do," he said, grinning down at her. "Will you humor me?"

She blinked, unwilling to steady herself just yet from her collapsed state against him. "Well, I suppose," she said. "But nothing overly rude."

"Oh, it's *very* rude," he assured her, his eyes sparkling.

"Then do it quietly!" she returned, tightening her lips. "I shall whisper if I must."

"I don't want you to whisper," he replied, already beginning to laugh. "I want you to announce."

She sighed, using his body to propel herself back onto her feet. "Very well, then. Do your worst."

He watched her, flushed and fond and still chuckling. "Tell me you love me," he requested. "Five ways."

For a moment, she just gazed at him, her chest aching. Sweetness and salt danced over her tongue and a scent hung in the air like caramel and vanilla.

"*Je t'aime,*" she said softly. "*Ya tebya lyublyu.*"

"Hm," he said, crossing his arms as though assessing her

pronunciation.

"*Tha gaol agam ort*," she told him. "I love you."

"You do?" he replied, taunting and smug.

"*Sic*," she said. "*Mea culpa.*"

"Good," he answered. "I love you too."

Chapter Twenty-Eight

ELIAS WENT BACK to the canape trays one last time in the hopes of pilfering one of the anchovy and parmesan tartlets, which he knew Hattie hated. He reasoned that if he ate the tartlet first and followed it with a little bakewell slice, she would never be the wiser.

"They aren't *actually* related," a nearby man with an impressive, waxed mustache said to another, shorter and clean-shaven, as he approached the tray. "What sort of siblings have different accents? Two of them are brown!"

"Well, perhaps they only share *one* parent," the other man replied uncertainly. "I could have sworn I was told they were siblings."

Elias chuckled, popping his prize in his mouth and turning to the men. "You think Willa Starling Selwyn had that many lovers, do you?"

"Oh, Lord Selwyn!" the man who seemed to have more of the facts said with horror. "Our apologies."

"None needed," said Elias, still amused. "Malcolm and Libba are siblings," he told them, pointing to the pair as they worked together to erect a heavy plinth that Libba would stand on as the alabaster statue that became a woman. "The rest are not. We were all the baroness's wards. She is my aunt via marriage."

The speculative man nodded thoughtfully. "Yes, yes, they do

look alike," he said of Libba and Malcolm, who could not have looked more different in that moment, with him ruddy and sweat sheened in his bright red-and-blue suit and her covered in talc powder and swathed in white gauze. "So you're all orphans, then?"

Elias shook his head. "No. Some of us. Or perhaps none of us. I'm afraid you will find no consistency here."

"Yes, so stop trying," the other man piped in a high octave, clearly aghast. "You cannot just ask people if they are orphans!"

"Why not?" his friend returned, frowning.

Elias chuckled and passed them by, moving to the temporary seating that had been erected in the corner of the pavilion to find a good place for himself and Hattie.

"Pomegranate?" Ruby's voice sang over the crowd. "And … cheese? Wait! *Chevre!*"

There was an eruption of cheers as she whipped her blindfold away with triumph and then let the guest holding out the spoon of combined flavors feed it to her, the goat cheese tinged red with the fruit juice.

Elias made a face.

It made him want another anchovy tart.

And thoughts of anchovies smothered in finely shredded parmesan were enough of a distraction that he didn't notice his parents taking the seats behind him.

"I can't believe we've never attended one of these before!" his stepfather exclaimed, startling Elias so badly, he almost dropped his bakewell slice. "What a lark! What nonsense!"

"Oh, Wallace, you have dirt on your knees," his mother said with exasperation. "What if that pig had hit you?"

"What if it had?" his stepfather returned with amusement. "A pig and a barrister in the same week? I'd have quite a story for the lads at the club."

Elias turned, blinking at them as his mother sighed and gave him a little shrug when their eyes met.

"Are you drunk?" he asked his stepfather, baffled.

"'Drunk'? Never!" the man said with a giggle. "I am merry, lad. Have you *tried* the punch?!"

"The numbers boy is quite something," his mother said over her husband, shifting awkwardly in her seat to draw Elias's attention over to her. "I drew scraps of paper with three other ladies and three gentlemen drew symbols from mathematics. He assembled a total in a matter of seconds."

"Yes, he does that," Elias said, a little stunned that she had participated at all. "They call him 'the Marvelous Human Abacus.'"

"He'd make a hell of a banker," his stepfather said, waving over a servant with a tray and taking up two cucumber sand-wiches.

"He does," Elias replied. "He is. Or was. He is now a part owner in a shipping firm."

"Shipping, is it?" said his mother with interest. "East India?"

"Something smaller," Elias said. "I haven't inquired."

"That sister of his is wearing very little," his stepfather said in half a whisper. "I've never seen such muscular flanks on a woman!"

"Nor should you," his wife snapped, snatching one of the sandwiches away. "What is she? Some sort of strongwoman?"

"Probably," said Elias, glancing at Libba, "but mostly an ac-tress, by trade."

"Actress!" his stepfather exclaimed in delight. "Oh, those are always most amusing women. Very liberated, you know."

Elias sighed. "Monica's act is my favorite," he said, pointing to her in the crowd. "She's second-to-last today. She will invite the crowd to choose from a variety of textiles and odds and ends, things like wine corks and old marbles and flaps of paper and scrap, and then someone will turn the hourglass, and she will fashion a garment from them on the dress form. Sometimes she will do two or three, depending on how much material is given to her."

"A paper and marble garment?" his mother said, clearly intrigued. "How long does the hourglass run?"

"Not long," said Elias. "I have seen her fashion a cravat out of newspapers that looked neater than the starchiest linen. It is a marvel."

"Bah, cravats," said his stepfather through his cucumbers. "I want to see the illusionist lad at work. He made one of the pigs temporarily disappear and I thought the Irish boy was going to flog him."

"Oh, an illusionist?" his mother said, sounding suddenly quite girlish. "Which one? Elias, which one?"

"Rhys," he said, pointing. "The Welsh one."

"Oh, I saw him earlier," she said, blinking. "He's very pretty, isn't he?"

"I beg your pardon!" her husband bumbled, stuffing the remainder of the sandwich into his mouth.

Elias could only stare at them.

Was this the first conversation they'd ever had? The first *real* conversation.

"You like illusions?" he asked his mother.

She opened her fan and gave it a nervous little flutter. "Oh, I do enjoy them," she admitted, blushing a little. "I've always wanted to believe in magic."

"And you," he said to his stepfather. "You like … pigs?"

"I like all sorts of things," the man replied with a sniff and a sudden brightening swell of his chest. "What do you like, boy? Hm? That wife of yours? Oh, ho ho."

"Oh, yes, your wife," said Elias's mother, as though realizing she'd forgotten a task. "What is her act?"

"She and Malcolm perform together," Elias said. "They each do a prepared sketch and then take requests from the crowd. People try to stump them."

"And are they ever successful?" his mother asked, leaning closer.

"Not that I've seen," Elias replied. "Though I remember there was a bit of a fuss one year when Hattie attempted to speak

Shelta to Miss Boswell with her family members present. Apparently, outsiders are not supposed to do that."

"'Shelta'?" his stepfather repeated. "What's that?"

"A cant," said Elias. "A secret language. The Parvee speak it in the caravan."

"Ooh," said his mother, her fan fluttering again. "Secret Traveller language, Wallace! How scandalous."

Elias opened his mouth to correct her and then shut it again.

Perhaps, just for today, it was not worth puncturing the atmosphere.

Clouds rolled across the sun as they passed into late afternoon, with people filling up the seats around the Selwyns as the interactive displays were taken down and Libba's troupe got into order for the performance.

"Do you see that bird with the cropped hair?" Mr. Selwyn whispered, leaning forward to nudge Elias's shoulder. "There by the harp?"

"Yes?" said Elias, looking at Libba's troupe member as she flung a long, blonde wig onto her head.

"I met her," said his stepfather, with the same self-satisfaction he might have used for a feat of great difficulty. "And she's a *nun*."

Elias turned to give a skeptical look over his shoulder.

"It's true!" he said. "Actors!"

Libba climbed up onto the podium and raised her arms, silencing everyone with much the same force of will she had used before, convincing even Wallace to withdraw and shut up.

"*Pygmalion* is an ancient myth," she began. "And one that I have always loved. It was a story first told me by Willa, the woman we are gathered here today to honor. And she did so in response to a childish question that I'd asked her, the day she'd offered to take me in."

Libba smiled, shaking her head and looking down. The tiny crystals she had glued over each of her constellation of beauty marks flashed in the late day sun. "I asked her who I should be to make her most happy, in gratitude for my new lot," she said.

"And Willa told me that we should never attempt to fashion another person to our desires, for that is not the way of love. This is a story about that exact folly.

"Today, we are performing a small piece of the full theatrical production of *Pygmalion*. If you enjoy it, I urge you to speak to my players after the performance. You may purchase tickets to the full production in two weeks' time at the Odalisque Playhouse on Ship Street, where we will be for the remainder of the year."

Elias turned to watch, resisting the urge to chuckle at the way Hattie was bustling across the pavilion with her skirts in her fists to take the seat he'd saved her next to his own.

She was panting, slumping down next to him and shaking herself. He turned, breaking his bakewell slice in half and offering her the bit with the cherry, which she accepted with a smirk.

Lem strode to the front of the stage as Libba and her players gathered around the plinth, crossing his massive, oiled arms over his chest and beginning to speak, his deep baritone echoing through the pavilion.

"Of a late summer night," he said, "in a lonely workshop, an artist creates. He has pled with the goddess to bring him love, and instead, only the muses have answered. And so he toils, for toiling is how he eases his pain."

The harp trilled, one of the young vagabonds stepping around Lem to bow to the crowd. The formerly golden-haired youth now somehow transformed into a distinguished older gentleman, with powdered-white hair and a mustache he certainly hadn't had this morning.

He took up a chisel and followed the music, approaching the plinth where Libba was now hidden behind several gray sheets of fabric that had been suspended on horizontal poles. Elias thought that they really did look like a chunk of marble or granite, even here in the light.

For every strike of the chisel, one of the troupe hit a drum and a sheet fell away, revealing more of the shape of the woman hiding underneath.

Libba, Elias could see, was holding a very difficult pose, with one leg raised behind her and her arms stretched toward the heavens.

No wonder she had such strong flanks.

The actress who may or may not have also been a nun strode forward, her long, false hair glinting in the light as she paced the circumference of the workshop.

"The goddess did hear," Lem's voice boomed. "And she did answer. For she, like us all, was moved by the creation of beauty."

Another sheet fell away, revealing Libba's talc-covered hand reaching to the heavens. The goddess passed near, touching the plinth, and her fingers began to wiggle.

It drew an awed gasp from the crowd.

A violin struck a chord, adding its wail to the harp as the artist sped in his endeavors, peeling away the remainder of rock that hid his beloved in its shell, pulling Libba out until her pose was fully visible to the crowd, and still, only her hand moved.

"The goddess," said Lem, "provides."

And Libba opened her eyes, winning another gasp.

What followed was something of a ballet, as far as Elias could tell, with Libba stretching and languid, moving in coils on her plinth before leaping from it into the arms of the sculptor. They followed the pulse of the music in long, controlled motions, choreographed to be somehow both passionate and stunning in their physicality.

"Elias," Hattie whispered. "It is the silent language."

And he nodded.

Because it was.

Libba was smiling now, though he was not sure if it was her own joy or the sculpture's as she tangled and leapt with the other actor, chasing the crescendo and the rapid tatter of the drum.

The man grasped her about the waist and lifted her high, as though presenting her to the audience. She spread her arms and then twisted around, grasping him about the shoulders and kissing his mouth as the troupe swept in and covered them with the marble sheets, bringing the scene to a close.

There was stunned silence. And then there was applause. And the sheets fell away as the troupe emerged to take a bow.

Elias thought it might have been a perfect moment. Utterly perfect.

If not for his parents' voices.

"Gracious," his mother said, her voice wobbled by the rapid flap of her fan. "Did you see that kiss, Wallace?"

"I did indeed, my dear," her husband replied meaningfully. "*Actors!*"

Part VII

Eight

Chapter Twenty-Nine

B Y THE TIME the sun had begun to set, Hattie was certain she'd wish to sleep for the next several days.

Her throat was parched, her feet sore, and her stomach very full as she leaned against a pavilion stake, watching Ruby create sparking flashes of fire from a sheet of paper and swishing them into a staircase shape.

It had been the first chemical trick Ruby had ever learned, Hattie recalled with a tired smile. And yet it remained one of her most requested performances.

Elias was standing next to her, clearly dazzled as the golden sparks reflected in the blue of his eyes. "She doesn't burn herself," he observed, sounding for a moment like that little boy Hattie had once met in a kitchen, many years ago.

"She does sometimes," she said with a little smile. "We all do."

It made him grin and wind an arm around her, pulling her close.

"Did you collect the keepsake cards?" Hattie asked. "All seven of them? I was concerned someone might take one."

"I have them here," he said, withdrawing the little stack from his jacket pocket and thumbing through them. "One, two, three …"

"Three," she echoed, tasting mint and sugar on the air. "Seven. There should be seven."

"You are mistaken," he replied with a chuckle. "There are eight."

She turned to him, frowning, as the crowd gasped and applauded the next fizzing eruption of light from Ruby's table. "No," she said. "There were seven. I counted."

He was still smiling at her and held the stack out. "You are the smarter one of the two of us," he said wryly, "but I do think I can count below ten."

She took the stack, an odd trepidation in her chest, and flipped through them.

Eight.

There were eight.

"Someone has added one," she said, turning them over in her hands, squinting at the print and script on either side of each in the low light.

"Or you just counted wrong," he said. "Stop that. You'll go blind."

She frowned again, handing them back to him. "I don't think blindness is so swift."

"But it might be," he replied, still teasing, still watching her in the late glow of dusk. "We can look at them again when we get home."

They were interrupted by Rhys, striding over with his tiger-striped trick box under his arm, his face twisted into a resigned glower. His kohl had smudged as the day had worn on and was in thicker, more theatrical lines around the spiky shadows of his eyelashes in the dimming light.

He paused in front of Hattie and then knelt on one knee, holding it out like a defeated general below a white flag.

"Yes, thank you," she said, snatching it up. "And the rest?"

"Monica will have it," Rhys muttered, scrambling back up to his feet.

To Elias, he simply regarded him for a moment and then said, "Your mother has wandering hands," before stalking away.

"I should have told him about the extra keepsake card," Hattie said absently, stroking the top of the box.

Elias was pulling a face. "What do you think my mother did to him?"

"Hm?" said Hattie, blinking away her reverie. "Oh, I don't know. Women are always trying to grope the young men at the showcase, though. It's far worse than the other way 'round. They're used to it, especially Rhys."

"Why 'especially'?"

"Because," she said with a shrug. "He is the pretty one."

That only deepened Elias's frown. "You think he's pretty?"

The applause stopped her from answering. Though now that she had a moment to think, she supposed that Rhys got the worst of it because one of his tricks was inviting the crowd to find where he'd hidden things he'd just made disappear.

Yes, in retrospect, Errol and Malcolm had a similar number of admirers, just fewer opportunities to be handled by them.

"If he's the pretty one," Elias began again, as soon as the applause had died down, "what are Mal and Errol?"

She wrinkled her brow, turning to study him. "The charmer," she said, "and the strapping one. You know this, don't you? Ruby is the vixen. Monica the angel. Libba the Valkyrie."

"And you?" he asked. "Me?"

She shrugged. "I have never asked."

"You asked about the others?" he clarified, raising his brows in disbelief. "It sounded like you chose those titles."

"Me? No. I'm useless at such things," she said with a laugh. "I am the one who is yours, I suppose. And you are the one who is mine."

"Hm," he said, looking unconvinced. "I suppose."

"The pretty one," he said again with a huff. "I suppose that's better than 'the Welsh one.'"

"Oh, he would certainly think so," she agreed.

"Why did he give you that box?" Elias asked, suddenly staring down at it with distaste. "I thought it would go in the rubbish after the showcase."

"Oh, you would like that, wouldn't you?" she replied, plucking at the remains of her erstwhile silk dressing gown. "No, I intend to repurpose what is left of my poor robe. That is what you get for thieving."

"I didn't steal it," he argued. "I improved upon it. The red one is much better."

"I must discourage such actions in the future, Elias," she replied with a raise of her brassy brows. "Lest you take it upon yourself to commandeer my other gifts from male royals."

"'Other gifts'?" he repeated as she turned to walk back into the crowd. "Hattie! What other gifts?! Harriet!"

She only smiled as she heard him following her.

And did not answer.

⚬❧⚬

ELIAS BID FAREWELL to his parents as the last of the props were being taken down.

He had intended only to walk over and thank them for attending and assure them that their allowance would be restored on the morrow, but his mother stopped him with a hand to his arm and a nervous press of her lips.

"Do you mind terribly," she said as her husband stifled a gigantic yawn behind her, "if we stay another night at the inn? It is just that it seems very late now to head back toward home."

"Of course," he said, blinking in surprise at the fact that it was a request and not a demand. "I can't imagine doing anything but sleeping after this myself."

She nodded, giving him a tight little smile. "Oh, good. Yes, that is good. And we will depart in the morning. I asked your Harriet if I might write to her and she said it was all right, though I think she is still a bit cross with me."

"Hattie doesn't get cross," he told her. "Not really. If you write, she will write you back."

"A wife who doesn't get cross?" his stepfather echoed, yawning again. "Marvels continue."

Elias rolled his eyes and waved them off, turning toward the carriage that awaited him with his wife inside.

When he crossed the drive and stepped into the thing, he found she had Peach in her lap and both had already begun to doze against the doorframe next to her.

It warmed him, and instead of slapping the roof as one often did, he leaned out and motioned to the driver so that he would not startle them back to the land of waking. And this way, for the whole of the ride, he could observe her in her slumber, cradling a tiny pig in her royal skirts.

By the time they'd arrived at the house, she had been jostled enough that she had started to wake on her own, her eyelids fluttering and her mouth pursing in clear disapproval at the interruption.

"Come on," he said as the doors opened. "You don't want to fall asleep in a corset."

She insisted on carrying Peach herself back up to the room, pig under one arm and tiger-striped trick box under the other, blinking blearily as she stumbled forward the whole way. Once inside their suite, however, she did relinquish both and submit to his assistance in getting out of the layered confines of her costume.

"You asked if I knew how to lace a corset," he reminded her as he slid the suede layer off her arms, the full skirt of her dress crinkling around her legs. "What if I didn't know how to unlace it afterward?"

"Then I should be very concerned for you," she replied sleepily. "And your motivations."

He laughed and then proceeded to demonstrate that his motivations were not a cause for concern at all, easing the grip around her ribs and freeing her from the press of fabric that had held her aloft all day.

"Polish," he said as she stepped toward the waiting bath, her chemise floating around her legs. "It was very … dense. Wasn't it? Chewy."

"'Chewy,'" she echoed with a dreamy sound of something like approval. "Yes, it is rather, isn't it? *Uwielbiam cię.*"

"Indeed?" he replied, watching her lift the chemise off and step into the warm water with a sigh of relief. "And what does that mean?"

She smiled at him drowsily, dropping her head to the side onto her shoulder, the braid sagging down over her ear where the pins had come loose against her scalp, tilting her crown.

"Ah," he said, his heart aching. "The feeling is mutual. Shall I unbraid your hair?"

"Once I am clean," she murmured, turning and sinking down into the water until her breath bubbled up from beneath it, submerged to her cheekbones.

He watched her with a fond warmth in his bones, removing his orange cravat and unbuttoning his marigold waistcoat, sighing at the freedom of his own ribs after a long day as he craned his neck from side to side.

He emptied his jacket pockets before sliding it off, carefully setting the fan of art cards on the bed and considering them as he shrugged himself down to his shirtsleeves and began to tug up the tail of it from his waistband.

Yes, there was no doubt. There were eight of them.

Not seven.

Eight.

He paused, reaching out to spread them into a larger spray across the coverlet, examining the destinations depicted on each card.

And he spotted the new one immediately.

Brighton, it read. *England.*

He frowned at it, pulling his shirt over his head. Blinking. Shaking his head. Giving his eyes a rub.

But it was still there.

Behind him, he could hear his wife emerging from the bath.

"Hattie," he said, pulling the new card forward with two fingertips and then lifting it up, tentatively, in front of his face. "You were right. Someone put a new one in with the old."

"Oh?" she said, and a few moments later, she appeared at his side, her skin damp and warm through the clinging fabric of her red dressing gown. "May I see?"

He passed it to her with a frown.

It was not like the others, each a small piece of art Willa had requested from the person in her correspondence, representing the place from which they were writing. Many of them were only identified on back, where the message was penned.

This one did not have art on it, just a rough sketch of a shingle beach and the name *Brighton* penned in bold calligraphy on the front, as though it were created in a hurry.

Hattie flipped it over, her eyes moving over the back.

"Not much of a message. It just says, *'Felicitations'* in the same calligraphy."

Elias could only make a confused mumbling noise and shrug. "A jest, perhaps?"

"Perhaps," she said, still frowning, her damp fingers toying with the corner. "'Felicitations.' It can mean 'good work' or it can be an expression of congratulations, I suppose. Perhaps it is a well-wisher from our wedding or a person who approved of the showcase."

He nodded, his spine giving a tingle. "That's likely all it is."

"Yes," she said, her tone entirely unconvincing. "Most likely."

Still, she did not stow it with the others, which she gathered up carefully and carried back to the salon.

This one, Elias noted, she lifted carefully and folded into a sheet of tissue that she withdrew from her bedside table before tucking it into the compartment within.

"Felicitations," she said again, softly to herself, likely unaware she'd spoken at all, then she looked at him and smiled. "Elias, you should wash while the water is still warm. And then come to bed, while I still am."

Chapter Thirty

A s was customary following a showcase, Starling's Rest had a day of nothing at all within its walls.

Breads and small bites were delivered from the bakery at dawn and laid out next to the leftover canapes on the dining room table, for anyone who wished to come and graze upon them throughout the hours of the day, whether they be performers, guests, or staff.

Beyond that, lights were only lit by the person who needed them, and all matters of service were to be delayed until everyone had enjoyed a proper sleep in and languished in the aftermath of such an ordeal.

Even Libba, who had derisively declared a few days prior, "For God's sake, it is *one* performance!" had not emerged from her cocoon, save to retrieve two full carafes of water, a hot compress, and an ungodly amount of fruit.

As for Hattie and Elias, they had agreed to take turns going down into the house proper to retrieve repast and anything else they might need and had spent much of the day alternating between sleep, idle chatter, and fiddling with the tandem puzzle box they had been gifted at their wedding.

"Perhaps if you just hold that latch there with the hook of your finger, I can wiggle the other bit out," Elias would say.

And Hattie would wish for death.

It was, in her estimation, an impossible task, and one he seemed hellbent on mastering regardless.

And it wasn't until her husband had gone down for post-luncheon tea that she realized he had taken the cursed thing with him. It was suspicious, as he knew very well that it was designed in such a way that he could not solve it alone.

And so she was hardly surprised to come upon him with Errol and Malcolm, each holding a corner and arguing about what to try next.

"Well," she said, crossing her arms and narrowing her eyes at the three guilty sets of eyes that had flown up to greet her in the dining room archway, "it appears you've found more brides."

Rhys sidled in behind her, wearing what appeared to be a pair of Libba's costume trousers from an old production of *One Thousand and One Nights* and the tatty remains of Hattie's tiger-striped dressing gown, his eyes now gray from lid to cheekbone from smudged kohl. "Afternoon," he said obliviously. "Any bakewell left?"

And then he'd walked around the table, peered at the box, and plucked a little triangular wedge of wood out of the center, which had collapsed it into a new shape for solving.

This had thrilled the other three men—and deepened Hattie's irritation considerably.

She had snatched up her tea and marched out, only to return for a refill to find both Lem and Monica now involved in the endeavor of the stupid, cursed puzzle boxes.

"You are holding it too tightly," Lem told Errol with a frown. "Muscle does not solve everything."

"It doesn't?" Monica asked, eyeing Lem's bulging biceps with skepticism. "Can we use tools? I've a knitting needle."

"No!" shouted both Elias and Malcolm in tandem.

And Hattie sighed. Loudly.

"Hands are tools," Lem observed, "but what if the removed pieces are also?"

"What?!" said Errol, looking down at the discarded pile of

wooden splints and shapes. "Oh, my God!"

"Hattie, *cariad*," Rhys's voice called from down the hall. "Come away from there before you crack a tooth."

And she did, though watching Rhys lounge in her mangled dressing gown was probably not much better, at least until he had begun to suggest avenues of revenge while attempting to toss little candied raisins into her mouth from across the room.

She caught four. She did not catch twelve.

When Ruby appeared a few moments later, the other woman caught all that were thrown in her direction. Ten, if anyone was counting, which Harriet was not.

"Did I tell you about the keepsake cards?" Hattie asked, once the raisins had been exhausted and clouds had given them a nice, blue tint to the parlor. "The new one?"

"'New one'?" Ruby asked, stifling a yawn. "Rhys, give me some of that Turkish delight."

"What Turkish delight?" he mumbled through a full mouth as he made it disappear in perhaps the most inelegant illusion of his life.

"Charming," said Ruby, frowning. "You've got a sugar mustache."

"Oh, you did finally grow one, after all," Hattie teased, getting a glower from Rhys.

Behind them, from the direction of the kitchen, there was a loud cheer of triumph, complete with whooping and exclamations of genius.

Hattie rolled her eyes.

"Where's my pig?" Ruby asked, turning to Hattie. "When you go get this mysterious missive, bring my pig."

"She's sleeping," Hattie said, though there was no way to know if that was true.

In truth, she just did not want to share. Peach had spent an hour this morning attempting to work out the mathematic, geometrical matter of how to get onto the human bed. She had failed, of course, with those stubby, little legs, but Hattie reckoned it was because the little pig had wished to snuggle her mistress specifically.

Certainly not the traitor with a wooden puzzle who had left their bed under false pretenses.

It was only the sound of the triumphant army coming toward the parlor that got Hattie up off the chaise and marching toward the bedroom, in search of both creature and cryptic missive.

By the time she had returned, it seemed most of their celebration had ended, and the burst of revelry had dissipated back into exhausted repose.

"What's this?" Libba asked when she appeared. "Are those my trousers?"

"No," lied Rhys, crossing his legs under him with a shimmer of metallic embroidery flashing like the garment itself was trying to tell the truth. "Not anymore."

Hattie set Peach down and watched as she made an immediate, enthusiastic run for Libba, who was the only person in the room still holding food.

"This is my croissant," Libba informed the pig, whilst breaking off a corner to surrender.

Elias was looking at the tissue-covered card in Hattie's hand with an expression of sudden concern. "Ah," he said to her. "We're doing that now, are we?"

"Everyone is here," she pointed out, and then she counted them to be certain. "Yes, eight. All of us."

"Nine, if you include our new sibling there," Rhys quipped, nodding at the pig and then holding his hands up in apology at the impatient look Hattie cut in his direction.

Elias sighed, crossing the room to stand next to Hattie, and took the card from her hands. "I brought some of Willa's keepsake cards from her various correspondences to the showcase yesterday, as you may recall," he said. "There were seven of them when I arrived. When we left, there were eight."

Hattie blinked. When he'd said the word *seven*, she'd seen the flash of yellow, heard the viola strings. When he'd said *eight*, she'd leaned closer to him, as though his storm clouds and smoke might shelter her.

"This one had been added," he said, holding it up, still swaddled in its wrapping. "Someone left it on the table during the festivities."

"Well, what is it?" Rhys asked immediately. "What does it say?"

"It says 'Felicitations,'" Hattie answered, frowning. "That is all."

Errol held his hand out, a polite and patient request to see the thing. Once he had it, he carefully pulled the tissue paper away and turned it over in his hands. "It also says Brighton," he pointed out. "It has a sketch on it."

"I told you," Malcolm said, a snapping, impatient quality to his voice. "I told you I saw her."

"Oh, do shut up," Rhys replied, frowning. "You didn't."

Mal rounded on him with a glower. "I'm not the liar here."

"Oh, please," said Rhys with a yawn. "You gamble. You do business. Your entire being is lies."

"All right," said Monica in a calming voice, stepping between the two. "Let's not bicker. Whom did you see, Mal?"

He didn't answer, only blinking at her like he'd been caught doing something naughty.

Hattie was watching him, her heart thick in her chest. She wanted him to say it. And she didn't.

"I saw her too," Elias said, from next to her, drawing everyone's attention around. "On the shore."

Hattie stared at him, her hand reaching out of its own accord to find his. "You did?"

He nodded, turning to meet her eye. "During the eulogy."

"Eulogy," Libba muttered. "Kangaroos."

"Libba," Ruby snapped. "Not now."

"You think she is not only alive, but in Brighton?" Errol said, still staring down at the card in his hands. "You think she came to her own funeral and didn't make herself known?"

"I don't know," Elias confessed with a shrug. "I don't know what to think. It's like you said. She was always unknowable."

For a time, they all simply existed in the silence.

Errol passed the card around, hand to hand, and let each of the wards examine it.

"It doesn't look like her handwriting," Rhys said.

"It isn't handwriting," Monica pointed out. "It is calligraphy. More like a drawing than script. It wouldn't match her natural penmanship."

"No one of note was ever known for their penmanship," Hattie said quietly, her healed hand seeming to ache from a burn that had long, long healed.

"Where did she *go*?" Libba asked, shaking her head. "When she initially left the house seven years ago. Where was she going? Did she tell any of you?"

One by one, they shook their heads.

Only Errol looked uncertain, frowning down at his hands as he sought out the memory. "She had her things packed," he said. "She told us she would be away for a while. She reduced the staff like she would for a longer trip. But that was all."

"How much did she pack?" Ruby asked. "How much did she take?"

Errol shook his head and shrugged. "Trunks, like always. She left from the wharf. I should have asked more questions."

"It never should have been only you who was here to do so," Malcolm said, frowning. "That wasn't fair."

Elias was looking at Hattie; she could feel him doing it, could feel somehow, without a single word spoken, the weight of what he was thinking. She turned and met his eye, considering it, considering that she might say what she had told him once in confidence. And somehow, she knew that he would not mind if she did or did not.

She took a gulp of breath, shaking her head. "I never thought she was dead," she said suddenly. "I never felt she was gone."

The others heard it. They looked at her.

"No," said Ruby, frowning. "Nor I. I tried to grieve, but … It felt dishonest."

"We cannot assume that she is alive just because of a phantom bit of art," Rhys said, his voice breaking. He shook his head, digging his fingers into his hair, and gave a humorless laugh. "It is not that I can't believe in miracles, but by God, I know how easy they are to fake."

"We don't know anything," Errol agreed, placing a hand on Rhys's shoulder. "We can only suspect and wonder."

Libba sniffled, rubbing impatiently at her eye with the heel of her hand and turning her head. "Fine," she said. "We will wonder. For a year, as she commanded."

"A year, yes," Monica repeated, looking thoughtful. "Perhaps something will happen when the year has ended, if we meet our end of the bargain."

"Perhaps nothing will happen at all," Rhys said sternly. "We must be prepared for that too, *chwaer*. Just as prepared."

"Agreed," said Monica, softening as she studied his face. "Agreed."

In the end, they wrapped the card back in its tissue but did not send it to the master suite for safekeeping.

Instead, it remained in the parlor, propped on the hearth, facing the sun.

Just in case.

Chapter Thirty-One

E LIAS COULD NOT sleep.

And judging from the amount of rolling about that was happening on the far side of the bed, Hattie couldn't, either.

It was odd, after spending so much of the day exhausted, to have any trouble at all, but he imagined they both had quite a lot on their minds, and for a time, he even thought he oughtn't interrupt her thinking, as disruptive as it appeared to be.

Finally, she sighed, flopped onto her side, and squinted at him in the dark.

"You are awake," she declared, as though he'd done something amiss.

He chuckled, turning his head on the pillow to face her. "So are you."

"Yes, well," she said sourly, "I am not the one who enjoys torment."

He laughed fully at that, moving to roll over to face her and prop his head onto his hand. "When I said that," he told her, "I did not mean *all* torment. Only one very specific kind."

"I don't believe you," she returned. "You enjoyed that puzzle box, and that was torture carved in wood."

He laughed again, harder this time, his chest shaking with the action as she glared. He could not help it.

"Libba and Ruby took it," he told her. "After we reassembled it. They are going to try next."

"Fine," said Hattie, flinging herself back onto the pillows and staring at the canopy ahead. "Let them. I never shall touch the thing again."

"Hattie," he said seriously, "I think I love you best when you are having a strop."

She only hissed in response, which made him grin so wide, his face ached.

"Especially," he added, "when it is my fault."

"Oh, shut up," she said, crossing her arms, which looked perfectly absurd, prone as she was and haloed in shuttered moonlight. "You are insufferable."

"Am I?" he asked, flattered despite himself. "I always thought the same of you."

She gasped, turning her head with her mouth already open to rebuke him, but never got to speak as he swooped down to catch her ire with his own lips, delighted at how it spiced her kiss. She froze as though she might shove him off and then chose to pull him to her instead, opening her mouth under his to invite him closer.

"Should I show you what sort of torment I meant?" he asked, rolling over her and bracing his arms on either side of her head, gazing down at the way her curls spilled out over the pillow. "The kind I enjoy so much?"

"I recall," she said sharply, "you leaving me in the hallway alone. Leaving me on my bed unkissed. I don't care to be stoked and doused again, Elias. I shan't tolerate it."

"Ah, you lack imagination," he teased, leaning down to kiss her jaw, her chin, her neck. "Sometimes the torment isn't a douse, only a very slow addressing of the flame itself. You know, that was always my intention for our first time. It is only that you ruined it."

"*I* ruined it?" she repeated, giving a little thrash under him that made him grin and nip at her throat.

"You did," he said, pinning her with his hips and running his hands along the silk covering her arms. "You made it impossible to go slow. You broke me."

"Hm," she said, mollified for the moment. One of her legs snaked out of her nightrail, wrapping around his hip and stroking along the backs of his thighs. "You seem plenty whole to me."

He exhaled, a sound of defeat and surrender. "You are doing it again."

"Am I?" she asked, sounding very pleased by the prospect. "Good."

"Oh, you are asking to be tormented worse than before, Harriet," he chided, reaching down to stroke the leg that was wrapped around him and following it up to the curve of her backside. "Do you really want to challenge me like that?"

"Of course I do," she replied. "It is not as though you've ever been victorious."

It was his turn to gasp in outrage.

"Alone in that hallway?" he mimicked. "Unkissed in your bed?!"

She grinned, her teeth glowing in the low light of the night. "Mere parrying," she said, rolling her hips beneath him until his breath escaped him in a sharp, little hiss.

"'Parrying'?" he repeated, dipping down to speak into her ear, soft and warm, their skin sliding against one another. "It sounds like you want to meet my sword again."

"Only if you are prepared to face torment in equal measure," she replied, her hands raising to stroke the sides of his face. "You are, after all, an excellent teacher in such matters. Did you think I might only learn one dialect of the silent language and not all?"

He flashed his teeth at her, searching her eyes in the dark. "I had not considered it."

"Foolish," she chided, dragging him down to kiss her again. "Perhaps this time, I will riposte instead. It seems, for a man who loves torment, that you inflict it far more than you experience it."

"Oho," he chuckled, running his hands up her thighs to ruck up the thin material of her nightrail. "You are mistaken. This very body of yours has been tormenting you since my very first blush of desire. It has been a long and arduous gauntlet of denial."

"By your own hand," she retorted, lifting her arms so that he could peel the fabric from her body. "Not mine."

"I assure you," he told her, pulling the gown away and setting it gently aside and then sitting back on his heels to observe her as he moved to remove the fabric covering his own form. "My hand tried its best."

"Elias!"

He grinned at her, pulling away the cotton that confined his chest and then lifting to divest himself of the pajama trousers. He lifted his chin in satisfaction at her intake of breath at the reveal of just how hard she had made him, at the proof that his claims were true.

He leaned forward, parting her legs and stroking the soft, supple skin on the insides of her thighs, just shy of touching her where he knew she wanted him to. "You never had to wait," he whispered, "until recently."

She made a frustrated little flutter in her throat, twisting her hips in an effort to force his touch higher, and received only a chiding click of his tongue in response.

"What about you?" she whispered, sharp and glinting in the dark. "With the way you stroke that wineglass at me. What if I were to touch you that way? You couldn't stand it."

"I already told you," he said softly. "That is unintentional."

She pushed herself up on her elbows, scooting her hips closer as he teased just short of pleasuring her. "Perhaps it was," she answered, reaching out to mimic what he was doing, to run her fingertips along the flesh of his thighs. "I do not for an instant believe it remains so."

He smirked, refusing to answer her one way or another.

"You know what you are doing," she breathed, inching up to cradle him at the base, feather soft and delicate as she demonstrated the motions she had watched him inflict on the poor crystalware. "Stroking the texture at the bowl of the goblet, stroking the length of the stem. Pressing your lips to the rim."

"'My lips,'" he repeated, ragged. "Are you going to do that part as well?"

She smiled slowly, running her little, pink tongue along the curve of her mouth. "I shouldn't," she said. "You haven't earned it. But, alas, I do wish to."

"Hattie …" he managed, certain his vision was going to darken if she continued to reference what he thought she was referencing.

"And when I have finished," she said, kneeling forward, her hair falling over his lap, "you will cease your torment. Won't you?"

"I …"

"Hm," she said, and then she pressed her lips to his cock with a curious flick of her tongue.

The world did go dark then, or perhaps it exploded in color. Elias could not rightly say. He gripped the blankets at his sides and tried to remember to breathe, watching her with the kind of silent awe one usually reserves for moments of epiphany or miracle.

The hot drag of her tongue over him was as exquisite as it was unbearable. The sweetness of her breath, the way he could feel her little gasps of delight rumbling through him as a physical thing.

He watched her until he was certain he could not hold back another second, at which point her name ripped from his throat, and she rose back up to sitting, a look of triumph glinting in those amber eyes.

She crawled backward, falling back onto her pillows with her arms raised in welcome as he tried to remember how to control his limbs, gasping for air and licking his lips and blinking the stars out of his eyes.

When he fell into her arms, he did so with gratitude, and just as she'd said, he held nothing back any longer. Though he still retained enough of himself to go slowly this time. He remembered to savor it because he hadn't yet.

He hadn't, and he desperately wanted to.

And, of course, if he didn't slow down, he was going to shatter. He wanted to shatter. Badly.

But he wanted her to shatter first.

"Talk to me," she begged. "Tell me what you want."

"You," he gasped, his limbs quaking with the force of his pleasure. "Only you. Forever. Just like this. God, Hattie."

"Oh," she sighed, arching up as though it had been a caress instead of a collection of syllables. "Say my name again. Elias, please."

"Hattie," he said. "My Harriet. I want you like I've never wanted anything. I am yours now. I have always been yours."

She shuddered, her hands clinging to his arms, legs locking around his as she unspooled at the sound of his confession. And she said his name as she found her bliss. She cried out and whimpered, "Elias!" at her moment of pleasure.

At which point, he understood why the reverse had impacted her so much, and he lost himself as well.

He lost himself completely.

And he kissed her as he found completion.

For a long time after that, they simply held one another, breathing and listening and smiling against the other's bare skin.

"I think perhaps you were right," she said, just as their muscles slackened and sleep began to take them. "Torment can be lovely."

He nodded, stifling a yawn. "Spoken by the woman who has always been mine. I am glad you agree."

She caught his yawn, burrowing closer into his side. "Elias, I think I will sleep for a while now," she said, no longer wired or tossing about in restlessness. "Perhaps when I wake, you can torment me a little more."

He nodded, resting his cheek in her hair, and surrendered to the call of sleep himself. "Of course," he murmured as he drifted away. "It would be my pleasure."

Epilogue

Six weeks later

THE SUMMER'S END festival had never been Hattie's favorite time of year. Perhaps she had not appreciated it properly, after the incident with Elias on the pier, even as time had covered that memory in a thin layer of dust, just beyond reach of her direct consciousness.

Still, it surprised her how excited she felt for this one, how roused her heartbeat had been by the scent of the fires being stoked and the call of the stall attendants and game masters as they'd flocked to their booths, inviting the denizens of Brighton out for one final lark before the shuttering of autumn.

The Starling wards walked together from the Rest down to the beach, accompanied by a few additional friends and one very well-outfitted pig.

"It is a waistcoat," Rhys said for the third time as he gestured at the garment affixed to the leash and the pig held in Ruby's hand. "Even with ruffles, it is a waistcoat."

"And so what?" Monica replied with a sniff. "She may be a dandy if she wishes. No one stops *you* from doing it, after all, Rhys."

Rhys had considered this, scratching at his curls, which were fluffy with humidity and salt air. "That is reasonable, I suppose," he said. "But I don't enjoy competition."

"Yes," Persephone Boswell agreed, winning a spin and glower

from her place, linked arm in arm with Libba. "We know."

Elias chuckled and pulled Hattie closer as they walked, the grit and grass giving way to the shingles and pebbles of the coast as they crossed through a wicker fence. "Anything you're desperate to do first?" he asked her, his color already high in anticipation. "I am aiming at the rope bout, myself. Love a trial of strength, especially in teams."

"Do *not*," she warned him. "Do *not* play at the throwing stand with Jasper Townsend."

"Aw, Hattie," Jasper called from behind them. "That's not sporting."

"No, it isn't," she agreed shrilly. "Ever."

"I'll play," Mr. Harcourt offered, a note of something slightly ominous in his tone. "Straight away, even, if you like."

"See? That's better," said Jasper, while Malcolm gave a knowing chuckle between the two men. "Last year, they had coconuts instead of wooden balls. Maybe again? You'll have to adjust for the weight, Harcourt."

"Noted," the barrister said, a wry smile twisting his lips.

"Speaking of coconuts," Rhys added, dragging out each syllable in a drawl.

"Yes, yes," Ruby snapped. "But next time you are paying for the ingredients. I'll bottle it up for you in a few days. God forbid you don't smell like an oasis for a few hours."

"God forbid," Miss Boswell echoed, though not quite as sarcastically as before.

"All right," Errol announced, clapping his hands together as they reached the edge of the festivities. "Shall we meet back here in an hour for the rope contest? I smell roasted neeps and don't want to arrive after they've all gone."

"Oh, honestly," Mal said with a nose wrinkle. "You're the only one on this beach excited about bloody turnips."

"Then why do they always sell out?" Errol asked, raising his brows and grinning. "An hour! No chocolate for Peach, and absolutely nothing with booze. You hear me?"

"I wouldn't," Ruby replied, blinking like an infant.

"Wouldn't share her booze and chocolate, she means," Rhys added with a snicker, which appeared to be the final signal that all should disperse.

"What do you think?" Elias asked once they were alone. "Sweet or savory? The hot fried fish is always very good."

"Both," she said immediately. "Do you like plum duff? Or Chelsea buns?"

"Are there people who don't?" He laughed, steering her toward the food stands. "My favorite, however, is the gingerbread. I know, I know, it isn't strictly summer fare, but it is the best thing here."

"I don't mind a gingerbread," Hattie said. "I wonder how it pairs with the fish."

They bought both and some lemonade with which to wash it down and spent some time wandering the games and stalls. Hattie tried her hand at hoopla and failed miserably enough that Elias knew not to attempt himself, lest he were successful.

"I can't be good at everything," she muttered, licking the plum powder off her thumbs.

"And bless you for that," he answered. "Oh! A hopping race! Shall we watch or participate?"

"Watch," she said instantly, grimacing at the people pulling burlap sacks up around their legs. "I've had enough humiliation for the hour, thank you very much."

"Well, then you'll want to be on the same team as I am for the strength contest," he told her with a twinkle. "To ensure it doesn't happen again."

"You?" she teased, grinning. "I was going to follow Lem."

Elias's smile faded and he looked around the crowd, squinting. "Lem shouldn't be allowed to participate," he announced. "For the sake of fairness."

It turned out that he needn't have worried, anyhow, for by the time they reached the rope that had been tabbed and measured for the pulling contest in a sandpit that had been built into the cradle of an old frigate sail, which was to be their arena, Lem was nowhere to be found.

"He's painting faces," Libba said with a shrug. "I told him not to work today, but he never listens."

"Face paint, you say?" Rhys exclaimed. "Where?"

"After," Errol told him. "Are we all together, or split?"

"Split!" Monica and Ruby both agreed.

Miss Boswell agreed to shepherd the pig during the proceedings.

"Typical," Rhys griped at her.

"A good illusionist values her hands," she replied sweetly. "I don't expect you to know much about that."

"All right, I don't want Rhys on my team anymore," Malcolm said with a sigh as he watched the other man turn various shades of puce as he failed to pluck a good retort from the sea air.

"Too late, Lennox," Elias gloated. "Take up your rope."

Hattie stood behind her husband, both because she knew she was mostly here for the spectacle of it and because this was the better vantage to observe his efforts. They had Monica, Mr. Harcourt, and Errol, while the other side had Libba, Malcolm, Rhys, Ruby, and the town vicar, who had wandered past while deliberations had been made and had volunteered to even their numbers.

The whistle blew and the pulling began in earnest.

Hattie dug her heels into the sand, her shoulders locking and arms aching. She cried out in effort, her feet pawing into the ground as she pulled and pulled and pulled.

The problem, of course, was that the others were doing the same thing.

"Heave!" Elias shouted.

But it was no use.

Perhaps it was because the vicar had God on his side, but it was only a moment later that they all went flying forward, directly into the sand, opposite a cheer of victory from the others.

At least, Hattie thought as she blinked away the daze of defeat, *I landed on Elias.*

That was a nice consolation, even if he was vexed by the matter.

"We'll win a game eventually," he assured her.

"We already have," she told him, using the opportunity to stroke her hands along his chest before he tutted at her and pulled her to her feet.

She shook out her skirt, giggling at all the golden grit that fell out of it in the process and allowing Elias to paw at her front to get the clumps of it away, so long as she was allowed to return the favor.

She sighed and stretched her aching arms over her head, bending one leg back and then the other.

"Shall we walk?" she asked. "Before you demand a rematch?"

"Fine," he grumbled, offering her his arm even so.

This time, she took him to a booth that she knew she could win. The riddles master had changed since her youth, and so she had not yet been banned from his stall. She would be, of course. It was only a matter of time. But until then, she could enjoy a feeling of victory this summer.

"If you feed me, I grow," the man said with a wiggle of his white brows. "If you quench me, I die."

"Fire," she said.

"Or thirst," Elias added. "If you eat instead of drink, it will grow. If you quench it, it will die. No?"

The man clapped. "The lady is correct, but the gentleman makes a compelling argument! How novel! Have a sweet."

They played four more riddles before Hattie squeezed her husband's hand and nodded back toward the shore, a bit jittery from the candy and not willing to yet damn herself from the riddle booth forevermore.

"I was doing well," he complained. "As were you."

"Yes, but how many comfits do you really want to eat?" she asked with a giggle.

"All of them," he replied flatly.

She smiled and tugged him toward the pier, *that* pier, the one he'd shoved her off of, once upon a time.

If he noticed their destination or found it amiss, he did not say, falling into step beside her and taking several deep gulps of the sea air as people gathered around the bonfire with driftwood and old furniture, squealing in excitement as they tossed in their tinder and watched it climb higher, smearing the very atmosphere with the scent of smoke.

The water looked green today, glinting and glittering like an emerald, the way it often did this time of year as the tide shifted and foamed toward the colder months.

He wrapped his arms around her and she leaned against her back as they watched and listened to both the ocean and the fire and revelry behind them, melding together into the sweet symphony of summer's final song.

"When is a baron not barren?" she asked, tilting her head up to look at him.

He narrowed his eyes, lowering his head to meet her gaze. "When he is a husband?" he guessed.

She shook her head. "Try again. No comfit for you."

He scoffed. "When he is … hm. Ah, are we returning to barren fields? When a baron is … what? Fecund? Fertile?"

"Indeed," she said, turning gently in his arms so that they were facing one another, her hands braced against his chest. "And when is a baron fertile?"

He stared at her for a moment, a wrinkle appearing between his brows as he considered what she was saying. "When he … erm … produces."

"Yes," she said. "Produces what?"

He paused, his eyes flicking down to her body and back up to her face. "An heir?" he guessed, thin and uncertain.

"Hm," she said, bouncing on the heels of her feet. "I suppose."

For a moment, he could only gape at her. "Are you certain?"

She shook her head. "Not yet. Only suspicious. When is a

baron not barren?"

Elias gave a short, incredulous laugh. "When he is—"

She grinned, planting her hands on his chest and shoving him quickly and firmly off the pier and into the water, where he landed with a resounding and satisfying splash.

She stood over the edge, watching as he emerged, thrashing and gasping and laughing through his shock and outrage, and before he could say a single additional word, she leapt in after him.

Afterword

Thank you so much for reading! The first book in a new series is always a mammoth of an undertaking, especially when establishing a world as vibrant and varied as Starling's Rest. I had so much fun getting these characters down on paper, and I hope you fell in love with Hattie and Elias as much as I did while writing them.

Hattie was my first expressly neurodivergent heroine, and it was such a joy spending time in her mind.

All of the Starlings will be getting their own romances, but next up is Liberty Lennox, who will enter into a scheme of ambition, folly, and fake fiancés opposite Jasper Townsend in *Little Miss Nobody*. If you like friends to lovers, theatrical farce, and the forbidden allure of a brother's best friend, this is the book for you. Look for it in summer 2026.

Thanks again for reading! And I hope to see you again in *Little Miss Nobody*.

If you have a moment, please consider leaving me a review on Amazon, BookBub, Goodreads, or Instagram. Reviews are my absolute favorite part of being a writer.

As always, if you have feedback, questions, or ever just want to say *hi*, shoot me a line at Ava@AvaDevlin.com. I love hearing from my readers.

A Guide to the People of Starling's Rest

(As recorded in observation of Baroness Willa Starling Selwyn's curious household, in the era of her disappearance)

Willa Starling Selwyn (née Starling), Dowager Baroness Selwyn
The Patron of Prodigies

A widow with an eye for brilliance and no patience for those who squander it. Willa married a destitute baron with her merchant father's fortune but was widowed soon after. She spent the rest of her life proving that genius, not birth, was the true measure of legacy.

The Heir

Elias Selwyn, Baron Selwyn
The Baron

Willa's nephew and heir to the Selwyn barony, Elias was meant to be raised among the other gifted children, but having none of their gifts, he found it unbearable. Determined to find meaning and belonging elsewhere, he begged to be sent off to school, where he earned high marks, built a reputation of his own, and eventually joined the British cavalry.

The Prodigies

Harriet "Hattie" French
The Polyglot

Once a scullery maid in a Brighton foundling house, Hattie was discovered when Willa overheard her shifting effortlessly between languages. By fourteen, she spoke half a dozen fluently and could pick up phrases in any new language within minutes. Vividly attuned to the colors and shapes of words, she grew into one of England's most celebrated linguists.

Malcolm Lennox
The Marvelous Human Abacus

Malcolm was discovered in a shipping-yard counting house, where his gift for numbers rivaled any London accountant's. A mixed-race prodigy in a world that would rather forget its debts, he hides sharp survival instincts behind a gambler's grin and a reputation for charm, odds, and fine wines.

Liberty "Libba" Lennox
The Chameleon

Allowed into Starling's Rest only due to her brother's growing fame in Brighton, Libba soon proved herself a talented actress. A born orator, dancer, and director with an uncanny gift for voices and gesture, she later moved to London to found a renowned acting troupe all her own.

Rhys Caradoc
The Illusionist

A Welsh pickpocket with nimble fingers and quicker wit. Willa hoped he'd take up medicine or clockmaking, but Rhys was born to mischief and trickery. His talent at illusions built a tenuous vocation, but an explosive reputation, well beloved in any port lucky enough to see him perform.

Errol Cagney
The Naturalist

Son of Willa's groom, Errol could gentle any creature from horse to hound. Encouraged into the greenhouse, he found equal devotion to plants. Patient, earnest, and unfashionably vegetarian, he remains the household's beating heart and its most patient listener.

Ruby Little
The Chemist

Once a seaside perfume-seller, little orphan Ruby dazzled Willa with her instincts for chemistry and her preternatural olfactory senses. Behind the glamor lies a formidable mind: she publishes scholarly papers under a man's name and sells her perfumes and fireworks displays under her own. She prides herself on being as reactive as her chemicals.

Monica Thresher
The Modiste

A laundress's daughter who repurposed rags into beautiful, intricate, and fashionable doll clothes. Willa brought her to Starling's Rest and cultivated a designer of rare imagination. Shy but far from meek, Monica sees the world in texture and pattern, her artistry stitched with devotion.

Other Notables

Julian Harcourt
The Barrister

A respected lawyer and longtime close friend of the baroness, now charged with executing Willa's labyrinthine will. Disciplined, skeptical, and devoted to order.

Jasper Townsend

The Best Mate

A Brighton shipyard lad raised on the docks, piers, and wharfs of the resort. Local fixture and Malcolm Lennox's lifelong best friend, a young man who may just have big dreams of his own.

Persephone "Seph" Boswell

The Shopgirl

A child of Irish Travellers whose caravan stopped on the Brighton shore every summer. Once a seaside magician performing tricks for coins, now the proprietress of Brighton's most curious curiosity shop. Sly, practical, and serenely unbothered, she delights in needling her old rival and fellow illusionist, Rhys Caradoc.

Lem

The Muscle

A London foundling who joined Libba's acting troupe as an enforcer and bodyguard but became a talented performer in his own right. He and Libba share a special bond of friendship and fraternity after their many years together.

About the Author

Ava Devlin writes romance that's steamy, sweet, and snarky. Her stories center around banter, longing, steamy entanglements, found family—and just enough rebellion to keep things interesting.

For over a decade, she's called New York City home, where escaping into the Regency is her favorite way to survive modern chaos.

She's been obsessed with love stories since her teen years, when she devoured every romance novel she could get her hands on. In her twenties, she moved to Britain, wandered through crumbling manor houses, and soaked up every scandalous bit of Regency history she could find.

Later, she lived in the French Alps as a governess (okay, okay, au pair)—basically her own Gothic subplot come to life.

These days, Ava writes books by day (and sometimes night), wrangles her mischievous rescue dog Hera, and spends too much time on the internet. She loves hearing from readers—especially if you come armed with book recs, Regency trivia, or dog selfies.

Instagram: ava_devlin_author
TikTok: @avadevlinromance
Facebook: AvaDevlinRomance